This is a work of fiction. Names, characters, places and incidents are either products of the author's imagination or are used fictitiously. Any resemblance to actual events, locales or persons, living or dead, is entirely coincidental.

10048, a novel by Frank A. Ruffolo

www.frankaruffolo.com

First Edition, July 2019

ISBN: 978-0-9836803-7-6 (printed version only)

Printed in the United States of America

10048

A Jack Stenhouse Mystery

CHAPTER ONE

Springtime in the Big Apple brings the people of New York out into the streets to celebrate their escape from another cold and generally nasty winter. However, at a little after three in the morning, most of the madding crowd is still asleep.

Some of them are awake, though. Blanketed by the morning darkness and its accompanying solitude, a lone black van creeps to a stop at the corner of Liberty and Greenwich Streets like a thief skulking through shadows. The side door slides open, and a man falls out onto the sidewalk.

As the van vanishes into the gloom, a disoriented and disheveled man picks himself up and stumbles toward the park around the Trade Towers Memorial. The unknown man, dressed in denim overalls, a tee shirt, and sneakers, staggers through the dark concrete canyon, unnoticed by two park officers on the graveyard shift who are busy dealing with a drunken homeless man who is refusing to leave the area. Bobbing and weaving like a dazed fighter, the mysterious man nears the South Pool and collapses alongside the retaining wall, out of sight of the officers.

Hours later, as the sun's rays poke between the buildings of the city like laser lights, a sliver of sunlight strikes the stranger's eyelids and jolts them open.

Breathing heavily, the man pulls himself up and sits on the retaining wall. Holding his stomach, he bends over in extreme duress. The man's eyes are tinted yellow, and they appear to be sunken and circled in black, almost like the mask of a raccoon. Suddenly, foam drips from the man's mouth and blood oozes from his gums, and he spews blood-filled vomit onto the pavement and all over his clothes. Moaning in agony, the man's tormented cries announce his location to a second set of police officers who are just coming on duty for the morning shift. The new officers converge on him at the same time as the crew from the night shift.

"Need EMT unit at the South Pool!" radios one of the newly-arrived officers. "HAZMAT condition. Repeat, HAZMAT needed! Possible case of Ebola!"

"SHIT!" exclaim the two overnight cops at the sight of the now unconscious man. "How the hell did he get in here?"

"Shit is right!" responds the officer on morning detail. "We're gonna have to shut this place down, and you guys are gonna have to explain why you didn't see him!"

As sirens wail, first responders from Ladder Company 403 and the First Police Precinct fill the promenade area near the South Pool with their ladder and pumper trucks, emergency vehicles, and police cruisers.

As soon as Ladder Company 403's pumper truck comes to a stop, Fire Captain Sam Lincoln jumps out to survey the situation. Following EMTs to the suffering man, he passes the two large pools where the Trade Towers once stood in their own Manhattan zip code—10048—and his mind drifts back to that fateful day of September eleventh, when Ladder Company 403 lost nineteen of their twenty-five man roster. Captain Troy Walsh and eighteen others of Company 403 died in the South Tower that Tuesday, and for the umpteenth time, Sam Lincoln is thankful he was off that day. He is quick to recall, however, that after seeing the carnage on TV, he couldn't remain home. He remembers how he stubbornly made his way into the city against the stream of thousands of panicked escapees, and that it took him over three hours to get to the fallen Towers from Long Island.

Sam is the only member of Ladder Company 403 who still works at the station from the crew that was on duty that day, and after things returned to a semblance of normalcy, he was promoted to commanding that station. Standing a safe distance away, he watches men in HAZMAT suits attend to the patient while he continues to replay in his mind the carnage and destruction he witnessed on that September morning.

After working on the now-comatose man, an EMT prepares him for transport to Mount Sinai Hospital while another technician removes his hazardous materials headgear.

Confused, Captain Lincoln stops the man. "What's going on?" he asks. "Does he have Ebola or not?"

As the emergency technician removes his HAZMAT suit, he says, "We don't know what's going on, Captain. He doesn't have a fever, and he looks like someone beat him up. It doesn't look like Ebola to us, but we're still going to need to quarantine this place until we can determine what it is. By the way, we can't ID him; he's not carrying any identifying papers."

Lincoln furrows his brow. "No ID, huh?"

"No, sir. Nothing but this gold coin. He was clutching it in his right hand. It looks old, like maybe from ancient Rome or something."

The Tech opens his gloved hand to show the coin to Lincoln, who grabs it from him.

"Are you kidding me?" exclaims Lincoln. "This is a gold aureus from the Roman Empire! Where the hell could he have gotten this?"

"Sir, you shouldn't be holding that. It could be contaminated."

"It's okay, son. I don't think it's dangerous." Lincoln puts the coin into his pocket and looks over at the mysterious stranger, studying the John Doe for a long moment.

While the man is being lifted into the emergency vehicle, Captain Lincoln glances at his watch and notes that it's now almost 7:15 a.m. Stepping away from the others, he grabs his cell phone and makes a private call. Then, he rejoins the crowd and directs his men to return to the station. He also informs the police officers and Homeland Security personnel still milling about that he is ordering 9/11 Memorial Park to be quarantined and closed to the public until further notice.

Looking around, Sam is not surprised when he

sees the familiar logos of local TV stations in the distance. It never takes long for the TV video trucks from competing stations to converge at news sites like swarming locusts. Scurrying around in organized confusion, the media crews work quickly to release their trucks' satellite dishes on antenna masts that poke into the sky like newly-sprouted seedlings reaching for the morning sun. Captain Lincoln knows he will have to make a public statement about the morning's event, so he prepares himself to speak with the reporters before returning to the firehouse.

"This is Skip Larson with WPIX. As our city slept this morning, 9/11 Memorial Park was placed under quarantine, and the entire area is now shut down. Tourists that have already begun to line up are being told the site is closed. An unidentified man, possibly infected with the Ebola virus, was found unconscious at the South Pool by NYPD officers in the early morning hours. EMTs responded in full HAZMAT gear and transported the man to Mount Sinai Hospital, the closest facility with the proper containment facilities for a disease of that nature. I questioned Captain Sam Lincoln from Ladder 403, but he had no comment on the matter, except to say that there will be a press conference after initial test results are released on the John Doe. Captain Lincoln does not believe the man has Ebola, but he stated that all precautions need to be taken until there is a definitive diagnosis.

"I will be at the press conference at Ladder Company 403's stationhouse to report on the results. Let's hope the tests show that the John Doe did not have Ebola.

"This is Skip Larson, on the case for you and News 11."

Sitting together on straight-backed chairs, Jack and Didi Stenhouse are bundles of nerves. They have been in the Lower East Side office of Dr. Gabriel Stratt for a while now, and they are getting impatient. Jack is particularly irritated; he can't stop fidgeting in his chair. The longer the fertility doctor takes to study the couple's test results, the higher Jack's anxiety level climbs. Not for the first time, he wonders, *What the hell is he waiting for?*

Finally, Jack can contain himself no longer. "Come on, Doc!" he blurts out. "The suspense is killin' me! What do those reports say?"

Stratt looks up over the files and pauses. Looking at the people before him, he notes that Didi is nervous, and Jack is, well, annoyed, so he says, "Mr. Stenhouse, we know you had a vasectomy over fifteen years ago. Now what has happened here is rare, but it does occur." He pauses again to look down at his notes, but when he looks up, he senses that Jack is about to jump over the desk, so he quickly adds, "Your vas deferens have regenerated."

Jack sighs and rolls his eyes. Damn these guys. They always use big words to impress others. "You know, Doc, I'm a simple man," he states in his usual, abrupt manner. "Just tell me in plain English. And call me Jack."

Nodding, the doctor walks over to two four-foot-high diagrams on the far wall. The one on the right shows the internal male reproductive organs, and the one on the left shows the female reproductive organs. Pointing at the male diagram, he says, "Right here, Jack. These are the vas deferens. When these tubes were cut years ago, your semen had nowhere to go. When the vas deferens are blocked, semen production slowly dwindles, and that system goes into hibernation. But the human body is quite adaptive." Returning to his desk, he reclaims his seat and continues. "Now typically, over time, this shutdown becomes permanent, and the severing of those tubes cannot be reversed. However, in some cases, the tubes spontaneously regenerate and reconnect themselves. From what I have observed in your case, this reversal occurred about a year ago, give or take a few months. Your body reacted positively to the reopening of the tubes, and semen production resumed. Now, it took quite a while to produce enough semen to allow you to impregnate successfully..." The doctor stops because he sees that Jack is sitting on the edge of his chair, clutching his wife's hand tightly and staring at him in shock. "But Jack," he continues slowly, "you are now fertile, and you have been for some time. Your sperm count isn't high, but it's high enough. I assume you and your wife have had unprotected sex recently, because she is now pregnant."

Gasps erupt from both Jack and Didi, but Jack soon recovers and leans over to give Didi a kiss. "Better hope it's a girl," he whispers. "I don't think you could handle two of me." When Didi responds with a grin that could light up a room, Jack turns back to the doctor. "Is this normal, Doc?"

"It's rare, but it does happen; it isn't abnormal. If your surgeon was a little careless, well, the body can be quite ingenious. Mr. Stenhouse, you're going to be a father, and it's obviously something you haven't planned. We offer counseling services that you and your wife can take advantage of, if you so choose. Now, Mrs. Stenhouse," the doctor continues, directing his attention to Didi, "you're about eight to ten weeks pregnant. I want to start you on a prenatal vitamin and schedule you for monthly checkups. Also, while you're here, I'd like to do a sonogram to make sure everything is progressing satisfactorily. Would you like to see your baby?"

Didi only nods her head, unable to respond because of the tears that are flowing down her cheeks.

"Good," says the doctor, rising from his chair. "I'll get one of my assistants to accompany you and your husband to our examination room. Mr. Stenhouse, do you want to seek counseling?"

Jack glances at Didi, then turns to Dr. Stratt. "No, Doc, I'm good. We're both good."

Smiling, the doctor pats Jack's shoulder and leaves the room.

When they're alone, Jack turns to his wife. "I'm sorry, Didi. I didn't think I could ever have children. When you took that home pregnancy test, I... I just hope you'll forgive me for having doubts about being the father. I love you awful."

"I love you, too, Jack. I always will."

A few minutes later, a technician beckons them

Frank A. Ruffolo

from the doorway.

"Let's go see our kid!" Jack announces happily.

The mystery man, now in a glass-enclosed isolation room at Mount Sinai Hospital, is being tended by a team of hooded doctors and nurses. When time passes and there is no improvement, the man's life signs deteriorate, and he dies.

After the attending physician declares the time of death, a nurse hands him the results of the patient's blood tests. Leaving his protective gear in the isolation room, the doctor takes the results to two NYPD officers who have been waiting in the hallway. Minutes later, Captain Lincoln speaks to the reporters still gathered at the South Pool.

"Ladies and gentlemen," says Lincoln, "I regret to inform you that our John Doe died a few minutes ago. Mercifully, his blood tests confirm that he was not infected with a contagious disease; his death was caused by acute arsenic poisoning.

"It seems that this man was murdered."

CHAPTER TWO

Rivetted by the fuzzy image on the screen, Jack and Didi stare wide-eyed while the ultrasound technician searches for her target—their growing baby. When she finds it, the specialist explains that their baby's fingers and toes are developing nicely, the eyelids are forming, and the heart is beating. Everything looks fine.

While mother and father continue to watch the moving image, Jack's phone suddenly rings and spoils the moment.

"Ugh. Sorry, Babe," says Jack, moving away from the examination table to answer the call. With the phone to his ear, he says brusquely, "Stenhouse here. Spill it." He listens for a moment and replies, "Yeah? I'll be there in forty-five. Gotta drop my wife off. Okay, I'll go right to the morgue."

Jack looks back at the screen while pocketing his phone. "Hey, Dee!" he declares with a wide smile. "He looks like me!"

Still on the table, Didi rolls her eyes while wiping away fresh tears. "Who was on the phone, Babe?"

"That was work. We gotta go; bad guys never take a rest."

After the technician ends the session, she leaves

the room to confirm Didi's next appointment, and Jack helps Didi off the table. While she adjusts her clothes behind a privacy screen, the doctor stops in to check on his new patients. "Did you see your baby?" he asks.

"Yeah! It was awesome!" responds Jack.

Grasping Jack's hand, the doctor draws him close. "Let me know if you need counseling," he whispers. "It'll be on me. Call anytime."

When Didi emerges from behind the screen, the doctor says, "I have some information I'd like to share with you before you leave. It shouldn't take more than five minutes. I also want to give you instructions and brochures that you need to read, some samples of prenatal vitamins, and a prescription."

Nodding their heads, the couple follows Dr. Stratt back to his office.

Later, on the way to Didi's boutique, the expectant parents can't stop talking about their happy news. When Didi begins to list all the things they have to do before the baby arrives, Jack laughs and tells her to slow down. "One thing at a time," he says.

After dropping Didi off at the boutique, he continues on to the morgue. On the way, he can't help thinking about the baby, but he knows he must concentrate on work, so to force himself to switch into work mode, he replays his recent phone conversation in his head before he walks into the autopsy room. When he sees the Medical Examiner hovering over the John Doe's body like a vulture feasting on his afternoon meal, he knows the day's pleasant thoughts have been thoroughly replaced.

"Doc," calls Jack. "Tell me what's going on with this guy. Looks like someone beat him up pretty good."

Dr. Ghoshin looks up over a pair of magnifying lenses like a high school librarian addressing a noisy student. "Mornin', Detective. Our subject showed up at the South Pool of the Trade Towers Memorial this morning. When they found him, he was unconscious and covered in vomit. The cops are trying to figure out how he got there without anyone noticing."

"Who responded to the call?"

"Ladder Company 403. They initially thought he had Ebola, but turns out it was arsenic poisoning. I'm calling it a murder. I don't think anyone would intentionally kill themselves this way; too messy. Besides, according to the initial blood tests, there's enough arsenic in his system to kill a horse."

Jack stares at the body lying in front of him. "Any ID on this guy?"

Ghoshin shakes his head. "No. I sent his fingerprints down to the First. They're working on them as we speak."

Knowing that there's nothing for him to do at this point, Jack says, "Okay, Doc. Let us know if you find anything unusual. I'm heading to the station now." Before leaving, he takes a photo of the unknown man.

Earlier, when Jack arrived at the morgue, he took advantage of one of the privileges of being a New York

City cop and left his red Road Runner double-parked outside the building with its blue light spinning on the dash. Now, as he climbs back into his car, he grimaces as he buckles up. "Crap!" he mutters under his breath. "Now that the Big Apple's fully awake, my ride to work's gonna make a stock car racer cringe." Sighing deeply, he starts up the beast, gives his usual two quick beeps, and is at the First Police Precinct in twenty minutes.

As the blue morning sky peeks between the tall buildings around the police station, Jack makes his way up to his desk in the Homicide Division, where he's greeted by his teammates, Detective Allison Giancarlo, and Sergeants John Burley and Hector Gomez.

"Hey, Jack!" calls Allison. "How'd it go with Didi?"

Jack gives his partner a sly smile. "Well, apparently, my vasectomy failed." Seeing the look of surprise on his partner's face, he adds, "I'm gonna be a father, Allison! Who the hell knew that could happen after all these years? Guess I won't be buying condoms for a while!"

With a squeal of delight, Allison hugs Jack while others around them laugh at his condom comment.

"Holy shit, guys!" shouts Sergeant John Burley, unable to resist a friendly jab. "There's another Stenhouse on the way! We're in deep kimchee now!"

Jack replies to the tease with a middle finger

aside his nose. "Okay, you had your fun," he says with mock seriousness. "Now, let's get to work. Any word on the fingerprints from the 9/11 Memorial guy?"

"No, he's a ghost," replies Hector Gomez.

"A ghost? What the hell?" frowns Jack, who hates metaphors. "Come on; spill it."

"The guy shouldn't exist. His fingerprints say he's Stanley Cummings, but Stanley Cummings was the owner of Precious Coins and Bullion. That was the fancy metals company and storage place for gold and other valuables that was located at the World Trade Center, on one of the lower floors of the South Tower. Cummings was supposed to have died in the building when the Tower collapsed."

"Hmm...that's odd," states Jack. "I dropped by the morgue this morning. The John Doe was roughed up pretty good, and the M.E. says he was poisoned."

"Well, I guess he wasn't very well liked," says Gomez. "The M.E. called here with more info after you left. He says the victim had contusions on his face, a broken nose, and three bruised ribs. Ghoshin sent his clothes and fingerprints here so Forensics can check them out."

"Wasn't Cummings the coin dealer whose inventory was never found after the Towers collapsed?" asks Allison. "I remember hearing rumors that over ten million dollars in gold and precious metals were lost. If that guy really was Cummings, by the way he died and how badly he was beaten up, maybe someone out there is still looking for his stuff."

"How's this for irony?" interjects Sergeant John Burley. "Ladder Company 403 responded to the Tower's collapse back then, and also this morning. On 9/11, that station lost most of their men in the South Tower, including their Captain, Troy Walsh. The current Captain, Sam Lincoln, is the only member of the station who was there at the time. Lincoln stayed at the scene this morning to announce the quarantine of the Memorial to the press, and then he went to the hospital to check on the victim."

Jack turns to the sergeants. "Okay, John. You and Hector go down to Ladder 403 and interview Lincoln and the attending EMTs. Ally, I assume we have an address on the Cummings family?"

"Yeah. His widow and two kids live on Long Island, in West Hempstead."

"Well, I guess we're headed out to the Island, then."

A short time later, Sergeant John Burley parks his car a short distance away from the crowd of reporters and satellite TV trucks gathered in front of the Ladder Company 403 firehouse. John is relatively new to Homicide, having worked his way up to his current position after six years on the beat. From their vantage point near the car, he and Sergeant Gomez can hear Captain Sam Lincoln providing the latest details about the incident at the South Pool. As they near the station, they listen as he states that he is releasing the quarantine so the thousands of patiently and impatiently waiting tourists can enter the Memorial area.

Inside one of the firetruck bays, the men come upon a group of firehouse crewpersons standing around, also listening to the captain.

"Hello," says Hector, as the officers flash their badges. "I'm Sergeant Gomez, and this is Sergeant Burley. We're from the First Precinct, and we need to talk to the EMT who treated the John Doe."

"That would be me," responds Michael Riley, stepping to the front of the group.

"Great. Is there a place where we can talk away from all this hoopla?"

Following the firefighter, Gomez and Burley enter a room inside the stationhouse containing several dining tables, a large flat screen TV, and a pool table. When the firefighter indicates one of the tables, the men take their seats. Then, Gomez turns on his recorder, and Burley clicks on a phone app to take notes.

"Okay, your name is?" asks Gomez.

"Michael Riley."

"Mr. Riley, how long have you been with Ladder Company 403?"

"I've been here for two years. But call me Mike. My father is Mr. Riley."

"Okay, Mike," responds Burley with a suppressed smile. "What was your first impression of the patient this morning? Did you find anything unusual?"

Michael leans back as he collects his thoughts. "Well, we were told that it might be an Ebola event, so we were pretty well covered up."

Gomez is confused and leans forward. "Hold on, 'we'?"

"Yeah, my partner, Sally Strom, was assisting me. She was in charge of all the emergency gear and supplies while I tended to the patient."

Gomez rises. "I'll go find Strom," he says. "John, you continue here."

"Okay, Mike, please continue," urges Burley.

Riley is calm and professional as he recounts the morning's events. "Well, Sergeant, I cleaned off the patient's face and took his vital signs and found that he didn't have a fever. He was bleeding from his nose and gums, however, and his breathing was shallow. His clothes were torn and covered in vomit and blood, which I assumed were his."

"Okay. Did you notice anything else?"

"Yeah. He had denim overalls and a tee shirt on, and he looked like he just came off the farm. Quite odd for a person in downtown Manhattan."

Burley doesn't look up as he enters some notes into his phone. "Okay, anything else that caught your attention?"

Mike thinks a bit and then opens his eyes wide. "Yeah, yeah!" he blurts out. "He was holding an old gold coin in his hand! I showed it to Captain Lincoln, and he said it was from ancient Rome."

That piques Burley's interest, and he looks up from his phone. "Coin, huh? And where is that coin?"

Shaking his head, Riley says, "I don't know. Captain Lincoln took it, and that was the last time I saw it. After that, we prepared our patient for transport, and left."

Burley's eyebrows shoot up to the top of his forehead. "Lincoln took the coin? The guy could have had Ebola! Was the captain protected?"

"No, he wasn't," shrugs Mike, "but I told him the patient had no fever and that I didn't think it was Ebola. He didn't seem to care that he wasn't protected."

Burley types more notes and saves them on his phone. "Thank you," he says to Riley. "If there's anything else you remember, please call us at the First."

Riley nods, and Burley hands him a business card. Outside of the room, Burley asks the first firefighter he encounters if he knows where Sergeant Gomez is, and he's directed to the stationhouse garage. There, he finds Gomez near one of the pumper trucks, questioning Sally Strom, the other EMT at the scene.

"She had nothing, really," Burley says after Sally leaves. "Mostly routine EMT operating procedure stuff. Except she did say that Riley gave something to Captain Lincoln."

"Yeah, I know," says Burley. "He said our victim had a gold coin in his hand. Let's go find Lincoln."

An hour later, Jack's Road Runner pulls into the driveway of a Cape Cod home on Woodfield Road in Long Island's West Hempstead, one of several bedroom communities near the borders of Nassau County and the New York City borough of Queens. Built in the fifties, the house is fronted by a brick porch shaded by a green aluminum awning behind rows of cheerful azalea bushes blooming in a rainbow of colors.

As Jack and Allison step up to the porch, a woman opens the inner wooden door before they can knock. Staring at them quizzically through the still closed screen door, she asks, "Can I help you?"

Stenhouse and Giancarlo display their badges and ID cards. "I'm Detective Stenhouse, and this is Detective Giancarlo," says Jack, pointing to his partner. "We're homicide detectives with NYPD's First Precinct. Are you Mrs. Stanley Cummings?"

"Yes," she responds warily, "but what do the New York City police want with me?"

"Mrs. Cummings, we'd like to talk with you about your late husband," answers Jack. "May we come in? We won't take up too much of your time."

"Oh, my. You want to talk about Stanley?" asks Mrs. Cummings with one hand resting on her chest in shocked surprise. "Ah, sure. Come on in."

The detectives follow the stunned woman down a carpeted hallway. On the way, Jack notes that Mrs. Cummings is wearing a fashionable blouse over skintight designer jeans and that her shoes and jewelry look expensive.

Entering the kitchen, Mrs. Cummings motions for the detectives to sit down at a corner table. Looking around, they noticed that the room looks as though it was recently renovated. The floor is dark brown hardwood, and there are sleek mahogany cabinets, marble countertops, a large stainless steel sink, and matching slate appliances.

Eliminating the customary niceties, Jack begins his line of questioning with his usual abruptness. "Mrs. Cummings, I know it's been over fourteen years since that terrible morning of 9/11, but we'd like to know if you can identify this person." Jack turns his phone toward Sarah.

When Cummings sees the image, she gasps, and her hand flies to her mouth. "THAT'S STAN!" she shouts, with tears welling up in her eyes. "But... My God, how did you get... Where did you get this picture? Why is he in that condition? What the hell is going on?"

"Stanley was found at the South Pool of the Twin Towers Memorial this morning."

"But...he died fourteen years ago! What are you saying? Wait a minute... Oh, my God! Was he the man on the news? Does he have Ebola? No, wait. What is happening here?"

Ever the stoic, Jack plunges onward, ignoring Sarah's questions. "Mrs. Cummings, it appears that Stanley did not die in the South Tower. That's why we're here. He didn't die all those years ago, but he did die this morning. Not from Ebola, but from being poisoned."

Sarah gasps again and turns pale. Rising from her chair, she walks over to the sink for a glass of water.

"Have you had any contact with your husband

since 9/11, Mrs. Cummings?" asks Allison softly. "Is there anything you'd like to share with us?"

Sarah closes her eyes and takes a drink of water to compose herself while Jack and Allison glance at each other and wait. After a few moments, she sits back down at the table.

"No," replies Sarah, looking down at her hands. "We thought he died. We had a funeral for him and everything, and we tried to get on with our lives. The boys are away at college now." Sarah's eyes suddenly go wide, and she looks up at the detectives. "Oh, now, wait a minute. Are you implying that I had something to do with him showing up today? We went through hell! If it wasn't for the victim relief package we got as a family, we would have lost this house!" Sarah starts to cry. "I don't believe this," she says, shaking her head. "Do we have to go through another funeral? Why didn't he ever call me if he was alive all these years?"

Jack looks at Allison, and then at Mrs. Cummings. "Mrs. Cummings..."

"Sarah. Call me Sarah."

"Okay, Sarah. We'll leave you now so you can process this. Take my card. If you remember anything that was unusual during the time you thought he was dead, please call us. We'll let ourselves out."

Before they leave, Allison turns to look back at Sarah. "We know this is a shock. Is there anyone you can call to help you through this?"

"Yes, I think I need to call someone. This is so unreal."

The detectives exit through a door in the kitchen that leads out onto the driveway. When they reach their car, Jack looks at the house to make sure no one is looking through the window. "Allison," he asks, "did you see the rock on her hand, and that watch? And look," he nods toward the garage, "she has a Porsche SUV, brand new."

"Yeah, I saw them," Allison answers, "and I also noticed her new kitchen. Damn, she must have cleaned up with that victim's fund."

"Bullshit," retorts Jack. "We need to dig deeper. Let's check the financials on her and her sons. Find out what colleges they attend."

Inside the kitchen, Sarah picks up her cell phone and dials a familiar number as Jack backs out of the driveway. Nervous and upset, she paces while she waits for the call to connect. When it is answered, she screeches, "The cops just left my house! They were asking about Stan!"

CHAPTER THREE

Having finished his remarks on the morning's events, Sam Lincoln is now hurriedly walking away from the reporters while purposefully ignoring the questions the nosy news teams are shouting at him. As he approaches the fire truck bays, NYPD Sergeants Burley and Gomez step in front of him to block his path. "Captain Lincoln," says Hector, "we need to speak with you."

"Yes, Sergeant...Gomez?" Lincoln says, reading the sergeant's proffered ID badge.

"My partner and I are investigating the John Doe found at the South Pool this morning. EMT Michael Riley told us you were there with him."

"Yes, as Commander of this unit, I was monitoring the scene."

Gomez tries to get a read on the captain but senses nothing out of the ordinary. "EMT Riley told us the victim was holding a gold coin and that he gave the coin to you. Where is that coin now, sir, and why did you take it from him? Weren't you concerned that it might be contaminated? At the time, it was thought the victim might have Ebola."

"Yeah, wow. I forgot about that," responds Captain Lincoln quickly. "Mike told me there was no fever, so I felt confident I'd be okay. I put the coin into my overcoat and dropped it in my desk drawer when I got back here. I have it in my quarters. Come with me."

The sergeants follow the Captain through the firehouse and up a flight of stairs to the second-floor living area where his private quarters are located. The room is plain but functional, with a bed, a desk, two flags—Old Glory and the New York State flag—on a mottled-green vinyl tile floor that has seen better days.

Lincoln opens the center drawer of his metal desk and hands a gold coin to Gomez. "Here ya go."

Gomez takes the coin and looks up at the captain. "Riley said you knew this was from the Roman Empire."

"Yeah, I'm an amateur numismatist," Lincoln replies with a shrug of his shoulders. "I knew it was an Aureus, a coin that was issued during the Roman Empire. It's quite valuable. I was going to hand it over to you guys, but during the confusion this morning, I forgot."

"We identified the John Doe as Stanley Cummings," interjects Burley. "He was the owner of a rare coin dealership that was located on a lower level of the South Tower of the World Trade Center. He was reported missing after the Towers fell and was listed as one of the people killed on 9/11. You were there that day. Any thoughts?"

Sam closes his eyes to search through memories that continue to pop up in his dreams. *Okay,* he thinks. *Remain cool. Just get this interview over with and everything will be fine.* Looking at the officers, he says,

"Yeah, I remember. Weeks after we finally got down to the lower levels, we found some coins and bullion that were in undamaged boxes under tons of debris. We brought them out, but I heard reports later on that millions of other valuables were still in there. If that guy was in the Tower that day, you think he got out and didn't tell anyone?"

"That's what we're going to find out," replies Gomez. "I'll need to take this coin as evidence."

Sam Lincoln waits in his room until the detectives have descended the steps outside. Then, he takes out his cell phone and dials a number he committed to memory.

"Look," he says urgently, "we need to talk."

Back at the First, Burley and Gomez complete paperwork while they wait for detectives Stenhouse and Giancarlo to return from their ride to Long Island. Gomez also uses the time to review new evidence from Stanley Cummings' clothes, while Burley researches the financials on Mrs. Cummings.

About noon, Jack and Allison finally walk into the Homicide Department. Allison stops to get two cups of coffee while Jack greets the sergeants at their desks.

"Sorry we're late," says Jack. "We got stuck on the L.I.E. Traffic never eases up around here. Any news on Stan Cummings—either the dead one or the alive one?"

"We got a lead on where Stan was probably hiding out," says Gomez. "Our forensic geeks worked on Cummings' clothes and found traces of *Carex barrattii* and *Vaccinium corymbosum* on his sneakers."

Jack takes a cup of coffee from Allison and shakes his head with annoyance. "Come on," he whines. "What's with all the Latin bullshit I'm getting hit with today? First Didi's doctor, and now you. Plain English, will ya?"

Gomez chuckles. "The first is a grass-like perennial also known as Barratt's sedge. The other is a type of blueberry. They grow together in the Pine Barrens in southern New Jersey, most likely in and around the town of Hammonton. The town calls itself the Blueberry Capital of the World."

"Oh, I know it," interjects Allison. "We took the kids out there last year. There's a large you-pick blueberry farm there, but it's not close. It took us almost two hours to get there."

Thinking quickly, Jack makes a decision and barks out orders. "Okay," he says. "Allison, contact the Hammonton police and tell them we'll be there in the morning to snoop around. Gomez, check the records of Ladder Company 403. See if you can locate anyone else besides Sam Lincoln who worked on the cleanup after 9/11. Find out if they have any info on the coin dealer and what may have been found under the South Tower."

Sergeant Burley looks up over his computer screen. "Jack, Mrs. Cummings got a fat check from the 9/11 fund, and about 200 g's from life insurance policies. She must have invested well because she's now among the one percent. It doesn't look like she has any other income, either. She isn't employed outside of the home now and wasn't in the past. And both her kids are going to Harvard. That expense alone would choke a horse."

"Good job," says Jack with a thumbs-up. "Now we're getting somewhere. Cummings survived the attack on the Towers and must have taken the gold with him, wherever he went. His wife is now living in fat city, so someone must know what he did—maybe his wife or employees of his business. Or maybe the first responders who found some of the gold."

"Yeah," chirps Allison. "But he must have pissed somebody off along the way. Someone with a grudge or someone who's looking for a bunch of their gold."

Jack finishes his coffee and throws the Styrofoam cup at a small garbage can, but misses. "Never said I was good at B-ball," he mutters. Looking up, he points at his team. "Okay, guys. John, you and Hector start gathering the names of surviving members of Ladder Company 403 and get pictures and bios of the ones who died and were never found after the attack. Then check on everyone who worked with Cummings." Picking his cup off the floor, he throws it into the garbage can.

"Jack," interrupts Hector, "I almost forgot. Stanley Cummings had this in his hand when he died. I got it from Captain Lincoln at the firehouse. He said it was from the Roman Empire."

Hector hands the gold coin to Jack, who stares at the brightly shining object. "Must be part of the stash," he muses. "Ally, see if you can get a list of the inventory Cummings had at his business before the attack. I know a guy with a pawn shop near Didi's boutique on the Lower East Side. He deals in rare coins. I'll show this to him and try to pick his brain. Allison, you and I are going to Jersey early in the morning, so meet me here at 6 a.m. so we can try to beat the traffic. After we return, we'll meet again as a group and update each other." Jack puts his hand on Allison's shoulder. "I'll drive tomorrow, and it won't take us two hours. Trust me." Jack slips the coin into a small plastic zip lock bag from his desk and dismisses the group.

On Jack's way off the floor, Lieutenant Nathaniel Conrad stops him. "Stenhouse," says his superior, "that reporter from WPIX is poking his nose into your case. He's coming here later today to get a statement. I'll try to brush him off with the ongoing investigation line, but he'll still snoop around. Oh, and the inspector got a call from the mayor. You're being watched on this one. Actually, we're all being watched. *Capeesh*?"

Jack frowns and lets out a low growl. "You mean Skippy's on the case? Fuck that bastard!"

Outside the building, Jack barely notices that it's a beautiful spring day in the Big Apple. The city's activity ebbs and flows like the tide, and as the traffic builds, he seamlessly negotiates the boulevards and avenues, the lifeblood of the city, on his way to Didi's boutique.

Congratulating himself on finding a parking spot right in front of the store, he jumps out of the car and pokes his head into the shop's doorway. Didi and her assistant, Sonia, are busy, so when Didi sees her husband, she throws him a kiss and returns to attending her customers. Always happy to see his wife, Jack is upbeat as he heads to Carl's Coin and Pawn, three doors down from Didi's store.

Standing in front of the pawn shop, Jack rings the bell and waits to be let in. When he receives the answering buzz, Carl Falzone, a short, bald Sicilian, waves at Jack from behind the counter. "Hey, good buddy! How've you been? How's that lovely wife of yours?"

Shaking the owner's hand, Jack replies, "She's fine, Carl. In fact, we're pregnant!"

"Oh, hey, that's great! Congrats, my friend! But good God! You—a dad? Oh, are you looking for a nice gift for the new mom?"

"Always the salesman?" smiles Jack. "No, I'm not looking for a gift. Not yet, anyway. I'm here on official business. I need you to take a look at a gold coin." Jack removes the coin from his pocket and hands it to Carl in the plastic bag.

The pawn shop owner's eyes open wide as he studies the coin. "Huh, this is Tiberius Caesar. Oh, wow, it's an Aureus!" Jerking his head up, he says, "This thing was minted around 20 A.D, Jack, and it's worth about nine grand! Where did you get it?"

"Did you hear about the John Doe who shut down the Twin Towers Memorial today?"

When Carl nods, Jack says, "He had it in his hand."

"No shit! These things are not common." Carl

continues to examine the coin until Jack holds out his hand.

"Look," says Jack, taking the coin back, to the dealer's dismay, "what I'm about to tell you cannot be repeated; not until we release more info."

"Okay. You know me, Jack. My lips are sealed."

Jack pauses slightly and then says, "That John Doe was Stan Cummings, the former owner of Precious Coins and Bullion."

Carl stares at Jack with his brows raised high, emphasizing his baldness. "That was the coin depository that was destroyed in the Tower! Millions of dollars' worth of gold was never recovered, and he died in there!"

"Yeah, well," replies Jack as he returns the coin to his inside jacket pocket, "he didn't die in there. Could this coin be part of that lost inventory?"

"Oh, for sure!" exclaims Carl with vigorous nods of his head. "They dealt in rare and valuable stuff. I even sold him some coins. But... He was at the Memorial today? How the hell did he get out of the Tower?"

Jack shrugs his shoulders. "Who knows?"

In a park on Long Island, Sarah Cummings sits astride the horse she rented at the New York Equestrian Center at Hempstead Lake State Park. Riding out of the paddock, she directs the horse onto tree-lined Eagle Avenue, then moseys him over to the footbridge over Southern State Parkway. The clomping sound of the horse's steel horseshoes on the asphalt and concrete changes to a low thump as she turns the horse onto a bridle path leading into the park. She needs to speak in private today, and she believes the horse trail along the quiet lake will do nicely.

Sarah leads her steed to the trail's entrance, a sort of tunnel created by towering trees on both sides, with leafy branches arching overhead. Keith O'Toole is already halfway down the path, waiting for Sarah on a black mare.

The horses seem pleased to see each other. They nicker softly, their chuffing blending into the pleasant sounds of warbling songbirds, buzzing bees, and muffled engine noises coming from cars traveling under the nearby highway overpass.

Keith automatically leans over his horse to give Sarah a welcoming kiss, but when he sees Sarah's expression, he pulls back in alarm. "What's wrong?"

Sarah steadies herself on her swaying horse. "I have bad news. Stan showed up at the South Pool of the Twin Towers Memorial this morning."

Keith rears back in shock, nearly falling off his horse. "He was the John Doe? What the hell?!"

"Yeah, but that's not all!" Sarah replies in a voice cracking with emotion. "The police were at my house!"

"Sarah," Keith says, lowering his voice to calm Sarah down, "no need to worry. If that was really Stan, they're just following up and checking out his family."

Sarah begins to cry, which quickly leads to loud sobbing. "But...but, what if they think I, or we, were involved?" she wails. "I don't know what to do! I'm going crazy with worry, Keith!"

Keith maneuvers his horse closer to hers and reaches out to grab her hand. "Look," he says, trying to catch her eye, "we have nothing to worry about. Just remain calm. I'm always nearby. Come on; let's take it slow. Let's talk about how we're going to tell the boys we're getting married."

Sarah wipes away her tears and sighs. Changing the conversation into the more pleasant topic of the couple's impending wedding seems to make the worries of the world melt away. For the time being, anyway.

Turning her horse around, Sarah urges him into a slow walk alongside Keith's mare.

Business is good at Didi's boutique, and Jack has to wait while she takes care of the last few customers of the day.

"Why are you here so early?" asks Didi as she rings up a sale. Jack usually picks his wife up when the store is about to close.

"I was checking with Carl on a lead. If I drive back to the First now, I'd get there at checkout time, so I decided to stay here."

After the customers leave, Didi turns to her husband and gives him a big, wet kiss. With a coy smile, she says, "It may be premature, Honey, but we need to start thinking about a nursery."

"Why? We don't know if it's a boy or a girl yet, so

how can we decorate a nursery now?"

Didi grins at her bewildered husband. "We could do it in yellows or greens, Jack. I don't want to know if it's a boy or girl before it's born. I want to be surprised."

"Hmm. Okay, Babe. It'll be our surprise." Jack hugs Didi and then steps back, holding her at arm's length. "Hey, are your tits getting bigger? Better be careful; you may fall over."

Didi ignores Jack's tease and pulls him closer. "You always know how to flatter a girl. Let's go home. If you're really nice tonight, I'll let you have a closer look at how big they really are."

As Didi releases herself from Jack's arms, she catches the eye of her assistant, Sonia, who winks as she hangs up the last of the clothing from the dressing room. "For a second there," Sonia says, "I thought I was going to have to throw water on you two."

Jack watches his wife as she and Sonia go through their nightly routine of shutting down the boutique, his thoughts turning from the front bumper of a '58 Caddy to an ancient gold coin.

At the headquarters of New York's First Police Precinct, Homicide Lieutenant Nathaniel Conrad and television news reporter Peter "Skip" Larson are conversing in Conrad's office when the lieutenant abruptly rises from his desk and walks around to where the reporter is sitting. Staring down at the unpopular newsman, Conrad glares at him with stern authority.

"Mr. Larson," he asserts, "we are prepared to work with the media on this case, and we'll release as much information as possible. However, this is an ongoing homicide investigation. We will only provide information when we feel it is appropriate. I will be your contact person in this matter. All statements about this case will come from my office. If you interfere with my investigative team, you will be dealt with swiftly. Do I make myself clear?"

Leaning back in his chair, Skip masks his trademark attitude of unruffled and tenacious control with a warm smile. "That's crystal clear, Lieutenant. I'll work through your office." Standing, the reporter shakes hands with Conrad and leaves.

Down the hall, Skip waits at the elevator bank for the car to reach his floor. When the door opens, he enters and turns around with the same earnest smile. However, as soon as the doors close, the smile disappears, and he mutters menacingly, "Yeah, right. I'll talk to whomever I please. This story is sure to get me an anchor desk."

CHAPTER FOUR

Allison Giancarlo dressed in a hurry today, so it's a good thing her work outfit is usually the same: a pantsuit with a plain, unadorned blouse. Allison prefers the unisex look when she's working, and only lets her feminine side show when she's with her husband and family. Pantsuits and short black hair keep things simple for the job she does.

Nestled on Allison's hip is a Glock 41, even though standard caliber issue for her department is a 9mm or .40 S&W. Allison is far from standard. She was the best marksmen in her academy class, and the .45 caliber Glock is her weapon of choice.

Sitting at her desk, Allison checks her watch and sees that it now registers 6:18 in the morning, but Jack is nowhere to be found. As she takes another sip of coffee, she wonders, *Where the hell are you, Jack? You're usually here by now, waiting for me.*

As if summoned, Jack suddenly appears in the department. Walking slowly, he heads toward his desk with a cup of black coffee in one hand and a can of Coke in another.

"Too much bourbon last night?" quips Allison with a smirk.

Jack's mirrored sunglasses are doing little to

shield the florescent lights from this morning's painfully bloodshot eyes. "Too much Didi," he mumbles as he sips his Coke and takes a gulp of coffee. "Let's get going before the traffic gets screwy."

"Well, talk about screwy," grins Allison, "you better get your Didi-time in now. All of that's gonna change in a few months. After the baby's born, you won't have real time for each other for at least seventeen years."

At Allison's comments, Jack extends a middle finger, rubs the side of his nose, and tosses the half-empty can of soda into the trash.

Watching Jack's can sail into the garbage can, Allison sighs and retrieves the offending item to place it into the recycle bin instead, which causes Jack to roll his eyes at his partner's continual attempts to make him environmentally-friendly. Although Jack and Allison torment each other mercilessly, they actually enjoy working with each other, and their fellow team members know this.

Sam Lincoln chose a booth near the front window of the coffee shop around the corner from the fire station for the urgent meeting he called.

While he waits for Keith O'Toole to get his coffee, he looks out the window and sees a bicyclist bizarrely dressed as Darth Vader riding by on a ten-speed. Sam smirks, for he knows that no matter how outlandishly the man is dressed, no one on the New York sidewalk will give him a second look.

When Keith finally slides into the booth with a latte and a muffin, Sam sees the worry lines on his companion's face, but he plunges ahead anyway. What he has to say is too important.

"Keith, we got a problem," he declares gravely.

"That's a fucking understatement, if I ever heard one," retorts Keith with a sharp shake of his head. "Sarah almost had a nervous breakdown yesterday. The cops went to see her. What the hell happened with Stan?"

"Fuck if I know," Sam grumbles into his coffee. "Look, we need to meet with the others to get our stories straight."

Keith puts down his latte. "I agree," he says. "I'll get the ball rolling and get back to you."

Sam taps his fingers nervously on the table. "Look, Keith. I think this is going to go south real quick."

"Come on," says Keith confidently. "They won't find anything."

Sam is not convinced. He stares hard at Keith over his coffee cup. "Yeah, well, one of us killed Stan," he states in a low voice, "and it wasn't me. Be prepared to leave town. Just in case." Grabbing his coffee, he leaves the table abruptly.

When Sam steps outside, he narrowly avoids being hit by Darth Vader, who is on a return mission past the coffee shop.

Inside, Keith remains seated at the booth. With his mind a whirlwind of conflicting thoughts, he stares blankly at the tabletop as if the solution to his problems could be found among the repeating pattern of the grain.

In the next state over, Jack and Allison have finally arrived in the town of Hammonton, and are now heading down Bellevue Avenue, a two-lane road lined with stores and small apartments. There are no concrete towers in this town, no skyscrapers. To the big city cops, it seems as if they've entered a land where time has stood still. When Allison closes her eyes, she can almost see a small boy running down the sidewalk rolling a steel hoop with a stick.

Turning onto East Central Avenue, Jack guides the Road Runner into the City Hall parking lot and cuts the engine. The officers look surprised by the government building in front of them. A long wooden porch and towering white columns make the building appear as if it were designed as a spacious southern plantation house instead of a functional administrative office.

Although Jack made great time getting to this small New Jersey town, the New York cops are still late for their meeting with Stuart Turner, Hammonton's Chief of Police. Walking quickly, they climb the steps to the front porch and push through the white double doors into a time warp. Around them are ornate crown molding, creaky hardwood floors, and a long counter with a swinging door. The room could easily be the set of a 1930s movie.

With sidewise glances at each other, they introduce themselves to the desk officer and then wait only a few minutes before the chief of police makes his way toward them.

"Mornin'. I'm Stuart Turner. What brings NYPD to Hammonton?"

Quickly sizing up the small-town chief, Jack notes that he's a tall, muscular man who looks more like a linebacker than a police officer. "Good morning," he says in reply, shaking the man's hand. "I'm Detective Stenhouse."

"I'm Detective Giancarlo," says Allison. "Is there a place where we can talk in private, sir?"

Scrutinizing the two city slickers, Turner smiles at them politely. "Sure," he says. "Follow me to my office."

Walking behind the chief, the group passes through a side door into City Hall, the headquarters of the town's police department. On the way, Jack and Allison glance again at each other when they hear how their footsteps resonate on the building's old wooden floors.

Hammonton is a small town of fewer than 15,000 residents. Not surprisingly, the entire population of this hamlet is less than half the number of the New York City police force. Commonly known as the Blueberry Capital of the World, the town is located in the Pine Barrens of New Jersey, a heavily forested area containing soil favorable for growing the town's famous product.

When the detectives enter Turner's office, they

have to squeeze around his desk to reach their chairs. The room is so tiny that it looks like it may have started life as a closet.

Turner seats himself heavily in his wooden chair and leans back to take the kinks out of his neck. "Okay," he says after a moment. "You said you want to talk about the man who died at the Manhattan Memorial. So talk."

Jack ignores the Chief's abruptness. He's accustomed to men who don't beat around the bush, being one of them himself.

"That incident yesterday at the Twin Towers Memorial points to your little town, sir," Jack begins. "We've been led here by certain evidence from the body. Here's a photo of the man at the Memorial. This is a small town, so we're hoping that you know most of the residents. Have you seen him before?"

Turner stares at the photograph of the dead man. "Yeah, I know this guy," he says. "It's Joe Stanley. He lives, or I guess I should now say he lived, out in the Barrens. He has...had, dammit...a small blueberry farm out there. He sold his harvest at our town's farmer's market for the last fourteen years. What happened? Who beat him up?"

"He was poisoned, and someone dumped him at the Memorial," responds Allison. "His name is Stanley Cummings. He was listed as one of the dead in the 9/11 attack at the World Trade Center. Did he file a report about an assault recently?"

"Stanley Cummings, huh? We knew him as Joe. A kind soul. We never heard one word from him," says

Turner. "I have no idea who would beat him up and kill him. And why the secret identity? Insurance? Cheating on his wife?"

"That's what we're here to find out," says Jack. "Stan was the owner-operator of a gold bullion depository in the lower concourse of the South Tower. Millions of dollars of precious coins were never recovered after the Tower fell, and it's been assumed all these years that they would never be recovered. However, we now believe that Stan got out somehow and that he took the stash with him. But to do that, he must have needed help; gold is pretty heavy. I figure he must have pissed off his crime partners over the years, so they ended up killing him."

"That seems plausible," says the chief.

"Can you take us to his farm? We want to look around. We'd also like to know when he purchased that farm and how he paid for it, and we're going to need a copy of any other records you may have on him."

"Sure, no problem. I'll have one of my officers get that info for you." Scratching his head, Turner adds sadly, "Damnation! Looks like big city crime has finally come to our little town. Never thought this day would come." As an afterthought, he says, "I'll take you to his place myself, unless you have an SUV or a four-wheel pickup. There are no paved roads out there."

With a sideways glance at Allison, Jack says to the chief, "Guess you're drivin', then."

"I got Shotgun!" calls Allison, causing Jack to lower his head and ask mockingly, "What are you, eight?"

Behind his desk, Turner rolls his eyes at the two supposedly sophisticated, big city cops.

Back in Manhattan, Sergeants Burley and Gomez have been working on digging up more information on the players in the Cummings case.

Neck deep in the last fourteen years of Sarah Cummings' bank statements and investments, Burley found that she received over $250,000 from a fund set up for the 9/11 victims' families, and $200,000 from a life insurance policy on Stanley. When he added those numbers to other data, he was surprised to discover that her current net worth totals about $2.5 million.

For his part, Sergeant Gomez has been working on the list of firefighters from Ladder Company 403. He put together the names of the nineteen who were lost at the South Tower, along with the names of six who survived that tragic time. He found that years later, three of the survivors died from various causes, all of which were attributed to the carcinogens they were exposed to during the search, rescue, and recovery operation, but three others are still alive: Salvatore Brusco, Keith O'Toole, and Captain Sam Lincoln. Gomez is trying to make appointments to interview O'Toole and Brusco.

While looking into the history of Ladder 403s involvement with 9/11, Gomez also stumbled upon the name of someone still alive who worked with Stanley Cummings at his World Trade Center business. When he contacted the man, he was in the hospital recovering from appendix surgery. The man said Stan was the only person who had access to the vaults, other than their clients with gold and other valuables stored at the company. He said the clients had to make an appointment before they could open their boxes. Several times, the clerk said, he saw a group of people from Kuwait at the company, and Stan told him they were members of the country's royal family. The man also said Stan supported local firefighters and many other charitable groups through his business. When Gomez asked him where he was on that terrible September morning, he said he was at home in New Jersey, getting ready to go to work. The man and his wife watched all of it unfold on television.

Allison is keeping the front passenger window open while Police Chief Stuart Turner maneuvers his SUV around potholes and ruts on the soggy dirt road in the Pine Barrens. She told Turner that she wants to catch whiffs of the forest's clean pine scent and hear the sounds of the birds challenging the four-wheeled-drive invader.

After a bumpy ride, the chief turns onto a small side path that ends in a clearing where a rustic log cabin and a black van sit adjacent to a field of blueberry bushes.

When Turner turns off the engine, everyone piles out of the car, with Jack the last to exit. The soft sounds made by shoes crushing pine needles and pine-cones does nothing to change the fact that there are no sounds of modern society here. Enveloped by the dense silence, Jack stares up at the trees.

"Quite a difference from the Big Apple, eh?" asks Stuart.

Jack nods as he studies the van alongside the house. "Is that Stan's?"

"Yeah, it's an AWD Mercedes Sprinter."

"Hmm...okay. Well, Stu, you should get your team out here to block this place off while they do forensics and crime scene analysis. This is out of our jurisdiction, so there would be way too much bullshit to get our New York guys out here."

"We're not like the First Precinct," notes Turner. "Hammonton doesn't have those kinds of resources. I'll have to call in the State Police, and then they'll take over the entire investigation."

Jack throws up his hands in frustration. "Politics, Stu, politics! It's all bullshit! Florida, New York, and even way out here?" He takes a deep breath to calm himself before continuing. "Okay, do what you have to do. Let me take a look at that van before we go inside."

Pulling out a pair of nitrile gloves, Jack walks toward the vehicle, stopping when a chipmunk scurries across his path. Smiling as it disappears as fast as it appeared, he reaches out a gloved hand to try the driver's door. When it opens, he reaches into his pocket for protective covers for his shoes.

With his hands and feet covered, Jack climbs into the van and reaches for the visors. Searching behind them, he pulls out the vehicle's keys and opens the glove box. Rummaging through the contents, he sees nothing of importance; just an insurance card and a registration form listed under the name of Joe Stanley, Stanley Cummings' alias. Twisting around, he looks into the back of the vehicle and notes that it is empty, save for spots of dirt and a few dried twigs and pine branches scattered across the floor.

Keys in hand, Jack turns back around in the seat to remove the protective coverings from his shoes so he can use them again in the log cabin. Then, he exits the vehicle.

"CSI will need these," he says, holding out the keys to Turner. The chief nods and removes a handkerchief from his pocket, spreading it out in his hand. When Jack drops the keys into the hanky, Turner folds the cloth around them and places the bundle into his pocket.

Together, the trio walks across a carpet of pine needles toward the covered front porch, all the while tracked by birds watching warily from the treetops.

"Go ahead inside," directs Chief Turner. "I'll call for CSI before I join you."

Stopping at the foot of the wooden steps, Allison and Jack put on their protective gear and then climb up to the porch. Lined up like sentinels gazing across the Barrens, are three old fashioned wicker chairs.

Reaching out, Jack tries the front door. It is locked, however, one of the porch windows is open slightly, so Jack raises the window higher. Sitting on the ledge, he swings his legs around and bends under the window frame like a NASCAR driver entering his vehicle. Within seconds, the front door opens to admit

Giancarlo.

Outside, Chief Turner calls for support from the State Police. That task done, he puts on gloves and grabs coverings for his shoes.

"Stenhouse, State CSI will be here in an hour or so," he says inside the cabin. "I guess you'll want to observe, so I'll stay until you're ready to leave."

"You guess right," responds Jack without looking up from searching under seat cushions.

The cabin is simple; only a few basic amenities are visible. A pot belly stove shares a great room with a small kitchen and utility area. The furniture is cheap secondhand and looks like it's from the seventies. It's not exactly the living conditions for a man with millions of dollars' worth of gold.

"I didn't see any power lines out here, yet there seems to be electricity," announces Allison, flipping a light switch. When nothing happens, she declares, "Must be a generator around here somewhere."

Jack pulls out his cell phone to check for a signal. When he gets three bars and a notice that he's in a Wi-Fi hotspot, he asks, "Hey, Chief, we're pretty far out in the middle of nowhere. How come I got Wi-Fi?"

"There's a large blueberry farm less than a quarter of a mile away. They paid to have power, cable, and cell service run out to the area."

Grunting in reply, Jack joins Allison, who has stopped at the bedroom door. Peering in over her shoulder, he exclaims, "Damn! Looks like a tornado went through there!"

Inside the room, clothes are strewn all over the floor, and the contents of drawers, with the drawers themselves, scattered around haphazardly. The bed frame is turned over, and the mattress is slashed in several places as if a Samurai warrior attacked it.

Stepping over the mess, Jack scans the inside of the closet and notes that nothing remains on the hangers. Beside him, Allison looks over the clutter and spies the edge of something shiny on the floor. Using her foot to move aside a bed pillow, she uncovers a Canadian Maple Leaf coin.

"Jack! I got a gold coin here!" she shouts. Bending down, she picks it up while shifting some of the nearby clutter with her shoe. "I also got Joe Stanley's driver's license and Social Security card!"

"Stan's killer must have done this," surmises Jack. "Let's leave everything else so Forensics can do their thing. But pocket that coin and those phony ID cards."

Allison heads for the kitchen to grab a paper towel to protect the coin and the documents and then joins Jack and Turner on the porch.

"May as well make ourselves comfortable while we wait for CSI," says the chief as he takes a seat on one of the wicker chairs.

"Sounds good," replies Jack. But instead of sitting down, he walks over to the edge of the porch and cranes his neck to look around the side of the house. "Hey, Ally!" he calls out. "I found the generator!"

With nothing to do but wait, the group chats

about trivial matters while they unwind in the peace and quiet. Before long, they hear the unmistakable sounds of vehicles hitting potholes, and gravel being crushed by tires. Soon, they see a State Police van and an official-looking SUV scattering squirrels and chipmunks in their path.

CHAPTER FIVE

Sergeant Hector Gomez has two interviews scheduled for today, both of them in Long Island's Nassau County.

Hector is an ex-Navy Seal with a Puerto Rican background and unique military skills. He entered the police academy after the Navy and was tapped to work undercover for Vice immediately after graduating. After five years, he switched to Homicide and made sergeant.

Hector's first interview is with Keith O'Toole in West Hempstead. After talking to Keith, Hector plans to drive to Salvatore Brusco's house on the north shore.

Hector sits in his car for a while, surveilling Keith O'Toole's house. His undercover experience makes him overly cautious, so he watches the house and the neighborhood before exiting the car.

Waiting inside the house, Keith's blood pressure is up. He's been nervous ever since Gomez called to make sure he would be available to talk.

When the doorbell rings, Keith freezes. He stares unseeing at the grandfather clock in the hallway as it begins to ring its full ten o'clock Westminster chime.

Standing outside, Gomez also hears the clock's song. Glancing at his watch, he mumbles, "Clock's a little fast."

Summoning up his courage, Keith opens the inner door and then swings the screen door out to allow Hector to enter his home. "Morning," he says with forced cheerfulness. "You must be Sergeant Gomez."

Nodding, Hector displays his credentials as he enters the house.

Keith O'Toole is the only occupant of this home. His wife left him childless and lonely when she died almost sixteen years ago. He tried dating, but had no success meeting women, so when he met Sarah at the firehouse, he was more than ready for companionship.

Keith directs Hector toward the living room and offers the sergeant a seat at one end of a black, L-shaped leather sofa. As Keith takes his place at the sofa's opposite end, Gomez scrutinizes his every move.

"Mr. O'Toole," begins Hector, turning on a small digital recorder to capture the interview, "I've come here to investigate the reappearance and suspected murder of Stanley Cummings, the John Doe who was found yesterday at the South Pool of the 9/11 Memorial. We haven't released the fact that Mr. Cummings was registered as one of the victims of the Twin Towers attack on 9/11, but we plan to do that soon. Since you were a member of the crew of Ladder Company 403 on 9/11, I'd like to ask you a few questions about the rescue and recovery operation that took place there. First, I need your name and address as a formality."

Keith cricks his neck to release some of his tension. "Yes. I'm Keith O'Toole. I live at 23 Bedell Terrace, in West Hempstead, New York."

"Thank you," Gomez responds courteously. "Since you were a member of the team that arrived at the second Tower on 9/11, can you tell me about the state of the floors located below ground level?"

Keith sighs deeply. He looks openly at the sergeant; however, his nervousness causes him to fold and unfold his hands repeatedly, and one of his eyelids keeps twitching. Sergeant Gomez notices Keith's uneasiness and makes mental notes while he waits for Keith to answer his question.

"We lost nineteen men that day," Keith responds with a faraway look in his eyes. "A few of us stayed at ground level to escort people out of the lobby, while the rest went up into the Tower." Keith rubs his twitching eyelid to try to convince it to stop moving. "Luckily, some of us were able to get out before the Tower collapsed completely. It was awful. Everything suddenly went dark, and we ran as fast as we could. We couldn't breathe. We were covered in dust and debris from the building, and probably from the victims as well. Minutes seemed like an eternity. After the building collapsed, the only sounds we heard were the personal alarms all of us carried. They're triggered if we fall or stop moving. I'll never forget that sound; it was an eerie symphony that echoed through the darkness like a death knell."

"Can you give me the names of the others who got out with you?"

"Yeah, Salvatore Brusco, Tommy Smith, Tony Arata, and Asa Wilkes."

"Thanks. Please go on."

"Tommy and I came out together. We looked like walking statues because like I said, we were covered in powdered concrete and dust, and God knows what else. We walked away from the building and waited for the air to clear and the sunlight to break through. I guess that took about thirty minutes or so. Volunteers came up to us with bottled water and washed us off a little. As soon as we could see better, we turned around and went back into the debris to try to rescue our own. Tommy and I found Asa, Sal, and Tony lying under some light debris. They were shaken up, but relatively unhurt. Unfortunately, most of the responders we removed from the debris died a few years later from complications related to all the dust and stuff we breathed in over the following weeks while we searched for survivors, and then for victims. Sal developed some major problems and lost a lung a couple of years later. He's still alive, though. All of us helped other firefighters, police officers, EMTs, and regular citizens who were lucky enough to have gotten free of the fallen Towers."

"Do you have any medical problems?" asks Gomez.

"No, not really, and I don't know why. I was just as involved as all the others. I'm grateful for that, but it bothers me that I'm not sick. Not yet, anyway," he laughs nervously.

Keith suddenly realizes that he hasn't actually answered the sergeant's question. "Sorry," he says, "I can't forget how awful it was. Now, about the lower floors. It was over a week before we could make an opening large enough to peer into and send cadaver dogs through. We also sent a robotic camera down there and saw the destruction on screen. Tons of cement and steel crushed the businesses that were there. The basement concourse contained offices and a small shopping mall of specialty shops."

"Can you describe the condition of the bullion depository that was operated by Mr. Stanley Cummings?"

"That business was located near the entrance to the subway. It was crushed like all the others."

"Did you see anything else when you looked into that level?"

Gomez notices that Keith hesitates a moment before responding. "We saw metal vaults and gold and silver coins strewn all over the place."

"Really?" asks Gomez. "What did you do when you saw that?"

"We retrieved some of the coins and gold that we could see, but most of the area was sealed over with solid concrete. So a lot of it must still be there. Sergeant, I have to ask...do you know how Cummings got out, and where the hell he's been all these years?"

"That's what I'm trying to find out," Hector replies while staring at the beads of sweat on Keith's forehead. "Was Sam Lincoln there with you?"

At that question, Gomez notes that O'Toole's eyes suddenly dilate and that the man takes in another deep breath. Gomez' training tells him that those reactions are involuntary and could be physical indications of O'Toole's state of mind.

"Yeah, Lieutenant Sam Lincoln," Keith responds quietly, avoiding direct eye contact with Gomez. "Well, now he's Captain Lincoln. Sam joined us later. He was off that day; had to take care of some personal business, I think. He was involved in the search and cleanup, though. He went down into the lower level before we sealed it up. He recovered whatever gold and silver he could reach."

"Did Sam know Stanley Cummings?"

To release more nervous tension, O'Toole rises from the sofa and walks over to the grandfather clock. Opening the door, he pulls the weights down to rewind it and responds to Gomez through the noise of ratcheting gears. "Geez," he answers, "I don't think Sam knew Cummings. I mean, not personally. All I know is that Stanley supported our station through his business." Keith closes the access door to the clock's inner workings and returns to the sofa. "Do you think Sam was involved in Cummings' disappearance?"

"No," says Gomez, staring hard at O'Toole. "I'm just trying to get background information. You said Sam went down into the lower level. Did anyone else go in with him?"

Trying to avoid Gomez' stare, Keith looks down at his hands. "No," he says quickly. "I was there that day. We were only able to open up a small crawl space, and Sam volunteered to go in. He said he was upset that he wasn't on duty when the planes hit. He wanted to do as much as he could to help out."

"Okay, Mr. O'Toole. How about Salvatore

Brusco? Was he involved in the cleanup?"

Now Keith restores eye contact and replies more calmly. "Yeah, Sal was there. He helped Sam out for a while, but then they sent him to work on Tower One. I haven't seen him in a long time. Not since his bout with lung cancer."

Gomez noticed the abrupt change in O'Toole's demeanor. "You said Stanley Cummings supported your station with his business? How did he do that?"

Keith stops to adjust a small pillow at his back. "Well, he was always bringing us breakfast and donuts and stuff, and every year, he bought tickets to the Fireman's Ball. He said he wanted to be a fireman when he was a kid."

"All right. Thank you, Mr. O'Toole. That's all for now," says Gomez as he turns off the recorder. "Here's my card. If you remember anything else after I leave, please give me a call. I'm also going to speak with Mr. Brusco, so I'll give him your regards. Don't be too surprised if I contact you again."

After Gomez leaves, Keith paces up and down the length of his living room, spending several minutes worrying. Then, he marches over to his phone.

"A cop was just here asking about Stan!" he shouts when his call is answered.

In the car on the way to his next interview, Gomez mulls over Keith's responses.

Something doesn't add up, he decides.

Stenhouse and Giancarlo are still in New Jersey. While the New Jersey State Forensic team scours the home belonging to Stanley Cummings, a.k.a. Joe Stanley, and its surrounding grounds, they relax on the front porch. After about an hour, Chief Turner exits the house and joins them.

"How's it going in there?" asks Jack.

Before Turner begins to respond, a forensic tech emerges from the rear of the cabin. "Chief," he says, ignoring the two visitors from New York, "we found this tin of arsenic in a small shed near the generator. It says it's for agricultural use only."

Turner sits down next to the detectives to inspect the tech's plastic evidence bag containing a white box. "I tried to get them to let you inside," he says, glancing at Jack and Allison, "but they used the 'no jurisdiction' line. Sorry. They didn't even want me in there, but I insisted since we're in my area."

"Yeah, well, if we need to, I'll get a warrant and confiscate all the stuff they find. Then, they can go pound sand."

At Jack's comment, Turner breaks out in a wide grin, so Jack asks, "What's so funny?" But when the chief doesn't respond, Jack shrugs and points to the evidence bag. "Does anyone around here sell that stuff? They'd have to keep records on arsenic sales, right?"

"I don't think anyone in our town sells it," replies Turner, removing his hat to scratch his head.

"Maybe they do in Philadelphia; we're only forty miles from there. Let's go back to my office now. We can check out the chemical distributors in Philly. Forensics can wrap things up here."

Just then, another thought occurs to Turner. "Or," he says thoughtfully, "that large blueberry farm is right next door. We should stop there to see if they purchase arsenic. People in this area sometimes use arsenic for varmint control, so maybe they gave some to Cummings. We help each other in the Barrens," he says, placing his hat back on his head.

A cautious ride along two dirt roads brings the officers to AJ&J Blueberries, about a quarter of a mile from the Cummings house. Chief Turner stops his vehicle at a guardhouse in front of a chain link fence surrounding the company's headquarters building and farm to talk briefly with the guard, who makes a quick phone call and then grants them passage to the main building.

Sergeant Gomez is enjoying the drive to Salvatore Brusco's home in Glen Cove. As he heads down Old Estate Road, a pretty, tree-lined street near Long Island Sound, he finds himself snaking through an upscale community of sprawling homes and can't imagine how a New York City firefighter could afford to live in this area. Looking at the large houses, he imagines that most of them are probably worth at least a million dollars.

Following GPS instructions, Hector pulls into a

winding driveway that leads up to a large house with a four-car garage. Exiting his unmarked sedan, he walks along a brick-paved path to the home's attractive front door and rings the bell.

"Yes?" responds Salvatore Brusco. "Can I help you?"

Sergeant Gomez offers his police badge and ID card for inspection. "Yes, you can. I'm Sergeant Hector Gomez, with NYPD. I called about an interview."

"Oh, um, yeah. Right. Ah, come on in," Brusco stammers, closing the door behind Hector. Pointing the way, he ushers Hector through a large foyer into a spacious living room with a floor-to-ceiling fireplace.

"Honey, this is Sergeant Gomez from the New York Police Department," Brusco explains when a stylishly-dressed woman walks out of the kitchen. "He's the one who asked to talk to me. Can you get us some coffee, please?" With his hand on Gomez' shoulder, he says, "Never knew a cop who didn't drink coffee. Come on. We can sit at the dining room table."

Mrs. Brusco heads back into the kitchen as Gomez follows Salvatore into the home's large dining room, where they take seats at an elegant table. Mr. Brusco is frail and unsteady but looks as if he was once proud and strong. It seems that firefighting and cancer have left far-reaching marks on this man.

"Sergeant," asks Salvatore, "what do you need from me?"

Gomez hesitates. As he breathes in a pleasant aroma of polished wood and fine leather, he takes a quick look around at the home's well-appointed décor and debates within himself whether to ask the question he's particularly interested in having answered. He knows that his task is to ask about Stanley Cummings, but what he really wants to know is how the hell this former firefighter can afford this house.

Deciding that it's better to stick with police business, he says, "Mr. Brusco, I need to ask you some questions that will take you back to September 11, 2001."

"Oh. Well, okay. Shoot."

"Thank you. I understand that you were a member of Ladder Company 403, one of the stationhouses that responded to the attack that day."

"That's right."

"I also understand that you assisted fellow firefighter Sam Lincoln in the rescue efforts at Tower Two."

Brusco inhales a deep and wheezy breath, standard nowadays for this man with only one lung. "Hmm, that stirs up memories," he says, lowering his head. "We lost a lotta good men that day. Yes, I was there."

"Did you know Stanley Cummings?"

At that question, Salvatore raises his head, and his eyes widen, and the color drains from his face. He pauses slightly, then answers, "Stan Cummings? Yeah, his business was located in the Tower. He was a frequent visitor at the station. He was always bringing us food. He died in the attack."

"Yes. He owned Precious Coins and Bullion in the

South Tower," says Gomez. "Cummings was reported to have died on 9/11, but he was recently found at the South Pool of the 9/11 Memorial. He's dead—poisoned."

Shocked by this news, Salvatore's breathing becomes more forceful. "He...he was the John Doe on the news?" he asks haltingly. "The reason they shut down the Memorial?"

Seeing Brusco's labored breathing, Gomez fears an abrupt end to the interview. "Are you all right, sir?" he asks.

"Yeah, I'll be okay," wheezes Brusco.

Relieved by Brusco's assurance, Gomez presses on. "Yes, Cummings is the one who was on the news," he replies. "What can you tell me about the rescue effort at the South Tower? You recovered some valuables from that location, correct?"

Mrs. Brusco interrupts the men when she brings in a tray of coffee and small cookies. Grateful for the distraction, Salvatore rises from his chair and walks around the table, ostensibly to try to improve his breathing. Gomez notes that the questions seem to fluster him.

"I can't tell you much," he says after a few moments of rapid breathing. "We opened up a hole, and Sam Lincoln crawled into the sub-basement. He surprised us when he started handing up coins and other stuff, so Keith O'Toole, another firefighter, went in and helped him. It took about an hour or so. Then, I was sent to the North Tower."

As Mrs. Brusco pours two cups of coffee, she eyes her husband and notices that he is still having trouble breathing. "Sal," she says, guiding him back to his chair, "you need to calm down." Turning to Hector, she explains, "He's been short of breath ever since he had cancer and had to have a lung removed. When he gets excited, he gets an asthmatic reaction in his remaining lung. I don't like to see him like this."

Salvatore pulls an inhaler out of his pocket and brings it to his lips, taking in a deep draw of the soothing medicine. "I'll be fine, dear," he whispers, patting his wife's arm. "Your coffee always does the trick. Sergeant, I started to have bouts like this after my surgery two years ago. But that's me. How did Cummings... I mean, where was he all these years?"

"We don't know that yet. That's why I'm here."

"Well, it's very strange that he showed up like that. I think I answered all your questions, though; I can't think of anything else to add. Did you talk to Sam Lincoln yet?"

Gomez senses that Salvatore wants to end the interview, but he still has questions. "Yes, we already interviewed Sam Lincoln," he says. "Mr. Brusco, I'm very curious. How can a former firefighter afford such a beautiful home? It's gorgeous."

Gomez watches with interest as Salvatore and his wife exchange pointed looks.

"We purchased this house many years ago, long before the price of houses went sky high," states Salvatore. "We came into some money unexpectedly, and we used that to help with the cost."

Gomez notices that beads of sweat have begun to appear on the couple's foreheads.

Standing, he shakes Brusco's hand. "Well, thank you both for the coffee, and thank you for your time and service to the citizens of New York, sir," he says. "I see that you need to rest now. Here's my card. My department will be in touch if we have further questions. Oh, and before I forget, Keith O'Toole says hello." Gomez turns to leave but stops mid-stride. "Just to confirm," he says lightly, "you said that both Sam Lincoln and Keith O'Toole were down in that hole retrieving valuables. Is that correct?"

"Yes, Sergeant. Both of them were down there."

"Okay, thanks again."

As Hector walks to his car, he hears loud coughing coming from inside the house, the sound clashing with the familiar suburban noises of power mowers and leaf blowers.

Suddenly, a thought sums up his impression of the couple he has just met in this fine, upper-class neighborhood:

One lies, and the other swears to it.

CHAPTER SIX

AJ&J Blueberries is a large corporation consisting of a blueberry farm and processing plant in New Jersey's Pine Barrens. During harvest season, the company opens a section of their farm to the public for self-picking.

"Hey, this is the place we took our kids!" asserts Allison as Turner turns his SUV onto a paved road toward the main building. "I didn't think it covered this much acreage, though. I guess I wasn't paying attention; too busy keeping the kids out of trouble while my husband drove."

Up ahead, the road splits in two. A sign at the fork points left toward a public u-pick area with a snack bar and gift shop, and right, toward the farm's commercial zone.

Directing the car to the business end of the operation, Turner drives past several farm vehicles the company uses to pull the large containers full of ripe blueberries to a processing plant further down the road. After pointing the vehicles out to his passengers, he explains that the plant is where the berries are sorted, cleaned, and boxed for distribution. The car stops at a small parking lot in front of a large, unassuming building.

Inside the building, the group enters the company's reception area, a small, uninviting room where no attempt has been made at décor or comfort. The room has no seating, and the only color is provided by vinyl, commercial-grade flooring set in a checkered black and white pattern.

To handle the introductions, Chief Turner walks up to a small sliding window in the room's far wall, but just as he is about to knock on the frosted glass panel, it slides open to reveal a woman peering wordlessly at him and the others.

"Good morning, Jane," says Turner. "I'm here with some detectives from the New York City Police Department. We need to speak with Mr. Stohl, please."

While the visitors wait for the receptionist to call Stohl's office, Jack turns to Turner. "I'm impressed by the size of the operation I've seen so far," he says. "I would never have thought that a business of this size would be out in the Barrens. The place is huge! Must be a lot of money in blueberries."

"There sure is," remarks Eric Stohl as he enters the lobby area. "Good to see you again, Stuart. How may I help you?"

Eric Stohl is the CEO of AJ&J Blueberries and has been in charge of operations at this farm for over ten years. Although he is only in his fifties, his gray hair makes him appear much older.

Turner shakes Eric's outstretched hand and introduces the detectives. Then, he says, "We need to ask you a few questions about Joe Stanley."

"Really?" responds Eric with raised brows. "He's our neighbor. He has that small house about a quarter of a mile from here. Is something wrong?"

"Mr. Stohl, is there somewhere we can talk in private?" interjects Jack.

"Sure; sorry. We can talk in my office."

Eric leads the group to a modestly sized room with plain and unadorned white walls that are in direct contrast to the room's furnishings. A large mahogany desk, several cushioned chairs, and a console holding a widescreen TV sit atop a plush Oriental rug that fills the room. The fine furnishings seem out of place, but Jack gets the impression they were selected to make the room appear less "industrial."

After Eric directs his visitors to the chairs, he moves to sit behind his desk, and Jack gets down to business. Wasting no time, he informs Stohl that he will be recording the session on a small digital recorder.

"Mr. Stohl," he begins, "your neighbor's legal name was Stanley Cummings. He was recently found unresponsive at the Twin Towers Memorial in New York City, and he died shortly afterward."

"What? That's terrible!" exclaims Stohl.

"Yes, it was arsenic poisoning. We found a can of arsenic at his house."

"Wow, you never really know people, do you?" muses Stohl. "We gave some arsenic to Joe...ah...to Stanley, I guess. We had a bad problem with raccoons eating our berries. The only thing that deterred them was fruit laced with arsenic. They're quite smart, so when they left us, they must have made their way over to our neighbor's place instead. That may have been when he came over and asked if we were having a problem with raccoons. We work together out here, you know?"

"Joe Stanley also had a blueberry farm, so didn't you consider him to be a competitor?" asks Allison.

"No, he's not a competitor. His farm is small. He serves a niche organic market."

"Okay, gotcha."

"Well, like I was saying, he came over for some guidance, and we told him what we did to get rid of the pests. He had no access to arsenic, so we gave him a can."

"That stuff is pretty toxic, isn't it?" asks Allison.

"Yes, we made sure he signed it out so we could keep our records complete. Do you think he committed suicide?"

Jack ignores Stohl's question. "Did you ever see anyone at Cummings's place? A farmhand, maybe?"

Eric furrows his brow and sits back in his chair. "I didn't interact with him directly; I'm usually pretty busy running this complex. I only talked with him a few times at the annual Blueberry Festival in Hammonton, but I did approve the poison transfer. Aaron Dawson, my facilities manager, would have met with him. I'll ask my secretary to contact him. He's out in the field right now, but it shouldn't take him long to get here."

Stohl phones his secretary to place his request,

and while he has her on the phone, says to his visitors, "Sorry for my lapse in hospitality. Would any of you like refreshments? Coffee, water...blueberries?"

All of them decline his offer, but Jack detects a possible problem. After the CEO hangs up the phone, he asks, "Mr. Stohl, it's not blueberry season, so how can you offer us blueberries?"

"Ah, you caught me, Detective," smiles Stohl. "During the offseason, we import them from our farms in Peru and Mexico."

Satisfied by the CEO's answer, Jack and Allison relax in their chairs while Chief Turner and Eric Stohl share small talk and local town gossip as they wait for Aaron Dawson.

A short time later, the facilities manager strides into the room.

"Mr. Stohl, did you need me?" he asks.

"Yes, Aaron. These police officers would like to speak with you. Don't worry; you're not in trouble. They have a few questions about our neighbor down the road. Gentlemen, you can use my office. I need to make a call to Corporate, anyway. Dawson, please show them out when you're through. If there's anything else they need, please contact me directly."

After Eric leaves the office, Aaron sits at Stohl's desk and listens as Chief Turner introduces the officers from New York. Then, the chief defers to Jack.

"Mr. Dawson," Jack begins, "we're here to investigate the death of your company's neighbor, the man you knew as Joe Stanley. His actual name was Stanley

Cummings, and he recently passed away from arsenic poisoning. Mr. Stohl said you had some dealings with him. Were you ever at his home?"

"Oh, my God!" exclaims Aaron. "Joe's real name was Stanley, and now he's dead? Nothing like that is supposed to happen in small-town America! Well, I guess evil has finally worked its way out here."

Aaron Dawson looks the part of a blueberry farmer. He has a dark, wrinkled face and rough and calloused hands. "Um, yeah," he responds to Jack's question. "I was at Joe's house a few times. Neighborly stuff, you know?"

"Did you ever see people at his house or notice anyone hanging around with him in Hammonton?"

Aaron rubs his hand over his face while he thinks. "There were a couple of times when I saw people at his place. He'd come over here periodically to buy small containers to sell his crop at the town's farmers market, so I thought they were helping with his harvest."

"Could you describe those people?" asks Giancarlo. "Any distinctive traits or features?"

"No, not really; I didn't pay much attention. Oh, wait. One of them used a pocket inhaler. He may have had asthma or something."

"Sir," asks Giancarlo quickly, "would you mind looking at some photographs of people who may have been connected with Stanley?"

"Sure, no problem."

"Good. We'll send them to Chief Turner; he'll

contact you when they arrive. Oh, one more thing. Your boss said you handled the exchange of arsenic to Cummings. Did anyone accompany him here the day he picked it up?"

"No, he was alone. Like I said, he stopped by from time to time to buy supplies. We occasionally talked about harvesting and horticulture. He was a nice guy."

"Okay, thanks," concludes Jack. "I guess we're done for now."

Dawson leads Chief Turner and the detectives out of his boss's office and back into the reception area, where Jack and Allison are handed containers of the company's South American blueberries.

Inside Turner's SUV, Jack munches on the fresh berries. "Ally," he asks between bites, "which photos did you have in mind?"

"Well, we already interviewed Sam Lincoln and Stan's wife, and Gomez is checking on more leads," responds Giancarlo after swallowing a mouthful of berries. "We can send him the photos of everyone we've already spoken to, and also include the ones we're still trying to get in touch with. There's a weak link out there somewhere. Man," she adds, eying several berries in her hand. "These blueberries are great! I wonder if the public knows they're not from Jersey."

"Detective," declares Chief Turner from the driver's seat, "the visitor's center is open all year round, so they have to import most of their berries in the offseason. And they also experiment with new strains, which, like single barrel bourbon, are quite expensive, so they only give them out to special guests. Those are the berries you're enjoying now."

When Turner pulls onto the road leading back into the Barrens, the car hits a pothole, and Giancarlo's berries fly up into the air like a spray of blue buckshot. Stenhouse had already closed his container, so at Allison's expense, he erupts into hysterical laughter, prompting Allison to flash him an angry finger.

Watching the commotion in the rearview mirror, the small-town chief shakes his head at the immature actions of his "big city" passengers.

"Police officials have finally released the name of the man found poisoned at the South Pool of the 9/11 Memorial. He was Stanley Cummings, the owner of a precious metals company that was located in the South Tower of the World Trade Center. He was reported to have died in the attack on 9/11, but it now appears that he disappeared that day with millions of dollars in gold coins and gold bullion, none of which has ever been recovered.

"Two questions need to be asked: Where has Stanley Cummings been all this time? And where is all of that missing gold?

"This is Skip Larson with WPIX News 11, always looking out for you and the truth."

CHAPTER SEVEN

While early morning joggers pepper Manhattan's concrete trails, and nearly empty city buses cruise the streets, Jack cradles Didi's head and her long flowing auburn hair as she blurts out BUICK! and regurgitates the contents of her stomach into their porcelain receptacle.

"Ohhh," moans Didi, "I'm thrilled to be pregnant, but this nausea is horrible!"

Jack strokes his wife's hair to comfort her as she dry heaves. "Dee, I remember my mother talking about having morning sickness when she was pregnant with me. She said the only thing that helped her was chewing a stick of Beemans Gum. There's an old-time candy store near the First that sells some of the older sweets like Dots and Fizzies and stuff. I'll drop by there today to see if I can get you some of that gum."

Dee wipes her mouth with a washcloth and says, "Just get me some ice water, Babe. I think it stopped for now."

Nodding, Jack pads into the kitchen dressed only in his tighty-whities while Didi enters the shower to wash off this latest bout of nausea.

While Didi is in the bathroom, Jack pulls on tan slacks and a collarless white shirt and grabs his blue blazer. Walking back into the kitchen, he makes himself some breakfast.

Having taken a liking to the blueberries from New Jersey, he pours a cup of black coffee into a bowl of cereal and adds some of the fresh berries on top. He is wolfing down his version of a warm breakfast when Didi emerges from the bedroom. Still queasy, she pours herself a glass of milk and speaks in a hushed tone.

"I'm not hungry this morning, Jack. Can you take me to work, please?"

Jack looks up from his cereal bowl and glances at the wall clock. "It's only seven, Babe, and Sonia usually picks you up. You don't open till nine. Are you sure you want to get there so early?"

Didi is still feeling uneasy. Her face has a pallor that changes from white to green, like the lime green spandex leggings and white thigh-length tee shirt she's wearing today. The shirt, a gift from Sonia, spells out "GUESS" in sparkly letters that stretch across her ample bosom. Didi belches and sighs, "I need a change of scenery, Jack. If I stay here any longer, I may start throwing up again. Please, let's go now. I already called Sonia to let her know that you'll be driving me today."

"Okay, no problem," says Jack as he gulps down the rest of his coffee. Grabbing his empty cereal bowl, he places it in the sink and unplugs the coffee maker. "Your wish is my command, Madam," he says, bowing to his wife. Then, pointing at Didi's tee shirt, he grins mischievously. "They're real, you know. Just sayin'."

Later, when Jack walks into the Homicide Department squad room, he notices someone standing at the whiteboard near his desk. The man seems to be studying the evidence and timeline that he and his team have compiled so far on their current case.

"Hey, Slick!" Jack bellows. "Who are you, and what do you want with my case?"

When the man turns around, Jack recognizes him instantly. "Oh, it's you, Skippy," he declares disapprovingly. "You're looking at evidence that isn't for public viewing. Go speak to Lieutenant Conrad if you want an update."

"Good morning, Detective Stenhouse," replies Skip Larson good-naturedly. "I'm just trying to get a heads-up. What's the story behind Hammonton?"

When Sergeants Burley and Gomez enter the department, they are not surprised to see Jack standing nose-to-nose with the WPIX reporter.

"Look, Slick," says Jack with his finger pointing into Skippy's chest, "this is confidential information. It's not for the public, and that includes your minions. My friends here are going to escort you over to Conrad's office, and you can wait there until he comes in. Or we can tase you, cuff you, and charge you with interfering with our investigation. Then, you can post bail before you become someone's bitch. It's your choice."

At first, Larson glares haughtily at Jack, but then he quickly changes his demeanor and breaks out into a broad smile. "Okay, Detective," he says pleasantly, "I'll do it your way. For now." Turning toward the two sergeants, he says, "No need for the escort, guys. I know where Conrad's office is." As he steps away from the whiteboard, he deliberately runs into Sergeant Gomez' shoulder.

Watching the reporter depart, the officers roll their eyes and sigh. Muttering loudly, Gomez calls out, "Shit for brains!" as Jack grumbles in frustration.

Not happy with the way his day has started, Jack is in a foul mood. "Where's Ally?" he growls. "Either she's running late, or we're fucking early! Do you guys have anything new from yesterday?"

Gomez meanders over to the office coffee pot, leaving Burley with Jack. "I reviewed Sarah Cummings's financials again," he says. "She's worth over two million dollars. She received more than 200 g's from the 9/11 victims' fund, and a total of a million dollars in payouts from life insurance policies and her husband's business insurance. However, that was fourteen years ago. Also, Liberty Life and Casualty Company contacted me about Stanley's policy. They want to know if he committed suicide. I don't know what they're going to do, but they weren't happy that he showed up alive after they paid out his death benefit. They're reviewing their options and may want to reclaim the money they sent to Sarah. The agent said they might want the whole damn thing back, or they may be satisfied with just getting back the interest on the payout."

Jack whistles. "That's a lot of dough."

"Sarah has two sons at Harvard," continues John.

"At sixty-five thousand a year with no scholarships or grants for either of them, that's a big chunk of money to pay out." Shaking his head, he asks rhetorically, "Where's all that money coming from? Could she have gotten lucky with some really good investments?"

Jack furrows his brows in thought. "Let's bring her in for more questioning. Take care of that today, okay?"

Burley nods but adds, "I'm not finished. One of the firemen who used to work for Ladder 403 is now acting as her financial advisor, and from what I've pieced together, he's also linked with her romantically."

"Oh?" considers Jack. "Who is that?"

"His name is Keith O'Toole."

When Burley spots Gomez returning from the coffee pot with only one cup, he asks, "Hey, where's my coffee?"

"It's in the pot," says Gomez. "You know, guys, I interviewed O'Toole yesterday. He was pretty nervous and avoided eye contact with me. I also questioned Salvatore Brusco, the other fireman from Ladder 403, and he got so upset that he had an asthma attack."

"Huh, that's really interesting," says Jack as Burley leaves to get his own cup of coffee. "Let's get them all in here, one at a time. Something's going on, and we need to try to break them. Let's also talk to Sam Lincoln again."

When Allison Giancarlo finally walks into the office, all heads turn in her direction.

"Sorry, guys," she says apologetically, "there was an accident on the Hudson River Drive. While I was waiting in traffic, I sent some of the photos over to Turner in Hammonton."

"Hey," says Burley, "I didn't want to ask while Skippy was here. How'd it go out there?"

Jack walks up to the whiteboard containing the information that Skippy was so interested in reading. "Stanley was running a small blueberry farm in Hammonton under an assumed name. We went to his house, and it was trashed. Hammonton is a small, sleepy community out in the Barrens. It's so small that the town's chief of police had to call in the state's forensics team to investigate the scene because he doesn't have much of a department out there. Not surprisingly, State kicked us out of the house. They said they'll send us the results when they're done with the investigation."

"Damn," declares Burley. "So we have to wait for that report. Hope they don't take too long."

"Yeah, but before State arrived, Allison found a gold coin and some fake ID inside the guy's bedroom. And when the CSI crew was poking around, they found a can of arsenic in a shed behind the house."

Sergeant Burley mulls over everything Jack has said so far. "Hmm," he muses, "looks like things are getting interesting."

"Yup," agrees Jack," and I have a feeling that those Jersey assholes won't cooperate very much. They'll probably want to protect their precious turf. I'll get a warrant if I have to, but I think we need to get Conrad or Rawlings involved with this one. The police chief helped us out a little, though. He drove us to a large blueberry farm bordering Stan's place, and we talked to the owner and the manager. They said Stan got the arsenic from them. They gave it to him to control raccoons, of all things. The manager also said he saw people at Stan's place from time-to-time, but the only thing he remembers about them is that one of them used an inhaler."

Jack stares at his crew. "So it looks like we have four potential suspects—Sarah Cummings, Keith O'Toole, Salvatore Brusco, and Sam Lincoln—and no real leads. We still don't know how Stan got out of the Tower, or where the hell the gold went."

Gomez suddenly remembers something. "Hey, one more thing," he says. "Salvatore Brusco lives in Glen Cove, in a huge house overlooking Long Island Sound. I checked the records on the house, and it's worth close to two million dollars. He and his wife claim they bought it before the housing crash back in the eighties, but I think that's bullshit. It's obvious that Brusco has money. He was wearing a Rolex, and his wife had on some pretty nice gems. Also," he adds, pausing for effect, "Brusco uses an inhaler."

"Well, money talks, and bullshit walks," comments Jack with a shake of his head. "Interesting about the inhaler, though. All right, let's talk to these people again. Get them in here today. Allison, check with Turner to see if he has any updates from the Jersey State Police and ask him if he looked at the photos you sent. While you're doing that, I'm going to step out for a few minutes. I need to get some Beemans Gum."

"Oh, no," remarks Allison sympathetically. "Didi

has morning sickness? I used Beemans with all of my pregnancies. You can get it online, and I hear that it can even be delivered by drone."

"Well, that's just great. All I need are drones flying around my place. Be back in a few. I'm going down to that old-timey candy store to see if they carry the gum."

Sergeants Burley and Gomez leave the floor together for their drive out to Long Island to enlist the assistance of Nassau County Police in rounding up Sarah Cummings, Keith O'Toole, and Salvatore Brusco for more questioning.

Forty minutes later, Jack is back at the whiteboard with a supply of gum in his pocket and a cup of coffee in his hand.

When Allison sees that Jack has returned, she walks over to the coffee pot and pours her partner a cup. "Here ya go, Jack," she says genially.

Jack looks at the cup already in his hand and smiles at Allison. "I guess I'm a two-fisted coffee drinker now."

"Oh," grins Allison sheepishly. "I didn't see that you already had one. Well, I know you'll drink both of them, so enjoy. Hey, I just got off the phone with Chief Turner. They were able to pull a fingerprint from the handle of the bathroom sink at Cummings' house. Our records department ran the prints, and they found a match. But get this...the match was found in the database of current and former New York City employees. The prints belong to a guy named Larry Grimes. He was one of the firemen from Ladder 403 whose body was never found. He's also on the list of the 9/11 missing. He has no family and wasn't married, so no one is looking for him too hard. It looks like we got another suspect, Jack. Another 'ghost.'"

Jack finishes his first cup of coffee and throws the empty container at the trash can with an overhead shot. When it goes into the can, he triumphantly pumps his fist in the air and takes a sip of his second cup of hot brew. After a few more sips, he says, "Another 'ghost,' huh? Let's go down to 403. We need to talk to Sam Lincoln again. By the time we're done there, Gomez and Burley should be back with Brusco, Cummings, and O'Toole. What did Turner say about the photos?"

Before answering, Allison moves Jack's cup into the recycling bin and takes a gulp of her own coffee. "Nothing yet on the pictures I sent, but he said he has a copy of the fake ID Cummings used to get a Jersey driver's license and to purchase his property in the Barrens. Since Cummings' estate was settled years ago when they said he was dead, that property will now be confiscated for being purchased illegally."

"Great, just what the government needs," deadpans Jack, "a blueberry farm. Come on; let's visit Mr. Lincoln."

Coming up behind Jack, Lieutenant Conrad levels his gaze at his subordinate when he turns around. "Had an interesting talk with Skip Larson," he says dourly.

"Yeah? Where is that nice man?"

"He just left. He said you weren't 'cooperative.' You must be mellowing in your old age, Jack. I would've bet money that you tasered that asshole. Look, I'll try to keep Skip in line, but don't be surprised if he makes a few comments on the air about you."

Jack stares across the office, looking at something that isn't there. "Fuck him," he spits out, "and the horse he rode in on."

In West Hempstead, Sarah Cummings discreetly pushes aside one of the vertical blinds over her dining room window to look out onto the street. Parked in front of her house is a video truck with its satellite dish poking skyward, and Skip Larson standing at the curb, watching the house. Muttering, "Oh, shit," over and over, she rushes to the phone on the kitchen wall. "Keith!" she shouts frantically, "a TV reporter is at my house! What should I do?"

Although the news shakes Keith, he tries to remain calm so he can guide a very anxious Sarah. "Look," he says, "don't answer the door; they probably want to ask about Stan. I'll call my lawyer and be right over. Don't do anything stupid, Sarah. I love you."

"What if he's out there when you get here?"

"No problem," assures Keith. "We'll deal with it together. Just remain calm and act surprised if he says anything. It'll be okay."

Ending the call, Sarah sits down nervously on a

chair in the kitchen. When the doorbell rings a moment later, she flinches and tiptoes to the front door, but doesn't open it. Instead, she cocks her head and listens intently, then looks out of the peephole. What she sees on her front doorstep increases her uneasiness: Skip Larson is on her porch with his cameraman, and he looks ready to begin his nightly broadcast.

"This is Skip Larson. I'm in West Hempstead today, at the home of Sarah Cummings. Her husband, Stanley Cummings, inexplicably appeared at the Trade Towers Memorial in downtown Manhattan a few days ago. He was declared missing after the 9/11 tragedy, and Sarah and her family received a sizeable settlement from the Victims Fund. Sarah doesn't seem to be home, or perhaps she doesn't want to speak with us today. I wonder what she thinks of her husband's reappearance. Does she know how he got out of the South Tower that day, or where he's been hiding all these years? Does she know the whereabouts of the gold that is still missing from her husband's depository?

"Earlier today, I tried to interview Detective Jack Stenhouse, the lead investigator of the 'second' death of Stanley Cummings, but he gave me the 'no comment' treatment and threatened to tase me and arrest me for interfering with his investigation. Detective Stenhouse's bullying tactics won't work on me; I will always pursue the truth.

"We'll remain at Sarah's house for a while to try to bring you the answers to all of our questions. Reporting from the Cummings home, this is Skip Larson, on the case for you, and News 11."

CHAPTER EIGHT

Jack and Allison wend their way through one of the open bays at Ladder Company 403, looking for Sam Lincoln. They finally spy him talking on his cell phone near a group of firefighters cleaning and polishing their trucks and equipment to keep themselves busy between calls. Flashing his badge at the captain, Jack prods him to end his conversation.

"Well, well, well," chirps Lincoln. "It's the First Precinct's Finest come to visit. How can I help you fine officers?"

An unsmiling Jack ignores Sam's "cheerful" greeting and stares right through the man. "Captain," he says somberly, "we need to talk in private." Lincoln nods and leads them through the stationhouse.

As they settle into the uncomfortable but utilitarian chairs in Lincoln's office, Jack stares at the American flag sitting proudly in the corner but doesn't allow the fire captain's patriotism to persuade him to pull his punches. He decides to open the discussion with a name the officers haven't mentioned before, hoping that his surprise question will reveal something about what the man may be thinking. "Tell me about Larry Grimes," he states curtly. Then he watches with interest as Sam seems to be thinking hard before responding.

After a lengthy pause, Sam says, "Larry died on 9/11. What else do you need to know?"

Jack keeps a cold stare on the firehouse chief. "We found out where Cummings spent his time after 9/11," he states slowly, still gauging Sam's reaction.

Jack waits for a comment or an involuntary reflex from the chief, but when there is none, he adds, "Forensics pulled Grimes' print off a handle at Stanley Cummings' house. Mr. Lincoln, talk to me about the morning of 9/11. Tell me what you found on the lower floor."

Lincoln grips the arms of his chair and stares at the ceiling. When he begins to speak, he doesn't make eye contact with Jack, but then slowly looks over at his inquisitor. "Grimes was one of the first guys who went into Tower Two," he says. "We thought all the men went up to the higher floors, but some of them may have gone down below. Grimes' body was never found. In fact, most of those we lost that day were never found. Like I said before, I was off that day and got there later. I was the one who crawled into the sub-basement area and retrieved some of the gold and precious metals. I found an open area where I could stand up, and that's where I saw some lock boxes scattered around with coins, gold and silver bars, and other stuff."

"I need to know a couple of things," interrupts Jack. "You said that Grimes was the first one there. If you arrived later, as you said, how do you know he was the first one on the scene?"

Avoiding eye contact again, Lincoln rises from behind his desk and walks over to a photograph of the

Manhattan skyline showing the Twin Towers in their former glory. "I was debriefed later in the day with the other members of our crew who made it out," he says while staring at the photo. "I was told that Grimes was running an errand before the attack and that they found his vehicle at the scene when the rest of the crew responded to the call. I never saw the car, although there were many crushed and damaged vehicles nearby."

"Did you see anyone in the crawl space when you entered it?"

"No."

"Was there any other way out of that area besides the hole you guys made in the debris? Was there any other way to leave without being seen?"

"No, Detective, I didn't see any other way out. The South Tower collapsed all around that floor."

"Then how do you explain Stanley Cummings' recent appearance, and Grimes' fresh fingerprints?" asks Giancarlo, inserting her two cents into the interview.

Lincoln sits back down at his desk. "I don't know," he responds vaguely. "I don't see how anyone who didn't leave before the Tower collapsed could have gotten out of that mess alive."

Jack is just about to question Lincoln about the gold Tag Heuer watch glistening on his wrist when the fire alarm sounds in the station.

Instantly, Captain Lincoln jumps out of his chair. "We're going to have to continue this another time," he declares with unmistakable relief as he runs out into the hallway.

With the interview now over, Jack and Allison also enter the hallway and quickly find themselves dodging single-minded fire personnel as they scurry around, grabbing their gear.

Heading down the stairway to the first floor, the officers see Lincoln staring up at them from the foot of the stairs. "Detective!" Lincoln shouts. "You need to move your car!"

"Oh, shit!" snaps Jack as he and Allison rush past Lincoln. "We'll be talking again soon, Captain!"

Back on the road, Jack recounts his impressions of the interview while he maneuvers his car into position behind a large truck so he can take advantage of the 'free ride zone' for better gas mileage. "Lincoln is lying," he declares firmly, "I just know it. He's hiding something."

"I agree," says Allison, keeping a watchful eye on the truck in front of them. "He was wearing a pretty nice watch."

"Yeah, I noticed that. Can't wait to talk to him again," comments Jack dryly.

Walking around the corner from his house to Sarah's, Keith O'Toole's resolve to help his fiancée increases when he spots the WPIX-TV mobile unit parked on her swale. Striding forward, he interrupts reporter Skip Larson's conversation with his cameraman.

"Mr. Larson, Mrs. Cummings is a friend of mine," proclaims Keith. "She told me you were here and asked me to come over right away. She's quite distraught about her husband. I can find out if she wants to speak with you."

Skip nods and smiles widely in anticipation of an exclusive. "Yes, that would be great! Thank you, Mr. … What's your name?"

"Keith O'Toole," responds Keith glancing behind him as he walks up to the house, past a mass of blooming azaleas in varying shades of pink and white. When he arrives at the door, he fishes a key out of his pocket and unlocks it, closing it firmly behind him.

An upset Sarah meets him just inside the door. "Keith!" she whispers. "I just got a call from the lawyer! He spoke to some friends at the police station in Mineola and they told him the New York City detectives want both of us to go to Manhattan to answer more questions. He's going to meet us here in about fifteen minutes. Is that reporter still out there?"

"Yes," says Keith, holding Sarah close and rubbing his hand over her back. "Now listen. Skip Larson from PIX is out front. I told him I'd find out if you'd answer some questions. We can let him in so it looks like you're going to cooperate, and then we can get him to leave if we tell him we need to talk to the police. Don't worry; everything will be fine." He kisses Sarah and turns back toward the door. Opening it slightly, he pokes his head out and motions for Skip to come inside.

The truck that Jack was trailing cut through the constant Manhattan traffic like butter, making the ride back to home base a short one. So, when the partners enter the squad room and see Sergeants Burley and Gomez already at their desks, Jack is both surprised and pissed in equal measure.

"I thought you two went out to the Island to round up suspects," challenges Jack. "Why are you back so soon?"

Gomez sighs and flees for the coffee pot, leaving Burley to respond.

"There was no need to drive all the way out there, Jack," Burley says. "Mrs. Cummings called while we were in the car. She said Skip Larson was at her house and that she and O'Toole agreed to do a quick interview with him. After that, they're coming here with their lawyer. They should arrive in a couple of hours."

"Okay," says Jack sheepishly. "Sorry I snapped."

"No prob. I guess we're all a little frustrated with this case. After I hung up with Mrs. Cummings, I got a call from a Sergeant Collins at Nassau County PD. He contacted Salvatore Brusco and got him to come in as well, and about fifteen minutes after that, Brusco called and said he was leaving his house. He should be here before Cummings and O'Toole."

"They're all coming in together? What the fuck?" swears Jack, irritated that the rest of his day promises to be pretty hectic. He quickly calms down, however. "Never mind," he says. "Ally, can you fill them in on what happened with Lincoln? I gotta hit the head."

Nodding her assent, Allison grabs a cup of coffee from Gomez before launching into her summary of their morning.

"We think Lincoln is hiding something," she says. "He wouldn't make eye contact with either of us, and he seemed to be searching pretty hard for answers that wouldn't come back to bite him. We need to look at his financial statements, and we need to check any contacts he may have had with our other suspects, including firefighter Grimes."

"You want to check out Lincoln's financials, too?" asks Gomez with an arched brow.

Allison takes a sip of her coffee. "Yeah, I guess so. Actually, we should check all the firefighters. They all seem to have a taste for fine watches. Lincoln was wearing a diamond Tag Heuer."

"Nice!"

"Yeah, it's interesting. Hey, Burley," she asks John, "can you send a photo of Grimes to Chief Turner in Jersey? Ask him to find out if anyone saw him hanging around there."

With a toss of his head, Skip beckons his cameraman to follow him into Sarah's house. When they enter, O'Toole leads them into the living room.

Glancing around, Skip takes a minute to assess the best placements for his subjects. Pointing to the sofa, he asks Keith to sit next to Sarah and then takes a seat in a nearby armchair.

With a meaningful glance at his cameraman, Skip picks up his mic to begin the interview.

"Today, I'm at Mrs. Stanley Cummings' house on Long Island. She has graciously allowed us to ask her some questions about her late husband, the man who mysteriously showed up at the South Pool of the Trade Towers Memorial just the other day." Thrusting the microphone into Sarah's face, he asks, *"Mrs. Cummings, is it true that your husband was the owner of the coin dealership in the South Tower, and that he was listed as one of the many who died on 9/11?"* When Sarah nods affirmatively, he asks, *"Where has he been all this time, ma'am, and what happened to all the gold that was stored in his company's vaults? The majority of it was never found."*

Squeezing Keith's hand tightly, Sarah responds in a clear voice. *"Mr. Larson, I don't know what happened with Stan or the gold, or with anything. The authorities told my family and me that Stan died that day and that they couldn't find his body. We grieved and held a funeral, and we eventually went on with our lives. This new development is very disturbing. I'm astonished at the thought that Stan deliberately deserted his children and me, and I can't understand how he could have just disappeared."* In a voice now cracking with emotion, she says, *"I don't know where he's been all this time."*

"Look, Sarah's upset," interrupts Keith, "and we can't spend any more time talking to you now. We have an appointment with the detectives who are investigating this mystery. They want to ask us some questions in Manhattan. I'm sorry, but you'll have to leave now."

Nodding reluctantly, Skip ends the interview inside the house, but continues his comments curbside, in front of his video van. Holding his microphone lightly, he looks into the camera and records the rest of his remarks for the evening's broadcast.

"Mrs. Cummings appears to be as shocked as we are. She says she had no idea that her husband didn't die in the collapse of the South Tower, and she insists that she knows nothing about the missing gold. Maybe it's still under all of that concrete and steel, or maybe Stanley Cummings stashed it away somewhere where we'll never find it.

"This is Skip Larson, on the case for News 11."

CHAPTER NINE

"Well," says Jack, standing at the whiteboard, studying the names and photos of all the suspects, "we have several potential villains here: Cummings' wife, Captain Sam Lincoln, Keith O'Toole, Salvatore Brusco, and Larry Grimes. They all seem to be connected to the missing gold, and because O'Toole and Mrs. Cummings are linked and want to be interviewed together, it seems that we can also put a romantic element into the mix. Damn! If we can just get some Rock 'n' Roll involved too, we'd have a first run movie!"

Pleased by his own wisecrack, Jack smiles to himself and continues to stare at the board while behind him, a young officer enters the squad room followed by Sarah Cummings, Keith O'Toole, and their attorney.

"Excuse me, Detective Stenhouse," the officer announces, "your visitors are here."

"Well, well, well," says Jack, catching Keith's eye. "I didn't expect to see you and Sarah here together. On a date, are we?"

"We just got engaged," responds Keith curtly. "We became close after Stan... I mean, when we thought Stan was dead."

"Oh, I see," says Jack with a tilt of his head. "We

do need to talk about Stanley and some missing gold. We'd also like to share some new revelations about this case with each of you, but we're going to do all of that separately. Mr. O'Toole, I'll be questioning you with Sergeant Gomez, and Detective Giancarlo and Sergeant Burley will question Mrs. Cummings. Please come with us."

At that, Keith's eyes widen, and he glances at his lawyer. "I don't want to leave Sarah alone," he objects before his attorney puts a silencing hand upon his arm.

"You can interview them together, or not at all," asserts the attorney. "I'll be overseeing the entire process, so if at any time I think the rights of my clients are being violated, I'll end this pretty quickly."

Although the attorney's power play was expected, Jack can't help but frown at the man's haughty attitude. Brushing past him, Jack stands in front of O'Toole with a deep and menacing stare.

"I really don't give a rat's ass what you want," he growls at Keith. "So, let's do this the easy way, shall we?" he says, turning his penetrating stare onto the lawyer. "By the way, nice watch, O'Toole," he adds, looking back at Keith. Then, beckoning to his team, Jack says, "Allison, come with me. Burley, you and Gomez can observe."

As the group walks down the hallway, a buzz fills the air, and all heads turn toward the commotion. A tall redhead in a black jacket and tight skirt ending two inches above her knees exits the elevator to low murmurs and whispers. The men in the corridor instantly notice that the woman isn't wearing a blouse under her jacket, and they all instinctively check to see if she's wearing undergarments. Her six-inch heels similarly draw their eyes to her legs, which seem to go all the way up to her neck.

Towering over most, the six-foot-three-inch beauty sashays toward Jack, his team, and their suspects. As everyone takes a long, appreciative look at the new arrival, Jack mutters admiringly, "Daammmnn! That's one tall drink of water!"

Breaking free of the crowd, Sergeant Burley, the Homicide Department's young and currently unattached stud, shoulders his way past everyone like a dog in heat. Making his way toward the mysterious woman, he gushes a breathless, "Hi," and is instantly enveloped by the heady scent of her perfume. "I'm Sergeant Burley. Welcome to the First. How can I help you?"

The redhead smiles as she sizes up Burley and looks into his deep blue eyes. Breathing in his Old Spice, her eyes stop briefly at the badge fastened to his waistband. "Hello, Hector Burley," she says. "Is Detective Stenhouse free, or does he charge?"

Hearing his name used in that clichéd line, Jack reluctantly moves his eyes off the woman's ample breasts. "That's me," he responds, "and you can't afford me. What's a nice girl like you doing in a place like this?" he asks, not caring that he's also using an outdated line. The woman has such a strong resemblance to Jessica Rabbit from the movie, Who Framed Roger Rabbit, that he can't help himself.

Groaning at the corny exchange, Allison tugs at

Jack's shoulder. "Hey," she insists, "you're going to be a father, remember?"

"Just window shopping," Jack confides as the tall redhead slithers toward him.

Knowing that Jack was ogling her chest, the woman reaches into her jacket pocket and pulls out a business card, straining the garment's buttons in the process. Handing Jack the card, she says, "Detective, I'm Sylvia Stone, a claims investigator for Liberty Life and Casualty. You're investigating a murder that we're interested in."

Standing nearby, Sarah Cummings' face pales, and she grabs Keith O'Toole's arm.

With the shapely woman in such close proximity, Jack's mind involuntarily goes into overdrive. As visions of his naked wife pass before his eyes, images of what may be beneath that jacket blur his thoughts. Knowing that he needs to appear professional, he struggles to shake off his risqué ideas. At long last, he manages to say, "Well, um...Ms. Stone...we're about to interrogate several persons that Liberty Life may be interested in."

"Detective Stenhouse, can we talk first? Somewhere private?" purrs Sylvia.

Surprised by the request, Jack hesitates. "Okay," he says after a moment. "Allison, start the interrogation without me. I'll join you later." Catching the eye of Sergeant Gomez, he adds, "Before you start observing, find out where Brusco is, huh?" Looking back at Ms. Stone, he says, "We can use my lieutenant's office. He's not here right now."

Allison watches Jack closely as he guides Sylvia through the door of Lieutenant Conrad's glass-enclosed office. Shaking her head in exasperation, she mumbles, "*Puttana*" under her breath, and turns to lead the suspects and their attorney to the interrogation room.

Inside Conrad's office, Jack motions for Sylvia to take a seat while he moves behind his boss' desk. Settling into the chair, Sylvia automatically crosses her legs, causing her tight skirt to rise four inches. Aware that Jack is staring, Sarah parts her lips seductively and then gets down to business.

"Detective," she says softly, "Liberty Life and Casualty paid out a large settlement to Mrs. Cummings upon the declaration of her husband's death in 2001, but we have recently re-opened the case. Our company needs to know the circumstances of Mr. Cummings' actual death so we can decide whether to revoke the payment we already made, or require Sarah Cummings to repay the interest we lost on the premature settlement. There was a clause in Mr. Cummings' policy that prohibited payment in the event of suicide or other dangerous or illegal activities that may lead to death, so you can understand our position. I've been assigned to investigate Mr. Cummings' death for my company, and I will help you and your team in any way possible. I hope we can work together and share the information each of us gathers. Can I count on your cooperation, Jack, and the cooperation of the First Precinct?"

Jack stares at Sylvia with unseeing eyes, as various scenarios once again flash through his mind. Sylvia smiles and waits for Jack to return to the conversation.

"Ms. Stone," he finally says, "I will need to obtain approval from Deputy Inspector Rawlings before I can allow a private citizen to partner with us in police business. Real life is not like what you see on TV."

Just then, Deputy Inspector Gene Rawlings enters the office. "I heard we had a visitor from Liberty Life Insurance," he says to Jack. Then, turning to Sylvia, he extends his hand. "Hello, Miss," he says sweetly, "I'm D.I. Rawlings. Welcome to my Precinct. What can we do for you?"

Jack stares at the inspector in surprise, as his customarily gruff manner is nowhere in evidence. *Yup*, he reflects with a sly smile, *it all boils down to T and A.*

Sylvia rises from her chair to clasp the deputy inspector's hand in a firm handshake. Then, she cocks her head flirtatiously and brushes her hair away from her face. "Inspector," she says coyly, "it's a pleasure to meet you. My, there are a lot of handsome men in this department!" she adds, unabashedly flirting with the older man. Continuing to toy with her red hair, she says, "As I was explaining to Detective Stenhouse, I was sent here to investigate the death of Stanley Cummings. My company paid out a large sum of money to his wife under false pretenses, and we must now determine our next course of action. Sir, my company would like me to work closely with the detective and his team of investigators, but Detective Stenhouse has just informed me that we need your permission before I can partner with your department. Would you agree to that? I promise I won't cause a stir."

It's very apparent to Jack that Sylvia knows how to get men to do whatever she wants, so he is not surprised when Rawlings responds, "Well, Sylvia you've already caused a stir, but I'm pleased to give you my permission. Stenhouse, effective immediately, you have another partner. Keep me informed on the progress you two make." Shaking Sylvia's hand again, Rawlings gazes into her eyes and says, "Welcome aboard, Miss... You know, I don't think I caught your name."

"No, you didn't. I'm Sylvia Stone."

"Okay, then, Sylvia. If there is anything I can do for you, don't hesitate to knock on my door at any time."

"Thank you; I will."

With his hand on the back of his neck, Jack shakes his head in astonishment at the amusing scene he has just witnessed.

When they are alone again, Sylvia directs her attention back to Jack. Leaning over the desk, she places both palms on its surface as if she were ready to pounce, giving Jack a full view. "So what do we do now, Detective?" she asks coyly.

Jack narrows his eyes as he looks up at Sylvia. Then he abruptly grabs the lapels of her jacket and pulls her closer, providing him with an even better look inside her valley of earthly delights. "Nice tits," he murmurs, "but I've seen bigger and better." Releasing her jacket, he rises from his chair. "Now that we got that over with, if you want to work with me on this case, you're gonna have to keep it strictly professional. Sexual innuendos may work well with others, but that dog won't hunt out in the streets. Not that I don't like a little T and A, but that kind of distraction on the job could get somebody killed. I suggest you get with the program. You *capeesh*?" Although Jack appreciates a good view, he's all business when it's time for work.

Stung by Jack's reprimand, Sylvia's face became as red as her hair. To compose herself, she takes a deep breath and gives Jack a wry smile.

"Okay, can't blame a girl for trying. Professional, it is." While Jack continues to stare her down, Sylvia self-consciously smooths down her hair and jacket.

"All right," says Jack. "Let's talk. Today, we're interrogating Sarah Cummings and Keith O'Toole, a firefighter who knew Sarah's husband. Sarah and Keith are now engaged. You can watch their interrogations with Sergeants Burley and Gomez in the observation room. After the interviews, Sergeant Burley will fill you in on the information we already have on Mrs. Cummings. Of course, we'll also need you to give us everything you have concerning this case."

"Yes, absolutely. You should know that Stanley Cummings also insured his business through my company, so that's another reason we're very interested in your investigation. We have a team checking into the Twin Towers' architectural design and tenant records. Our goal is to find out how Stanley got out of there, and to locate the valuables we insured. So, let's get to work."

Nodding, Jack opens the door to let Sylvia exit the office. *If I weren't happily married,* he muses internally, *I'd be all over you like white on rice.* As if Sylvia had read his thoughts, she tilts her head, flicks her hair, and winks as she passes him by.

Following Sylvia into the squad room, Jack

watches in amusement as two officers stop and stare as she glides past. When Jack reaches them, he overhears one of them say, "I'd eat a yard of her shit just to see where it came from." Smiling, Jack offers each of them a high five.

At the sound of the hand clasps, Sylvia turns around and sees Jack and the two officers standing together with their arms folded over their chests—all of them staring at her derriere.

CHAPTER TEN

When Sylvia said she would concentrate on business, she meant it. She is so focused on watching the interrogation through the one-way mirror that she doesn't notice that Gomez and Burley aren't paying attention to the proceedings like she is. Instead, they are standing behind her, soaking in her fragrance.

Inside the interrogation room, Jack is also focused. He is listening intently as Giancarlo questions Sarah Cummings, seated protectively between the couple's lawyer and her fiancé. Sarah, Jack notes, is gripping O'Toole's hand as if her life depended on it.

Frequently consulting her notes, Giancarlo grills the nervous woman.

"Mrs. Cummings, we have obtained your sons' records from Harvard. Those records indicate that both of their tuitions have been paid in full, without the assistance of loans or scholarships. Can you explain how you can afford to send both of your children to such an expensive school?"

"I, uh…" begins Sarah, until her lawyer stops her with a hand on her arm and a shake of his head.

Noting the attorney's cautionary motions, Allison changes tactics.

"Mrs. Cummings, how have you managed to

build your net worth up to an approximate sum of more than two million dollars? We know that you received payments from your husband's insurance settlement and the 9/11 Victim's Fund, but when we add them to your net worth before September 11th, they don't bring the total anywhere near two million dollars."

To gather her thoughts, Sarah stares at the ceiling and wrings her hands. Before speaking, she gives Keith a sidelong glance.

"A few months after I was told that Stan was considered among the dead from the attack, I went to Ladder Company 403 to express my gratitude for all they did that day and during the cleanup, and I found myself sitting next to Keith in the break room. We talked for a long time. He said he intended to retire because of what he had seen; the memories were intruding into his life in too many ways. He said he thought he might do something in the financial field because he used to help the other firefighters with their finances. I told him about the rough time I was having trying to decide what to do with my money since I was a newly single parent, and he volunteered to look over my situation. Keith was such a great help to me," she says, smiling at her fiancé. "With his guidance, I was able to invest well over the years, and we became close. You probably know that we're now engaged."

Allison is not impressed by Sarah's story. "So, what you're telling me," she states dryly, "is that you invested the modest amount of money you had so well that it grew to an enormous amount in less than ten years. Did you invest it legally, Mrs. Cummings?"

"That is an outrageous question, Detective!" huffs the attorney as Sarah gasps in shock. "What do you base it on? My clients are not on trial here; they have not been accused of doing anything illegal. They have willingly volunteered to help you investigate the death of Sarah's husband, so be careful with your line of questioning."

"Are you saying I knew where Stan was all this time and that we stole the gold from his business?" asks Sarah indignantly. "Are you crazy, Detective? I'm done here," she vows as sweat beads up on her brow. "You can question Keith if you want, but I'm done."

Agreeing with Sarah, the attorney smiles, and each of them sits back in their chairs with their arms crossed over their chests.

Sarah is relieved she spoke out and hopes she won't have to answer any more questions. Not today, anyway. She is still nervous, however. She restlessly flicks the nails of one hand with the nails of the other, and this catches the attention of both detectives.

"Be careful, Mrs. Cummings," says Jack. "I'm sure you don't want to ruin your manicure. Look, we haven't charged you with a crime. We're just trying to gather as much information as we can. However, we could change our minds and charge you with impeding our investigation. How does that sound?"

At that, the attorney rises from his chair and scolds Jack amid annoying clicking sounds from Sarah. "Charge her, or release her," he demands. "She's finished talking. I'm going to take her out of the room now. Detectives, I warn you not to talk to Mr. O'Toole while I'm gone, and I caution you to think twice about what you will be asking him, and how you will be phrasing your questions."

Jack and Allison confer quietly until the counselor returns. When he reclaims his seat, Jack picks up the interrogation.

"Sooo, Mr. O'Toole," he begins, "how can a retired fireman afford a Rolex watch? We looked at the financial histories of all the firefighters from Ladder Company 403 who were on duty on 9/11, and we were surprised to see that all of you are fairly well-off now. How did you guys get the gold out of there?"

"I don't know what you're talking about, Detective," responds Keith quickly. "I invested well and helped Sarah invest well, so..."

Rising, the attorney interrupts Keith. "Once again, Detective, my clients have done nothing wrong. Therefore, since you haven't charged them with anything, this outrageous interview is over."

"One last question, please," counters Jack. "Mr. O'Toole, what did Larry Grimes do on the morning of the Trade Towers attack?"

Keith looks at his lawyer, who nods his okay. "He was on cook duty that day. Captain Walsh told us that he left the station to pick up supplies. That was the last time I saw him."

"Okay, now it's over. We're leaving," states the attorney as he grabs Keith's elbow and guides him out of the room.

Following the suspects out, Stenhouse and Giancarlo walk toward the observation room, where Stone, Burley, and Gomez have been watching the proceedings.

"She's hiding something," declares Allison as soon as they enter the room. Staring through the mirror at the empty interrogation table, she says, "She got some gold from her husband, I just know it. This whole thing stinks."

"Sylvia," says Jack, "all the firemen we believe are involved in this shit are well-off now, and O'Toole is knee-deep in it. We need to get something on them. Can you get the Trade Tower building plans from your group? Allison, try to get maps of the subway system and the Trade Tower stations."

"Okay, will do," respond Allison and Sylvia simultaneously.

"Thanks," says Jack. "You know, Keith slammed shut harder than a clam in there. Maybe Brusco's our weak link. When is he due here?"

Allison looks at her Timex. "He should have arrived a long time ago. I'll see if I can contact him to find out where he is."

Jack inhales deeply and exhales slowly through his nose. "Look, I gotta leave for a while; I have to bring something to my wife. I'll be back in an hour or so. I want to interrogate Brusco personally, so if he shows up while I'm gone, hold off until I return."

"Look, I'll get all the plans and maps," says Sylvia to Jack and Allison. "I want to show you that I can be a good team player."

"Okay," says Jack.

As Sylvia leaves the room, Allison notices that Jack is staring at her legs, so she gives him a poke. Then, when she sees Burley gazing longingly at Sylvia's backside, she rolls her eyes skyward and sighs.

When the redhead is finally out of sight, Jack turns his attention back to his crew. "I gotta make a run to Didi's. See you all later." He heads for the door but only makes it halfway through before he stops and turns around. "Oh, I almost forgot," he says, scratching his head. "Gomez, contact Turner in Jersey to see if he got a hit on Grimes' photo. And Burley, get your head out of Stone's ass and get Lincoln in here, STAT."

"That goes for you, too, Jack!" shouts Giancarlo, to snickers from Hector and John.

Across town, Didi is on her lunch break at the boutique, but she isn't eating much. The only nourishment she can keep down lately is wheat crackers and ice water. As she takes small bites of her crackers, she stares at a photo of her husband. With a sigh, she murmurs, "I love you, Jack, but I feel so sick right now."

"Well, that's why I'm here, Babe."

Startled, Didi whips her head around. "Jack!" she gasps. "You scared the crap out of me! What are you doing here at this time of day? Is anything wrong?" Rising from her chair, Mrs. Stenhouse greets her husband with a kiss and an unexpected belch. "OH!" she exclaims. "Eew. I'm sorry, Honey."

"Don't worry about it," responds Jack. "Still feeling bad, eh? Well, I got some of that gum I was telling you about. Allison said it helped her."

With the speed of a striking rattler, Didi grabs the bag from her husband, opens one of the packs, and places a stick into her mouth. "Oh, Jack, it's so soothing," she sighs after a few chews. "Thanks, Hon. Maybe I can start eating regular food soon. Want some crackers?"

"No, not without some Easy Cheese," laughs Jack. "Look, I can't stay. I just stopped by to give you the gum. Gotta catch some bad guys, ya know?" Reaching out, Jack gently squeezes one of his wife's large breasts and kisses her on the forehead.

With a playful swat, Didi bats Jack's hand away and follows him to the front of the store. Watching him get into his car, she waits until she hears the familiar two quick beeps of his horn before she waves, even though an old man walking his dog blocks Jack's view.

Jack makes it back to the First about ten minutes after Salvatore Brusco arrives at the station.

"Brusco is in Interrogation Room Two," announces Gomez, "and Giancarlo is with him. He was late because of an accident on the L.I.E."

"Okay," says Jack.

"I also talked to Chief Turner. The Chief and Aaron Dawson, the facilities manager you met at the blueberry farm, remember seeing Grimes with Stanley

Cummings at the town's Farmers Market."

"That's just great," says Jack with a tilt of his head. "Now, we have another 'phantom' we need to locate among the living. Where's that redheaded Jessica Rabbit look-a-like?"

Gomez chuckles. "She went to get the architectural plans for the Trade Towers and the maps of the subway system. Oh, by the way, Skippy interviewed Mrs. Cummings and O'Toole, and he made a comment about you on the air."

Jack is unimpressed. "Screw him and the horse he rode in on," he grumbles. "Hey, I'll make a bet with ya. The next time we see Stone, I bet she changes her appearance."

"You gotta tell me why you know that," challenges Gomez.

With a loud laugh, Jack heads to the interrogation room. As he opens the door, he sees Salvatore Brusco taking a puff from his inhaler.

"Mr. Brusco, are you okay?" asks Jack as he takes a seat next to Allison. "We have several questions for you, if you're up to it."

"Yes, I'm okay," answers Brusco in a thick and wheezy voice.

"All right. First, we checked your financial records, and they agree with your explanation of when you purchased your house. You did indeed buy it before the prices went sky high during the housing crisis, but that doesn't explain how you came up with the down payment, and how you can afford a Rolex."

Brusco answers slowly. "My wife got a settlement from a car accident," he says, wheezing. "That's how we came into some of the cash. The Rolex was a gift from my kids when I retired. They knew it was something I always wanted. I was pretty sick there for a while, so I guess they decided to give it to me while I was still around. You can check with our lawyer about the settlement, and you can call my sons if you want to."

Jack stares at Brusco. "I need to ask you about a fellow firefighter, one of the men who was reported lost on 9/11. His name is Larry Grimes."

At the mention of Larry's name, Salvatore appears uncomfortable and takes a minute to respond. "Yes, Larry," he says after a few coughs. "He came over to us from you guys. He was with the police bomb squad before he transferred to the fire department. He thought he was moving into a less perilous profession," he adds with a grimace.

Jack glances at Allison before asking his next question. "Salvatore, did you see Larry Grimes enter the Tower that day?"

"No, no," says Brusco. "He left the station before we got the call. A couple of the guys rotated kitchen duty, and that day, it was Larry's turn. He told Captain Walsh that he needed to run to the store to get some last minute things for dinner. Walsh told him to take his command vehicle, and the shit came down while he was gone. I arrived at the scene on one of the last trucks, and I remember seeing the chief's car already there. I figured that Larry drove there from the store and that he was already inside. When the Towers fell, I

Frank A. Ruffolo

got buried by some debris. I'm lucky that it wasn't too deep, because after the air started to clear, I could see light through the dust and stuff. My head and arms were clear, but I was pinned down by something. I removed my face mask at that point, and that turned out to be a big mistake. What I breathed in caused me to lose a lung. Keith was the one who found me and got me out. We got some water from people in the street and then we went back in and started digging."

Jack continues to study Brusco. "What about Grimes? Did you see him at the Towers?"

"No, Detective." Brusco tries to swallow but coughs instead. After he clears his throat, he asks, "You got any water? My mouth is pretty dry from all this talking."

While Allison leaves the room to get some bottled water, Jack continues.

"Salvatore, you told one of our sergeants that Sam Lincoln crawled down into a cleared space in the basement and started bringing up gold and coins through a small hole in the debris. But how did he do that? It would have to take hours to get all of that stuff out of there."

Salvatore thinks while he continues to clear his throat. When Allison returns with a cold bottle of water, he downs half of it like a thirsty marathon runner at the end of a race.

"Oh, that's better," he says, placing the bottle on the table and replacing the cap. "Yeah, it did take a while. From what I could see, the crawlspace into the vault area was pretty narrow, but there was an open place inside it where you could stand up. I guess it was about thirty feet wide. When I looked into the hole, I saw coins and papers and stuff, along with damaged vault drawers. If I didn't know better, I'd say a bomb went off in that area. They sent a cadaver dog in first, and then Keith and Sam went in. After a while, they started to hand stuff up. I helped for a while, and then a transit cop relieved me. They sent me to the other fallen Tower."

"Thanks, Mr. Brusco," says Allison. "This information is very helpful, but we may need to talk again. You have our number. If you remember anything else, please don't hesitate to call."

"One more question before you go," interjects Jack. "We were told that a man who may have had asthma visited Stan Cummings at his hideout. That man wouldn't have been you, would it?"

Brusco knits his brows together in surprise. "Me? No! I don't even know where Cummings went! Where the hell was he?"

Jack pulls a map out of the Cummings file and points. "Right here in the Pine Barrens of South Jersey."

"Ha. Like I said, it wasn't me. If I went anywhere near a pine forest, my asthma and allergies would kill me. You can check my medical records and see for yourself. My doctor is Jeffrey Kleinhoff in Glen Cove. He says if my asthma gets any worse, I'll have to move to Arizona. It's a little too humid for me up where I live near Long Island Sound."

After Brusco leaves, Jack says, "Man, I felt sure that guy was involved, but I don't think he knows anything about Cummings and the missing gold."

"Yeah," sighs Allison, "but Grimes left the station ahead of everyone else. Maybe he didn't go to the market after all. And Keith was in the vault with Lincoln."

Jack pinches his nose as if he were trying to stave off a headache. "Right. That's some good info. However, now we're going to have to question O'Toole again, and getting anything else out of him or Sarah Cummings will be next to impossible—unless we charge each of them with something. And then we'll have to deal with their lawyer. Well, next up, Sam Lincoln. Let's get something to eat before he gets here."

CHAPTER ELEVEN

The partners decide to go to The Burger Joint, one of their favorite restaurants. Agreeing to walk the few blocks, they almost instantly regret their decision. The beautiful spring day has brought out more than the usual number of Big Apple pedestrians, and the sidewalks are exceptionally crowded.

As they squeeze past another person blocking their path, a commercial jet flies overhead and Jack looks up, his mind drifting back to the terrorist attack on the city. He remembers that he was on his way to a class at the police academy in South Florida when he heard that the two planes hit the Twin Towers.

Their favorite Burger Joint is also more crowded than usual, so the pair decide to sit at the counter instead of waiting for a table. After placing their orders, they huddle close to review their case.

"Jack, I remember hearing that ten to fifteen million dollars of gold was missing from the Tower after 9/11, but that was its value in 2001. I did some checking, and gold was only worth about $275 per ounce at that time. It's worth five times that now."

Jack sips an Arnold Palmer with a blank stare. "That's not the only thing. That much gold would have to weigh a few thousand pounds. There's no way they could have taken all of it out of there that morning; there wasn't enough time. It had to be taken out before the attack, way before the attack. I think Stan was stealing from his own business and that he had help from Ladder 403. There has to be some connection between them. Why don't you go to the fire station after lunch? Snoop around there while we're questioning Lincoln at the First. That way, Lincoln won't be able to run interference with his crew. If you find anything, I'll take another trip out to Brusco's to ask him about it; maybe he'll give up some more information. When I questioned him about Stanley, he got a little flustered. He knows something else, and we need to find out what it is."

After the food arrives, Allison brings up Sylvia Stone. "What do you make of that redheaded *puttana*?"

Jack laughs aloud and nearly chokes on his fries at Allison's colorful choice of words. "Sylvia? What a piece of work! I can't believe she tried to use sex to weasel her way into the investigation! She's supposed to be investigating Cummings' death for the insurance company that paid the benefits on his life and business! But she won't be flaunting her assets at us again. I made sure of that real quick."

"What the hell did you do, Jack?" asks Allison, leaning over from the next stool.

Jack chuckles. "Well, she wanted me to see what she had under that jacket, so I obliged and took a peek. No big deal. Not bad, but no big deal. Then I told her to cut it out. Right after that, Rawlings butted his head in, and she twisted him around her little finger. He gave her permission to help us and ordered us to share info with each other. His little brain was speaking for his big brain, if you know what I mean. Hey, maybe if you want a promotion, you should dress up like that, too. Whaddaya think?"

Allison replies with a choice verb and pronoun, and the rest of the meal is spent chatting about Allison's children and Didi's pregnancy.

When they're finished, Jack pays at the cash register and takes a toothpick from the counter dispenser. Placing it on his lower lip, it looks and feels to him like an unlit cigarette. Jack stopped smoking a few years ago, but every so often, he gets the urge to smoke again. When that happens, he does whatever he can to combat the feeling, and today, the toothpick is doing the trick.

When Jack and Allison exit the restaurant, they stop dead in their tracks on the sidewalk, each of them frowning at the sight before them. Parked in front of the store is a WPIX video truck, and Skip Larson is hurrying in their direction.

"Detectives Jack Stenhouse and Allison Giancarlo are the lead investigators of the mysterious death at the Trade Towers Memorial," says Skip into a handheld microphone. *"What new information can you share with the people of New York?"* he asks, thrusting the mic into Jack's face.

Annoyed by the pushy reporter, Jack takes the toothpick from his mouth and flicks it past Skip's ear. Then, he winks at Allison. Because Allison knows her partner well, she responds to Jack with an enthusiastic grin. *Boy, this is going to be good*, she says to herself.

Stepping back a bit from the main players, Allison watches as Jack snatches the microphone from Skip's hands and turns toward the cameraman. Pointing at the video camera on the man's shoulder, he barks, "Shut that thing off, NOW!"

Skip takes a step back but gives his video man the signal to turn off the camera. When the man complies and retreats toward the van, Jack walks up to the weaselly newsperson. Grabbing the belt around Skip's waist, he pulls the man toward him, and forces Skip to shove the mic into the open space between his pants and his abdomen. Then, he grabs Skip by the lapel of his sports jacket and pulls him even closer. When they are nose to nose, Jack snarls, "Just so you know, Skippy, that's what a hard on feels like. The next time you interrupt me during my lunch break, you'll need to have that microphone surgically removed. Now, if you want more info, talk to Conrad. Got it?" Releasing his grip on the reporter, Jack calmly adjusts Skip's jacket and pats the side of the stunned reporter's face. "Have a nice day," he adds, with just a hint of malice.

Mortified, Skip pulls the microphone out of his slacks and rushes into the van, slamming the door behind him.

Allison hurries to catch up to Jack as he pushes his way through the crowd of people who stopped to watch the drama. "Dammit," she says worriedly, "I didn't think you'd go that far. You know Conrad is gonna hear about this. I hope none of the onlookers took videos of that exchange."

"Frankly, my dear, I don't give a damn," quips Jack in a weak imitation of Clark Gable.

A couple of blocks later, Allison separates from Jack. She heads to the fire station while he continues on to the First.

When Jack enters his department, he spots Hector Gomez drinking yet another cup of coffee, and Jack's caustic side, which has just been given a boost, kicks in.

"Don't you have anything better to do than drink nonstop cups of coffee? What have you been doing while I was gone?" he asks sharply. "Where's Burley?"

"He's with Lincoln in Room Two, waiting for you," Gomez responds, ignoring Jack's harsh tone. Then, grinning mischievously, he adds, "The word around here is that you inspected Sylvia Stone's credentials. Did you find them up to snuff?"

"Hmpf. They weren't what I expected, but I like my women the same way I like my coffee—the larger the cup, the better."

Caught in mid-gulp, a vigorous coughing spell replaces Gomez's hearty laugh as his body attempts to keep his beverage from flowing out of his nose.

Wickedly pleased by Gomez' predicament, Jack strolls confidently out of the squad room and enters Interrogation Room Two, where he takes a seat next to John Burley.

"Sorry I'm late, Captain," Jack apologizes as he stares narrowly at Captain Sam Lincoln. "I just got back from lunch. We called you into the station to go over a part of your testimony that we don't understand."

"Oh? What part is that?"

"You told us you were the only one who crawled through a hole your colleagues made in the debris and that you found yourself in a very confined area where you retrieved precious metals and coins from the wreckage. However, we received some contradictory information. We were told that the area where the vaults were found was actually quite large. In fact, it was large enough for at least two people to work in—you and Keith O'Toole. Would you like to comment on that, Captain?"

Not missing a beat, Sam Lincoln leans forward and says, "You're right, Detective. I didn't think it mattered to you if more than one person retrieved the stuff. Keith was with me near the vaults, and we handed what we found up to the others."

"So you were lying before, and now you're telling the truth?"

"Look, Stenhouse," replies Lincoln pointedly, "don't try that crap with me. I wasn't lying before. I just thought it didn't matter who found the gold and who brought it up out of the hole. I shortened the story; gave you the Reader's Digest version. We dug until we hit the opening. I climbed in first to determine whether it was safe, and Keith followed. Together, we brought up what we found. Brusco was up at the surface when we started to retrieve the coins and bullion, and later that day, he was assigned to the other Tower. Period. End of story. Anything else?"

Jack narrows his eyes at the suspect. "Yes," he says sharply. "How was Stanley Cummings connected with Ladder Company 403? Was he involved with your firehouse before 9/11?"

"Well," Lincoln says after a short silence, "he was a business owner in the area, and he bought a table at the Fireman's Ball almost every year. He also gave us a large contribution when he won the bid on a Ladder 403 fire helmet at one of the silent auctions. Why do you ask?"

Jack's expression becomes as stiff as the busts on Mount Rushmore. "Captain, how these interrogations works is, I ask the questions, and you supply the answers. Now, I'm going to ask you another question. How were you able to identify the coin that was found on Cummings the day he died?"

"Ah, the Roman Aureus," smiles Sam. "Like I told you before, I'm a coin collector, and that coin is quite rare. I happened to see the same one recently on that reality show about the pawn shop in Vegas. You know the one? One of their customers came into the store and tried to pawn it. That's how I learned about it. Now, look, I'm a busy man. If there's nothing else you want to bother me with today, I need to get back to work."

Trying hard not to show his frustration with the firehouse captain, Jack breathes deeply and exhales silently. "What can you tell me about Larry Grimes?"

"He was one of the firemen who died that day. He transferred to us from the police department; he was in your bomb squad division. He thought fighting fires would be less risky than diffusing bombs. How's that for ironic?"

Jack smirks. "Yeah, I heard that before. Okay," he

continues, placing both palms on the table, "we're done for now. However, as the old cliché goes, don't leave town. By the way, Captain, we found Grimes' finger-prints in the house that Cummings was hiding out in."

Lincoln looks sharply at Stenhouse, his face ashen.

"What's the matter, Captain?" asks Jack inno-cently. "Are you afraid of ghosts?" With Lincoln's mouth hanging open in surprise, Jack dismisses him from the room.

On the way back into the squad room accom-panied by John Burley, Jack hears his name shouted across the office by Lieutenant Conrad.

"STENHOUSE! IN MY OFFICE! NOW!"

Chuckling, Jack shrugs his shoulders. "Wonder what's up now."

Standing outside of police headquarters, Sam Lincoln waits until the flow of officers in and out of the building quiets down. Then, he makes an urgent, hushed phone call.

"Keith, they found Grimes' fingerprints in Jersey. Meet me at Garvies Point at seven."

CHAPTER TWELVE

Detective Allison Giancarlo is happily following her escort up the staircase to the second floor living quarters at the Ladder Company 403 stationhouse. The muscles of the young firefighter in front of her look as if they're trying to escape from a polo shirt that's two sizes too small.

When she arrives in the living area, Giancarlo immediately sees what she's looking for. Displayed on the wall between two rows of beds are several photographs of the fire station's crew at various community events, including the Fireman's Ball.

Zeroing in on photos from the event, she grins when she spots a happy couple with their arms linked together. To be on the safe side, she scrutinizes several more photos before she returns to the one that caught her eye.

Satisfied that the image will help with the investigation, Allison turns to the strapping young man beside her and unknowingly gives him the once-over. When the firefighter sees that his physique is appreciated, he smiles and expands his chest proudly.

Uh-oh, thinks Allison, realizing what she did. Clearing her throat, she asks, "Why is there a photo of Mr. and Mrs. Stanley Cummings on your wall?"

"Oh," says the fireman, disappointed that he may have misread Allison's intentions. "Mr. Cummings made a large donation at the silent auction at the Ball that night, and he's also made numerous donations to the station over the years. He even renovated our kitchen; he replaced all the appliances."

"Really? Do you have any other photos of the Cummings' from the Ball or any other function?"

"Sure do, ma'am. There's a file on Lieutenant Jerguen's laptop. He's the photographer for our station-house, and he has all the pictures from that event and from just about every other occasion, too."

Noting Allison's interest, the young man walks over to the fire pole in the corner of the room. Calling down to the floor below, he asks Jerguen to come up-stairs.

Not happy that she was just called "ma'am," Allison brazenly admires the young man's backside. *Window shopping is not a crime*, she reasons.

"The Lieutenant should be right up, Detective," says the young man. "Can I get you a coffee or a bottle of water?"

Grateful that he didn't say "ma'am" again, Allison responds with a smile. "No, I'm fine, thanks."

A few minutes later, Ladder Company 403's un-official photographer ascends the stairs.

"Lieutenant," says the younger firefighter, "Detective Giancarlo wants to see all the photos of Stanley Cummings. Can you show them to her? I have to go back to work." Addressing Allison, the firefighter adds, "The lieutenant will take care of you now. Nice to meet you, ma'am." With that, the muscular guy leaves the floor.

Stifling a sigh, Allison says, "Hello, Lieutenant. How long have you been with this station?"

Lieutenant Jerguen is only in his mid-forties, but he is nearing retirement. His twenty years of eating smoke have taken its toll—the lines on his face have increased dramatically, and his gray hair ages him well into his fifties. "I've been here for about five years; I came over from a station in Queens. I inherited this laptop from the previous photographer, so everything you need should be on it."

Sitting on a bed with the laptop open on his lap, Jerguen clicks on a file and taps a few keys. Motioning to Giancarlo, he says, "I accessed my pictures folder. You can use that table over near the pole, or you can sit here on the bed to look through it."

Allison looks over at the table but decides to sit next to the fireman. It is a laptop, after all. Looking through the photos, she chooses several of interest and points them out to Jerguen.

"These may be what I'm looking for. Can you print them out for me?"

"You know what?" he says. "I'll do you one better. I'll copy the whole file to a flash drive, and you can have them all."

A short time later, Allison drives back to work with her Bluetooth activated to make a call. "Hey, Jack," she says, "I have some photos you're gonna want to see. How'd it go with Lincoln?"

Munching on potato chips, Jack answers between chews. "Not too well," he says, "but I did get a rise out of him. We'll compare notes when you get back."

When Allison arrives, she steps off the elevator and strolls over to Jack, who is standing next to the whiteboard, shuffling through a sheaf of papers in his hand. Leaning over his shoulder, she sees that he's looking through reports from Cummings' autopsy and the New Jersey CSI team.

"I got some new info, too," she says, before looking up sharply when she hears her boss shouting, "GIANCARLO! MY OFFICE!"

"Your turn," laughs Jack as Allison shoots him a nasty look.

While Jack watches, Conrad closes his door firmly behind Allison and proceeds to have a one-sided conversation with his subordinate. The discussion looks heated, as Conrad's fists are clenched, and the veins in his neck look like they're about to burst.

After a few minutes, the door opens, and Conrad leads Giancarlo back to Jack's desk.

"Now that I've formally stated our official position on Larson to the both of you," the lieutenant declares, "the next time that little shit interrupts you, taser the SOB. Now, I have to explain all this shit to Rawlings!"

Seated nearby, John Burley waits to burst out in laughter until after Conrad leaves. Looking over at the sergeant, Jack knits his brows together in a frown. "Let us all in on the joke, why don't you?"

Smiling widely, Burley taps his phone screen a few times and hands it to Jack. "You're a star, Jack!" he exclaims. "You and Skippy already got over 100,000 hits on YouTube!"

"What?" exclaims Allison, running over to share the screen with Jack. "Oh, no!" she moans while Jack roars in delight as a video rolls.

When the clip ends, Jack wipes tears of laughter from his eyes. "Oh, hell! That was so much fun, wasn't it?" he smiles at Allison. "But now, let's get back to work." Handing the phone back to Burley, he walks over to the whiteboard as if nothing has happened.

"The reports say Cummings was poisoned," he states matter-of-factly. "The M.E. analyzed the contents of Stan's stomach and the sputum that stained his clothes and determined that he ate arsenic-laced chili. He says the level of capsaicin in Stan's system was through the roof. He presumes that the murderer chose chili because the spices and the hot peppers probably masked the taste of the poison. The CSI guys said they found traces of arsenic on the kitchen floor of Stan's house, so some of it must have spilled before it was added to the pot. They also found a small bird pepper on the countertop. That's one of the hottest peppers on record."

"So Stan was a pepper-head," comments Allison, "and the murderer cooked him his final meal. That points to Grimes, O'Toole, or Lincoln."

"Ally, when I told Lincoln that we found Grimes' fingerprints in the house where Stan was hiding out, he nearly passed out."

Allison smiles. "You need to take a look at the photos on the flash drive I got at the firehouse. Cummings and Ladder Company 403 weren't exactly strangers."

"Oh, yeah? Hook it up to your laptop. Guys, we have a slideshow to look at."

As the photos of various firehouse events roll by, Allison informs the crew about what she discovered during her visit to the station, conveniently leaving out any mention of the young fireman who assisted her.

"Cummings donated lots of money to Ladder 403 and supported the Fireman's Ball," she says. "Hell, he even outfitted their kitchen. Here," she says, pointing at several photos, "you can see Stanley and Sarah enjoying an event with Captain Walsh. Stanley, Keith O'Toole, Sam Lincoln, and Larry Grimes are together in this other photo, and that one shows Stanley and Sarah with O'Toole and Walsh. That last one was taken about a month before the Ball, around the time the kitchen was done."

"Hey, do you see what I see?" Jack blurts out, pointing to one of the photos.

His partners bend closer to the screen to take another look at the photo Jack indicates, but none of them sees anything unusual. Persistent as always, Jack asks again, "Come on! Allison, can't you see it?"

Giancarlo looks again, and then her eyes widen as the realization hits her like a slap in the face. "Holy crap! It's O'Toole and Sarah together!"

"Yeah," says Jack with a satisfying smirk. "Keith

was, and still is, tapping Stan's wife!"

Neither Burley nor Gomez notices anything, so Jack obliges by pointing out to the sergeants what they're missing. "Guys, look at Keith's left hand. See? It's around Sarah's waist, and her hand is on his. They're standing pretty close together, and she's resting her head against his shoulder. Those poses assume a fair amount of familiarity, so it's highly likely that they were having an affair at that time, and it obviously continued after this picture was taken. That alone gives O'Toole a good reason to get rid of Stanley Cummings, right? Now, all we have to do is place him at Stan's house in Jersey. Then, we'll have our murderer."

You know," says Allison walking over to the whiteboard, Stanley was pronounced dead on 9/11, so in the eyes of the law, he's no longer alive. How do you arrest someone for murdering a person who's already 'dead'?"

The team looks at each other blankly until Jack proposes, "A life is a life, and this one was taken under suspicious circumstances. I'll call the D.A.'s office to clear up the legalities. In any case, someone did kill 'Joe Stanley.' Now I think we should concentrate on figuring out how the gold was removed. We should also try to come up with ideas about where it's being held now." Jack stops and glances at his watch. "But it's getting late. Allison and Gomez, you can head home now; tomorrow's another day. Burley, we all saw you sniffing around Stone. Give her a call; find out what she's up to." Jack scratches his head. "We got three suspects, and if you include Mrs. Cummings, four. We got firefighters helping a 'dead' man steal from his own company, and one of them was tapping his wife. We have a mystery person or persons who beat up a 'dead' man, and one of our suspects is another 'ghost.' Whiskey Tango Foxtrot!" Jack exclaims, shaking his head. "I'm going to call the D.A. now. Let's meet again early in the morning."

"Uh, I don't know about anyone else, but I won't be here tomorrow," states Allison dryly.

"Oh, yeah, it's Friday," Jack realizes awkwardly. "Then we'll meet here on Monday at eight. Burley, tell Ms. Stone to be here, too."

CHAPTER THIRTEEN

Stepping through a patch of oak and maple trees at Garvies Point Museum and Preserve on Long Island's north shore, Keith O'Toole descends a weathered wooden staircase and inhales the welcoming aroma of the sea. Off in the distance, a Boston Whaler skips merrily over the waves of Long Island Sound on its way to somewhere in a hurry.

Looking up and down the rocky beach, Keith spots Sam Lincoln sitting on a decaying tree trunk buried partly in the water and partly in the sand. Sam spots Keith at the same moment but doesn't acknowledge his visitor. Instead, he turns away and stares across the water while the sea laps at his feet and kisses the shore like a lover.

Strolling across the deserted stretch of sand, Keith drops down onto the log next to Sam but doesn't say a word. The two men look out over the water, silently pondering their thoughts.

As the rays of the setting sun bounce off the Sound like sparkling diamonds, the seagulls squawk while they dive for fish, but the men remain silent.

When the sun descends further and dusk approaches, Sam sighs and begins to talk.

"I asked you to meet me here because the cops

found Stan's house in Hammonton," he says in a shaky voice. "They also got Grimes' fingerprints. If they find Grimes, we're all fucked."

Turning his head sharply, Keith stares at Sam with his mouth hanging open in surprise. "First Stan, and now Larry?" he shouts furiously. "What the hell is going on? Wait... Are you saying we should kill Grimes?"

"Well, I didn't kill Cummings," Sam shouts back, jumping up from the tree trunk. "I thought you did! ... Did you?"

Keith gives Sam a look of disgust that tells Sam that Keith had no part in Stan's death. Somewhat mollified, Sam sits back down, but Keith rises and paces back and forth in front of the fallen tree.

"Hey, they won't find Grimes," Keith utters somewhat unconvincingly as he runs his fingers through his thinning hair. "Just stay cool and don't answer any more questions. If they bother you again, tell them to call your lawyer."

Sam cradles his head in both hands and stares down at the water lapping at his toes. Then, he looks up, pale as a ghost. "What if Lucchese did it? If that bastard had anything to do with it, no lawyer will be able to do shit for us!"

With the weekend now upon him, Jack takes advantage of his time off and awakens later than usual. He's usually off on Saturdays, but since it's the boutique's busiest day, Didi still has to go into work at nine.

After driving his wife to work, Jack's Saturday plans call for nothing more than washing and waxing his four-wheeled passion until it shines, and then relaxing in front of the TV until he needs to pick Didi up. Saturdays are Jack's days to unwind, and he takes full advantage of them whenever he can.

On Sunday, the couple eats a light breakfast before driving over to Our Lady of Victory Church. Jack dresses in his customary jeans, polo shirt, and Tony Lamas, while Didi wears black leggings, flats, and one of Jack's white dress shirts. Didi has been wearing a lot of Jack's shirts lately; they're comfortable and long enough to cover her bulging belly.

When the couple sees Father Lucarelli greeting his parishioners at the church entrance, Didi says, "Hold up, Hon. I gotta take this gum out of my mouth before we go in." Fumbling through her purse, she plants her well-chewed piece of Beemans into a rolled up tissue.

Standing on the top steps, Father Lucarelli beams at the Stenhouses. "Good morning! I haven't seen you two in a while! As a matter of fact," he adds conspiratorially, "I haven't seen you since your marriage. You know, Jesus has been waiting for you. We're glad you're here."

Reaching out, the priest shakes Jack's hand and then turns to hug Didi but stops in mid-embrace. "Is something new?" he asks. "You look exceptionally radiant today, Mrs. Stenhouse."

Jack fully intends to wait for his wife to explain,

but when she doesn't reply quickly enough, he blurts out, "We're pregnant, Father!"

"Oh! Congratulations!" the priest nods enthusiastically. "You're starting off right!" With one hand over Didi's belly, he blesses her precious cargo with the sign of the cross and then blesses her and Jack. "Now I hope you two—actually, you three—continue to join us every Sunday. And don't forget to stop by the Parish Center after Mass. The Knights of Columbus are selling coffee and donuts. Today, I'll treat you." Thanking the priest, Jack and Didi follow him into the church.

Stopping inside the doors, Didi dips her fingers into the holy water font and makes the sign of the cross on her forehead as Jack begins to do the same. However, when Jack's cell phone belts out his ringtone, and the unwelcome sound echoes loudly off the marble floor, his hand freezes in mid-motion. Berating himself for forgetting to put his phone on silent, he walks toward the door while fumbling to remove the offending object from his back pocket.

"Stenhouse…" he answers as the church door closes behind him. "All right, good," he replies, listening to the caller while wandering around the church steps. "See you tomorrow at eight." When the call ends, he turns the phone off and reenters the church.

"Who was that?" asks Didi as Jack rejoins her.

"It was Sylvia Stone, an investigator from Liberty Casualty Insurance. She's helping with the Stan Cummings case."

"Oh? Sylvia, huh?" says Didi, grabbing Jack's arm like a suspicious wife. "Should I be jealous?"

"No, Babe," laughs Jack. "She ain't got nothin' on you. I made sure of that!"

Didi searches her husband for clues as to what he means but eventually sighs in resignation. "You're impossible, Jack, but that's why I love you. I'd ask you what you did, but lucky for you, we're in church."

Smiling like the Cheshire Cat, Jack pinches Didi's posterior before he opens the interior doors and leads Didi toward the last row of pews.

CHAPTER FOURTEEN

The next day, Jack is the first to arrive at the station. He begins the day by studying the updated whiteboard while sipping a large cup of coffee.

"Mornin', Jack," announces Allison, accompanied by Sergeants Burley and Gomez. "Just coffee today? Must have been a quiet weekend."

"Didi was tired last night. Well, she's tired every night. She went to bed early."

"And so it begins," laughs Allison.

Jack ignores the jab. "Sylvia called me yesterday," he says. "She said she had some news about the Tower." Glancing at the wall clock, he adds, "It's already 8:15. Where the hell is she?"

"I'm right here," says a voice. Turning toward the sound, the group watches Ms. Stone approach them with several large rolls of papers under her arms. They are surprised to see that the sultry insurance investigator is dressed conservatively today in a black pants suit with a pink shirt and matching tie.

Jack looks at Gomez. "Told ya," he says with a smirk.

"Told him what?" inquires Sylvia.

"Nothing," replies Jack. "So what do you have

there, Ms. Stone?"

Before Sylvia can reply, the group's attention is diverted to Lieutenant Conrad's office door, which opens to reveal Skip Larson leaving for the elevator in a hurry. As the reporter punches the button for the ground floor, he turns and waves at the watching crew, prompting Jack to mumble, *Shit for brains*, under his breath.

"Okay, let me show you what I brought," says Sylvia after the elevator doors close. Unrolling the plans for Tower Two onto Stenhouse's desk, she points to a specific area. "Stanley's store was located here, between these supporting walls, all of which contained beams of reinforced concrete and steel. I spoke with a structural engineer yesterday, and he said it was almost impossible for those walls to fail as badly as they did. The vaults should have been protected, but they weren't."

"Hold on," interrupts Allison. "Larry Grimes was a demolition expert in the Army, and he was deployed to Iraq during Desert Storm. After he got out, he worked for the police bomb squad before he became a fireman. Brusco said it looked like a bomb went off in the area where Stan's business was. That would give credibility to all those people who say they heard or saw explosions going off in the Towers! Maybe Grimes blew it up to cover their tracks!"

Jack thinks for a second. "That would be the perfect setup. No one would think to look for explosive residue or remnants of a bomb in the aftermath of 9/11. What are these other papers?" he asks Sylvia.

Sylvia opens a large schematic drawing over the plans for the Tower. "These are the routes of the subway system. Here's the station that was under the Twin Towers. There was a corridor leading from the basement to the subway platform at the Cortlandt Street station. This track went east on the Yellow Line, and this one went west on the Red Line that runs under Broadway." Pointing to another area, she says, "This side section was damaged before 9/11, and they closed it off. It didn't reopen until the new Trade Tower building was completed."

Jack studies the subway routes, then leans in for a closer look. "What are these dotted lines running under the current subway line? They look like they're where the original Trade Towers were located."

"Hmm... They could be some subway lines that were proposed and never built," suggests Sylvia.

"Hey, I have an idea!" exclaims Gomez. "They could be the tracks that were built back in the twenties and eventually abandoned. Maybe an old line is still down there!"

Allison's face suddenly perks up. "You know," she says eagerly, "the curator of the Transit System Museum has route maps of the original subway system. Maybe he could tell us what this means!"

"Great job, everyone!" praises Jack, raising his head from studying the plans. "Allison and I will bring these down to the museum. The rest of you, try to dig up some info on Grimes."

Hector and John nod dutifully, but Sylvia wants no part of remaining behind. "Stenhouse," she bristles,

"Rawlings said I'm your new partner, so I'm coming with you and Detective Giancarlo."

Knowing that Sylvia is right, Jack rubs his temples to keep a stress headache from exploding across his forehead. "Fine," he says, still rubbing, "but we do the talking. Now, I'm gonna have to get a large coke to drink with my coffee so I can put up with all of this estrogen."

Burley and Gomez grin at Jack's comment, but Sylvia and Allison are indignant. Both women smack him wherever they can reach, forcing Jack to hold his arms up as a shield against their assaults.

"Good morning. We have breaking news about Stanley Cummings, the mystery man from the 9/11 Memorial. Evidently, he spent the years after the attack growing blueberries in southern New Jersey. We still don't know how he got out of the fallen Tower, or where the gold from his business is now. I'll be on the case until all the facts are revealed, and I will keep all of you informed as more details emerge.

"Until next time, this is Skip Larson, News 11."

Located across the Brooklyn Bridge from the police station, the New York Transit Museum should be an easy twenty-minute drive for the team, however, navigating through the ever-present Manhattan traffic is like shoveling shit against the tide. Jack does his best to maneuver his Road Runner around the cars and trucks blocking his path and somehow manages to bring the threesome to the museum just after eight a.m. The facility opens at ten, but Allison arranged for them to talk to the museum curator before the doors open.

Since it's unusual for someone to make an appointment to tour the museum, Curator Seymour Livingston's curiosity has gotten the best of him, and he is waiting by the door when the group arrives.

As the man unlocks the door, Jack can't help but think, *With that ring of hair circling the guy's head like a halo, he looks like he just stepped out of Sherwood Forrest. He'd look just like a monk if he were wearing a brown cassock instead of a three-piece pinstripe suit.*

Following the curator, the group walks through the main exhibit hall to the man's office at the rear of the building. When their guide indicates a large conference table, they open their maps and spread them out on its surface.

"Mr. Livingston," begins Jack, "thank you for agreeing to meet with us so early this morning. I know you talked to Detective Giancarlo, so you already have an idea of why we're here. We need your help in deciphering some symbols on this map, specifically, these dotted lines."

Seymour takes a quick look at the area in question. "That's easy," he replies. "That was the location of a station and subway line that were built in the twenties. The station was abandoned, and the new route we have today was built over it."

"Why was it abandoned?" asks Sylvia.

"When the old route was almost complete,

water from the Hudson entered the area through the bedrock. The workers tried to contain the seepage but to no avail. If you wait a few minutes, I'll go down to my archives in the basement and get you the plans so you can see for yourselves."

When the curator leaves, Jack declares, "Yup, I bet that's where Grimes is, and also where the gold is."

"If that's true, how did he get it down there?" asks Allison, not quite sure whether she should hop on Jack's train yet.

A few minutes later, Seymour walks back into the office with a stack of old construction plans and maps of the subway system in lower Manhattan. Unfurling large yellowed documents, Livingston lays them alongside the newer maps the officers brought with them.

"So what we have here is the old route that looped around from Cortlandt Street West to Cortlandt Street East," he begins. "Now, as you can see on this current map, they rerouted the subway tracks further south, and then ran them west and south of the Trade Towers. Now, I also brought you this photograph of some of the stations that were built back then. They were very charming. They had great archways covered by white tile and marble, like the one they just renovated under City Hall. Another of the original stations is under the Memorial's pools, but it probably wasn't as ornate as the one they just renovated."

"This is interesting, Mr. Livingston," comments Allison. "Can that lower level be accessed today?"

Always excited to talk about the history of the

New York subway system, Seymour brightens at the question. "Well, Detective," he says, unfurling another set of plans and placing it on top of the others, "if you look at this newer map, there are lower levels and underground shopping areas that access the current subway system. The Trade Towers were located directly between these two lines," he says, pointing at the map. "You can get to them from the lower floors at the Cortlandt Street Stations on the west and east."

Seymour pulls another map from the bottom of the stack. "Look here at the two Cortlandt Street stations. These red X's indicate access points to the line that was built below the current tracks and eventually abandoned. The tracks are indicated here by these dotted lines." He then places an even older map of the former line next to the current one. "At the bottom of this loop, which is just south of the 9/11 Memorial Park, there is another station that was going to be opened on that abandoned line. It's marked by this blue square. The access points to that line are located in utility rooms along the tracks. They can be reached via footbridges that run along the tracks at the points where the trains exit and enter the stations. The utility rooms contain electrical panels that control the lights on the station platforms and the other lights that illuminate the walkways. The access doors to the abandoned line are at the far ends of the utility storage areas. Now, the footbridge along the subway tunnels is very narrow, and it's only about four feet higher than the train tracks. If you go down there, take care while you're out on those ledges. If a train comes by, it will pass only a few inches from where you're standing. And if you go down to the lower level, remember that it's probably flooded."

"Mr. Livingston, how far from the current stations is the one that was abandoned?" asks Jack.

Seymour studies the map for a moment and then looks at Stenhouse. "It's between the two Cortlandt Street stations, approximately one hundred yards from each of them."

"What are these triangular markings along the older route?" asks Jack, looking again at the old map.

Seymour smiles smugly, reveling in his extensive knowledge of these old diagrams. "Those symbols show the amount of rise and fall in the old line. The route dips low where the abandoned station sits, and then comes back up farther west of it. That was probably part of the reason the track flooded. The water that collected at the bottom of that abandoned loop is deeper than other areas of the track."

"Makes sense now," says Jack. "Thanks for your time, Mr. Livingston. You were very helpful. All right, people, looks like we're going underground."

Jack waits until the group is out of the museum curator's earshot before he turns his attention to Allison. "Let's stop at the station to get Gomez and Burley. With luck, we'll find Grimes and the gold at one of the Cortlandt Street stations today and wrap this whole thing up in a big, red bow."

Walking beside them, Sylvia beams as she listens to Jack. Turning toward her, Jack gives her a thumbs-up. "You did good, Ms. Stone!"

CHAPTER FIFTEEN

Back at the First Precinct, Sylvia and Allison freshen up in the ladies' room while Jack fills his boss in on what they learned about the abandoned subway line.

As Sylvia washes her hands, she glances furtively at Allison as she tries to gather up the courage to ask a question that's been on her mind.

"Um, Allison, what's the story with Stenhouse? I mean, I like to get a bit of background information about the people I'm working with, and his reputation precedes him. I tried to get a rise out of him yesterday, but it didn't go very well."

"Jack is an in-your-face hound," replies Allison while Sylvia looks in the mirror and fixes her face. "But he also believes in the phrase, 'Don't shit where you eat.' He mellowed a bit after he got married and found out that he's going to be a father, so that's probably why whatever you did didn't work with him. Besides, you'd have to compete with his wife, which is next to impossible." Allison gives Sylvia a long look. "As attractive as you are, you're no match for her."

Sylvia is a little put off by Allison's comment. "Hey," she responds coolly, "I think I'm pretty good-looking, and so are you. Has he come on to you at all?"

"Oh, hell, no!" says Allison amid a burst of laughter. "I told you; Jack doesn't sniff around at the office. Besides, I *really* can't compete with his wife. Her nickname is Didi, and that should say it all."

Shrugging her shoulders, Sylvia follows Allison out of the restroom.

In the squad room, Jack removes the subway map from under his arm and unrolls it onto his desk with a flourish. "Okay," he begins, "I got the Lieutenant to give us four uniformed guys. Gomez, you and Burley take two of them to Cortlandt Station West. Go down to the tracks and enter the lower level. Giancarlo and I will take the other two guys to the Cortlandt station on the Broadway line. Remember, because we'll be underground, we may be out of communication with each other until we're all on the same floor. Giancarlo and I will probably get to the Broadway station before you get to yours, so when you enter the lower level, call us on the radio. We'll wait to hear from you before we proceed. If Grimes is down there, we'll flush him out to you, so be ready. Oh, one more thing. Get some vests and some hip boots. It's probably flooded down there."

Jack looks at each of his officers. "We set?" When he hears no questions, he gives a thumbs-up. "Okay, good. Let's roll."

"Whoa, wait a minute!" calls Sylvia from a few desks away. "What about me? You gave everyone something to do except me. If it weren't for my help today, you might not have gotten this far as quickly!"

Stenhouse doesn't give a shit about Sylvia's pride. With a snarl, he says, "Look, this isn't a TV show!

People can't just tag along on police business whenever they want to." Grabbing the subway map, he turns to walk away but catches a look from Allison. The look reminds him that his boss gave permission for Sylvia to work with them.

With a sigh, he turns back to Stone. "Okay," he says reluctantly, "I'll permit you to join us. But when we find the access point, you *will* stay behind until I consider it safe for you to enter. I'll give you a radio; keep it turned on. Wait for me to let you know when you can join us." To emphasize his point, he places his face up against Sylvia's. "YOU GOT IT?" he demands.

Agreeing to the instructions, Sylvia nods but won't let Stenhouse bring her down without a dig of her own. "Not going to take another peek, Detective?" she asks with a smirk.

Jack laughs heartily. "Not much to see there, ma'am. Now, let's go."

Catching Allison's eye again, Jack grins and heads into the hallway. Sylvia follows, not at all happy at being restrained, and embarrassed once again by Jack's comeback to another of her attempts to attract him.

"Look!" shouts Rawlings angrily, lowering the hammer on Skip Larson in another conversation about the reporter's commentaries. "We gave you access to the information we uncovered in this investigation, but you need to keep that door closed until we say it's okay to open it to the public! Another report like the last one, and we'll arrest you for impeding an investigation! Am I being clear enough for you?"

Skip hears only a dial tone when Rawlings ends the call abruptly. "Fuck it!" he yells into the dead phone. "You can't tell me how to report the news!" Seething, his mind begins to work overtime to plot the best ways to get around the lieutenant's directive.

A few moments later, a loud voice stops his devious scheming.

"SKIP LARSON! Get your ass over here!" bellows the station manager.

Just as Jack predicted, he and his group arrive at the Broadway line before the others get to the Cortlandt West station. There is no parking on the street near the subway entrance, so Jack pulls his Road Runner onto the sidewalk, behind a squad car that is already there.

Passersby watch curiously as the officers don bulletproof vests and hip boots. Ms. Stone also watches, but from a distance. She has mixed emotions. Although she wants to be involved, things are looking dangerous. For the moment, she's content to remain on the sidelines.

Following behind the two uniformed officers that Conrad pressed into service, the group heads down the steps to the station platform. Dressed in their bulletproof vests and toting semi-automatic shotguns, the sight of the battle-ready cops causes subway riders to scatter in waves before them.

Stopping in front of the door to the lower level, Jack turns to the team. "Remember," he says with a note of caution, "we'll be on a narrow footbridge that runs parallel to the tracks, so stay close to the wall. If a train comes by, it's going to get a little hairy."

Slowly and carefully, the team descends the stairway and then walks about thirty feet on a narrow bridge through a dimly lit tunnel, all the while assaulted by unpleasant odors of oil, mold, and urine.

Before they reach another door, Jack stops and cocks his ear. Motioning for quiet, he looks up and down the dark tunnel, and what Jack hears soon becomes apparent to the others. What began as a low rumble rapidly becomes louder and louder, and in the darkness, a distant light grows larger and more pronounced. Backing up against the wall, Jack shouts, "Lean back! We got company!" Soon, a seven-car subway train rushes past with only inches to spare.

As the train passes, a rush of hot air causes loose debris to wash over the officers. Coughing against the dust, they look through the train's windows at startled commuters, who stare back at them in surprise.

After the last car passes, the officers take deep breaths of relief.

"Wow, that was close!" the beat cops exclaim.

"Holy cow!" shouts Allison. "I hope we don't have to go through that again!"

"No shit!" agrees Jack as he grabs the handle of the next door and pushes it open. The team quickly follows, all of them wanting to get away from the tracks as soon as possible.

Inside the door, they find themselves in a narrow, dimly lit hallway. High up on the wall are a transformer array and an electrical panel with a large red handle.

"Seymour Livingston was right," says Jack. "This must be the master control panel for the lights at the station platform. I guess they place these as high as they can in case of flooding."

Another door is at the far end of the long corridor. Bare overhead light bulbs cast a yellow hue as the officers walk toward a steel mesh door with a faded red sign covered in grease and grime. Spitting on his fingers, Jack wipes away the oil and dirt to reveal the sign: "Official Access Only. Do Not Enter."

Shrugging his shoulders, Jack disregards the warning and pushes on the door's handle. When it moves easily, he becomes suspicious and removes a flashlight from a loop on his vest. Shining it on the old door and its hinges, he says, "Crap. Looks like this door's been lubricated. Someone's using it."

"Jack!" calls Allison, returning from inspecting a storage room in an adjoining corridor. "I think we should use these!" Approaching the group, she holds out several hardhats with lights attached to the brims.

"Good find!" confirms Jack. "They'll give us light while our hands remain free."

While Jack's team continues to explore below ground at the Broadway Line, Sergeant Gomez and his team are making their own descent into the depths of the subway system at Cortlandt Street West. Wisely, Gomez and his team are waiting for a train to pass the station before they enter the narrow walkway adjacent to the tracks.

In the corridor under the Broadway Line, Jack and his team have donned the protective headgear Allison found. When everyone is ready, Jack pulls open the metal door and leads the way down a rusty steel staircase into deep darkness.

"Watch your step!" Jack calls as beams of light from their headlamps dance around the walls and floor. "Watch your footing! These steps must be almost a hundred years old!"

The farther the group travels down into the darkness, the cooler and clammier the air becomes, and the more they hear creaking and cracking sounds from the staircase as it quivers under the weight of the four police officers. Allison jokes, "I sure hope all this rust is strong enough to hold these steps together!"

After a few more minutes of slow travel, they reach a solid metal door at the bottom. When Jack pulls it open, a rush of musty, damp air wafts past.

Stepping through the door, the group enters another unlit area. "There's no electrical panel here," notes one of the uniforms as four beams of hardhat lights bounce from ceiling to wall to floor, causing rats to squeal and scamper away from the topsiders' intrusion into their inner sanctum. "This seems to be a storeroom of some kind."

Noticing a light switch on the wall, Jack flips it on, and a couple of bare light bulbs overhead flicker as more rats squeal their disapproval. "Look, there's a watermark on the wall. It's only a few inches high, so this area probably doesn't get too wet. This may be a utility room near the old platform."

Allison grunts in agreement while one of the cops touches the floor and walls to test Jack's theory. "Yeah, it's damp in here," he says.

The other officer spots another door at the other end of the room and opens it, releasing a sickly smell of stagnant water and mold into the room.

Pointing his headlamp through the open doorway, Jack sees another walkway ahead, with submerged subway tracks on the ground below it. He also notices that the watermark on the wall under the footbridge is only about three feet under its floor. "Well, Livingston hit all of this right on the nose," he remarks. "There has to be a foot of water on those old tracks, but the walkway is dry. All right, let's wait here until Gomez contacts us."

After spending an uncomfortable fifteen-minutes in the dark, dank space, Jack is relieved when he receives a call from Sergeant Gomez.

"Jack, you there?" crackles a disembodied voice.

"10-4, Hector. Did you guys find miners hats in a storage room?"

"Miners hats? What do you mean?"

"Look for a storage room at the top level. There should be a bunch of hardhat lamps in it. If you find them, you won't need to use your flashlights. We're about to make our way down to the old station platform. Call us if Grimes comes your way."

"Okay, Jack. I'll send one of the officers up to check on the hats. Good hunting."

Motioning to his team, Jack calls for silence as he leads the way along the ledge. The surroundings are dark and dank, and the only sounds they hear are dripping water and startled rats.

Creeping along, they soon notice that the floor is declining slightly, and when they make their way around a bend, they encounter tiny lights along the tunnel's walls that illuminate their way, albeit faintly.

Still in the lead, Jack spots a glow of yellow light in the distance. Stopping the group with an upturned fist, he whispers, "That's the station platform. The water is getting deeper now, so Grimes may be around here somewhere."

CHAPTER SIXTEEN

When Larry Grimes received the call from Sam Lincoln about the cops finding his fingerprints at the Cummings house in New Jersey, he panicked. Desperate to protect himself, he acquired several sticks of dynamite and placed them in strategic areas of the tunnel. *This is just in case the cops show up*, he reasoned.

On his way to conduct another inspection of the explosives to make sure they'll work if he needs them, he steps down to the station platform from his makeshift bedroom and stops. Hearing rats squealing in the far tunnel, he cocks his head to listen more intently and notices lights bouncing on the walkway along the tracks. Fearing the worst, he pulls out the detonation device to the dynamite timers that he always keeps on hand, and scurries toward the walkway that leads to Cortlandt Street West. Although he is nervous, he is confident that it will take only one press of his glowing red button to rain hell onto his underground home and erase all evidence of his existence there.

Jack slowed the group down when he heard the rats and ordered the officers to try not to annoy any more of the pests. "Those things can tip Grimes off that we're here," he whispered. "Be as quiet as you can."

At the opposite end of the tunnel, Gomez and his team have also slowed down. Creeping along the footbridge from the direction of Cortlandt Street West, they heard rats swimming toward them and sat down quietly on their footbridge.

While they're waiting for the rats to pass by, Hector hears something else, and his heart begins to race. "Someone's coming," he whispers urgently. "Turn off your lights!"

Unaware that the officers are on the footbridge, Larry Grimes is headed directly for Gomez and his team.

Outlined by the dim tunnel lights, Larry's silhouette appears on the ledge at the same time he and Hector make eye contact. Seeing the officers behind Hector, Larry knows he's been found. Raising the red detonator button high above his head, he shrieks hysterically, "I'm not going to jail for this! I won't hesitate to take you all down with me! I'd rather die first! I'll kill you all, I swear it!"

Instantaneously evaluating the threat to himself and his men, Gomez unholsters his weapon and fires, the sound of the gunshot in the tunnel, deafening.

When the .40 cal projectile hits the previously missing man in the left shoulder, two things happen in quick succession: he drops the detonator into the watery blackness below, and the bullet's impact flings him into the rusted bars on the outside of the access ledge. The weight of Grimes' body shatters the fragile structure, and he falls headfirst into the black, stagnant water.

"Shit!" yells Hector as he re-holsters his weapon. "Take this!" he shouts to Burley, handing him his cell phone. "I'm not ruining my phone for this jackass!" Then he jumps feet first into the murky water.

As Gomez swims around looking for Larry, the sound of his gunshot slams past Jack and his crew five hundred feet down the tunnel.

Immediately, Jack thumbs his radio. "Gomez! Gomez!" he shouts.

Tense seconds pass until the radio crackles to life.

"Jack! It's Burley! We found Grimes, but Gomez had to fire at him. Don't enter the platform! Grimes said he'd blow it up, so there may be trip wires, and the guard rails on these ledges are unstable! Grimes broke through one and fell into the water!"

"He was going to blow the station up? What the hell happened?"

"He must have heard you coming! He headed right toward us with a detonator! Gomez defused the situation with a great shot, but Grimes fell into the water, and Gomez went in to retrieve him. Call the EMTs and the bomb squad."

"Will do. Is Grimes alive?"

"Yeah, I think he's okay. He struggled with Gomez at first, but it looks like he only got hit in the shoulder. Don't know how safe this water is, though. Both of them are soaked in it."

"Good job, guys!" shouts Jack into his radio. "We'll call the bomb squad and EMTs from the upper level. When they arrive, we'll guide them down here. They're going to have to evacuate the stations until the situation with the explosives is neutralized."

While Jack's team high-fives each other, Jack stares down the tunnel at the utility room for the abandoned station. Looking down at the tracks, he notices that the water line is only about ten inches below the top of the ledge in this area. As they head back up to the street, Jack reflects on the forethought of the station's builders. *It's a good thing they put the control panels so high up on the wall. This place must get dicey when the tide comes in.*

At the other end of the tunnel, Hector is still directing Larry to swim toward a ladder so they can get out of the water. When Grimes is close enough, Burley grabs him by the arm and pulls him up. Howling in pain, Grimes shouts at Hector, "You shot me! You shot me, you fucker!"

With their suspect in tow, the group makes their way back through the tunnel.

At the surface, a dripping wet Gomez walks over to Grimes, who is handcuffed and seated at the end of the subway platform at the Cortlandt Street station. Leaning over, he says, "Be glad I didn't kill you. You're now under arrest as a suspect in the murder of Stanley Cummings. You have the right to remain silent. Anything you say can and will be used against you in a court of law. You have the right to have an attorney present during questioning. If you cannot afford an attorney, one will be provided for you."

Larry looks up at Sergeant Gomez in disbelief. "You know you shot me, don't you? You shot me!"

Minutes later, EMTs and backup police arrive

from the First Precinct. The officers force upset commuters up to street level and block the subway entrance with police tape. As emergency technicians tend to Grimes and offer Gomez a blanket, more assisting police officers clear the station, sending the annoyed public out into the city streets.

As soon as Sylvia Stone sees Jack, she grabs his shoulder. "When can I go down, Detective?" she asks, but then quickly corrects herself. "I mean, when can I come with you? No! I mean, when am I allowed to join the team?"

Blushing furiously, Sylvia watches miserably as Jack bursts out laughing so hard that he can hardly respond. "Oh, shit!" he finally says, catching his breath. "Okay, okay! You can join us on the lower level but stay on the access ledge until the bomb guys clear the station. And be careful! Don't lean on the railing! I don't want to have to go in for a swim, too." Still laughing, Jack leads the bomb squad down the stairs with a red-faced Sylvia following close behind.

With their lights dancing in the darkness, Jack and the bomb technicians head down the tunnel with Allison and Stone. Because of the bulky specialists' uniforms, the way is slow going. Dressed in full protective gear, the techs have to shuffle sideways, with their backs up against the walls of the narrow walkway.

On the surface, more uniformed officers have been sent to each station. New Yorkers are notoriously nonchalant about just about everything, so despite multiple warnings about possible explosions, the crowds outside each location continue to grow.

Under the feet of the disbelieving public, the officers have finally arrived at the abandoned station. Illuminated by the dim lights, the new arrivals take a minute to marvel at the abandoned building. Once-white tiles, now yellowed by age and dampness, still adorn walls accented by elegant, red brick archways.

"Wow," comments Sylvia, "with the archways and tile, this looks like the old City Hall station, except there's no stained glass."

As the team climbs a short staircase up to the platform, Jack points out several waterline marks along the far wall. "Water must be coming in from the bay," he says. "It rises and falls with the tide."

Leading the bomb squad, Sergeant Frank Callavito directs the group's attention to several charges located at the archways leading to the upper level of the station. "Dammit!" he calls out. "There must be fifty pounds of dynamite here! We're now under the South Pool of the 9/11 Memorial. If these things go off, they'll take the pool with them!" Looking around, he sees more charges up the staircase. "Stenhouse, we got another fifty pounds on the upper landing!"

Stooping to examine the dangerous setup, Callavito says, "Looks like a simple job, though. Won't take us too long to neutralize them. I'll get my guys to remove the explosives as quickly as possible so you can re-open the upper stations."

"Good idea," smirks Jack. "Betcha those people up there are pretty pissed off. But hey, it's better to be pissed off than pissed on."

Not wanting anyone to be too close to where the bomb guys are working, Jack motions for Allison and Sylvia to return to street level.

When the last of the dynamite leaves the station, the bomb techs give the all clear, and the police officers handling crowd control allow the angry public back into the subway. As the people stream in, Allison and Sylvia head back down to the lower level.

When Jack sees the women heading his way, he directs them to search for Larry's holdout. Eager to help, Sylvia quickly finds a disorganized area equipped with a cot and a hot plate in a far corner of the run-down building. Inspecting the setup, Allison remarks, "This looks adequate for the short-term, but it surely can't be his permanent residence. Grimes must live somewhere else."

Jack was also doing some snooping. "Hey! Come and see this shit!" he calls to them.

Standing near the old station's token booths, Jack points to a large pile of coins and silver and gold bars scattered around the floor and lying in battered boxes.

Gasping in shock, Sylvia takes out her phone and immediately begins to snap photos of the stash. "I'm going to have to catalog all of this before we move it," she says, clicking away. "Hey, look over there! There are some uniforms piled on that box."

Jack takes a closer look. "Hmm, these are transit

worker uniforms. Grimes must have worn them when he was moving the gold down here. When CSI gets here, I have a feeling they're gonna find a lot of familiar prints all over the place. You know," he says to Sylvia, "All of this is now evidence in our case, and we're gonna have to get it out of here quickly. It's low tide now, but when the tide changes, this platform will be under water again. You can help us inventory it back at the First."

CHAPTER SEVENTEEN

Sergeant Gomez and Larry Grimes have been brought to New York-Presbyterian Hospital. Larry is having his wound cleaned and dressed, and both men are receiving injections of tetanus and penicillin as a precaution against contaminants in the subway water.

Since there is no need for Hector to remain at the hospital any longer than necessary, he will be released as soon as the proper paperwork is completed. Larry, on the other hand, will be admitted for at least twenty-four-hours for observation. Hector's bullet exited Larry's shoulder above the water line, but he fell into some pretty foul stuff.

"Hey, John, thanks for sticking around," says Hector when he sees his pal in the hallway outside of the examination room. "Can you drive me home? I really need to get some clean clothes. Um... Is something wrong?"

John is looking at Hector with a strange expression.

"You know protocol. I got to take your weapon and badge. You'll get them back after the investigation. We both know it's bullshit, but I have to do it."

"Yeah, I know. Don't worry about it. You gotta do what you gotta do." Following the rules he knows he must follow, Gomez hands over his Ruger and badge.

"One of the patrolmen will give you a ride back to the First," says John. "You can shower there. After you file your report, pack up whatever you want from your desk and go home. I.A. will contact you."

"Well, I can sure use the rest of the day off," Hector says with a resigned sigh. "In any case, I'll be able to wash this subway funk off. By the way, how's Grimes?"

"Your suspect will be fine," says a patrol officer who joins them in the hallway. "It was a clean wound. They're keeping him overnight, so we'll station a cop outside his room. They'll rotate a new one in at the end of each shift."

"I'm going to visit him now for a brief talk," says Burley. "When he's released, we'll book him at Central. Then we'll bring him to the First for questioning— that's if he doesn't lawyer up first."

Gomez gives his partner a bro handshake and leaves the E.R. with the uniformed officer.

Sergeant Burley starts walking toward Grimes' room but stops when he sees Lieutenant Conrad heading toward him.

"Is Gomez okay?" asks Conrad.

"Yeah. A uniformed is taking him to the First to file his report. Here are his gun and badge. I don't think we'll find his discharged bullet. It went clean through and is now somewhere under four feet of black water."

"What the hell happened down there?"

"We split up into two teams. Jack and Allison

came in from the east, and Gomez and I came in from the west. We took up a defensive position on our end to head Grimes off if he tried to leave the tunnel. We thought Jack would get to him first, but Grimes must have heard him coming from the other direction, so he ended up fleeing straight toward us. He was carrying this." Burley hands Grimes' deactivated detonator to Conrad. "Hector saw Grimes thumbing the red light, so he took the shot."

"Shit. It could have gone south real quick," states Conrad grimly.

"Yeah, but Hector didn't hesitate. The suspect fell into the water still holding the detonator, so Hector went in after him and was able to get both the suspect and the trigger out of the water before anything exploded. They're holding Grimes here overnight. He'll be processed in the morning, but I'm going to see if I can get a statement from him now. Oh, one more thing. Stenhouse said there were tons of explosives around the station, so Grimes wasn't bluffing. That's all I know. Have you heard anything, sir?"

"No, I came here right after I heard the call for EMTs. Good work, John. I'll congratulate Gomez when I see him. Rawlings and I.A. will want to speak to him, but after they see this detonator, I don't think they'll give him a problem."

Later, the tide starts to come in and the level of black water begins to rise while the CSI crew is still sweeping the abandoned station for evidence.

"Stenhouse!" calls Sylvia from the ticket booth area.

Rushing up the stairway with Giancarlo in tow, Jack just misses bumping headfirst into the insurance investigator.

"We need to get this stuff out of here," says Jack. "The water is rising fast."

"I know; that's what I want to talk about," replies Sylvia uneasily. "We'll need a large team to take all this stuff out of here. It must weigh close to eight thousand pounds."

"Jeez!"

"After the attack on the Towers, they said between ten to twelve million dollars of the coin dealer's inventory was lost in the explosion. But this stash is probably worth close to one hundred twenty million in today's dollars."

Jack processes Sylvia's extraordinary numbers in open-mouthed surprise.

"That's incredible!" exclaims Allison. "How the hell did Cummings get involved with all of this?"

"What are you talking about?" asks Lieutenant Conrad as he climbs the stairs from the station platform.

"We have a problem, sir," says Jack. "We're going to need a lot of men to remove all of this gold and silver, but we're going to have to wait until the tide goes out. This place is going to get very wet very soon. There are more valuables here than we previously thought. You're looking at about one hundred twenty million dollars' worth of evidence, and Ms. Stone estimates that it weighs about eight thousand pounds."

"Holy shit!" exclaims Lieutenant Conrad.

"And sir, if you intend to stay down here much longer, you better get some waders. That water is going to go over the ledge soon. That goes for you, too," adds Jack to Sylvia.

CHAPTER EIGHTEEN

After waiting several hours in the hospital corridor, Sergeant Burley finally gets permission to speak with Larry Grimes. While a police officer stands guard outside, Burley enters the room to find a tired Larry hooked up to monitors that are busily sending his vital signs to the nurse's station. The nurses are concerned about Larry's increasing body temperature, an early sign of a possible infection.

"Oh, it's another officer," says Grimes irritably. "Black lives matter, you know. Did you come to shoot me, too?"

"Only if you force me to," responds Burley, unimpressed by Larry's snide remark. "As far as I'm concerned, my life matters more than anyone else's. My name is Sergeant John Burley, and I need to ask you some questions. Are you up to it, Mr. Grimes?"

Larry nods and struggles to sit up.

"Thank you," says John. "First question. Why did you kill Stanley Cummings?"

With an annoyed huff, Larry says, "Sergeant, I did not kill Stan. Look, I said I would cooperate with the police, but my attorney's going to request full immunity in exchange for my cooperation. The doctors said I should be released in twenty-four hours, so I know you'll have someone waiting to bring me down to the station. That's where I'll tell you everything…as long as my counsel is with me. Not now. I also need protection. It's not safe for me to talk to you here, and that's all I'm gonna say right now. Now please get the hell outta here. I don't wanna be killed in this hospital."

Surprised, Burley is about to ask Larry why he thinks someone wants to kill him, but before he can say anything, he is pushed aside by a doctor and nurse who have barged into the room. The monitors hooked up to Larry have alerted them that their patient's blood pressure is rising, along with his temperature.

"Grimes, I'll wait until your doctor is finished. I still have a few questions."

The doctor gives Gomez a pointed look and then addresses his patient. "Mr. Grimes, the water you fell into was very nasty. We're going to push Ceftobiprole into your IV now. It's an antibiotic that should quickly knock out any infections that may be brewing. We're going to monitor you throughout the night, and if you show improvement in the morning, you'll be released." Turning to Gomez, he says, "Sergeant, Mr. Grimes needs to rest now. If all goes well, you can speak with him again tomorrow."

Dutifully, Sergeant Burley turns to leave the room, but something tells him to take another look at the patient. When he does, he catches Grimes smiling widely at his retreating back before the door closes on him with a whoosh and a thump.

When Sylvia returned to ground level, she contacted her superiors at the insurance company to describe the situation in the flooded tunnel. They were happy to hear that such a large quantity of precious items was discovered, and they agreed to grant Sylvia's request for emergency help in removing them. A couple of hours later, they hired Jancko Armored Couriers to assist local police in their efforts to retrieve the valuables.

Dressed in full hip waders, the courier's employees are now working with members of the police department and Ladder Company 403 to remove the stash. Set up as a human chain, the Jancko employees are handing off the precious items to volunteer police and firefighters stationed along the route up to the street. More Jancko employees are placing the valuables in an armored vehicle parked at the subway entrance.

Down below, the water in the abandoned tunnel is now over the access ledge and is lapping at the floor of the abandoned station's platform. The air in the tunnel is thick and dank as the water from Hudson Bay fills the area.

Slowly and carefully, Jack makes his way back down with a pair of hip waders that he wants to keep dry. Calling out from the short stairway at the upper level, he says, "Allison! You and Sylvia need to stay here to oversee the extraction team. CSI will be here with you. I'm going back to the First to fill out some reports, but before I go, I have something that Ms. Stone is gonna want. Tell her to come over here, would ya?"

When Sylvia appears, Jack quips, "Don't say what you're probably thinking. Here, you'll need these." Jack hands the pair of hip waders to Sylvia. "You two can hitch a ride to the station on the armored truck."

When Jack returns to the upper floor, all he wants to do is breathe cleaner air and remove his swat vest and hip boots. However, when he sees a convoy of media trucks parked outside like a committee of vultures waiting for their turn at the carrion, and Lieutenant Conrad in the middle of a sea of outstretched arms, he sighs dejectedly. Still dressed in his waders, the lieutenant is talking into a field of microphones pointed at his face.

Fervently hoping that he won't get roped into the same media circus, Jack makes a mad dash for his Road Runner, but Skip Larson sees him and approaches at a dead run. Sighing again, Jack jumps into his car and barely manages to get away before Skippy can reach him.

Overjoyed at successfully evading his nemesis, Jack honks his horn and gives Skippy the bird as he speeds away.

Left behind on the sidewalk, Skip Larson doesn't let the missed opportunity stop him. He merely turns around and waits with dogged determination for an exclusive interview with Lieutenant Conrad after the media feeding frenzy ends.

"This is Skip Larson on Cortlandt Street with Lieutenant Nathaniel Conrad from the First Police Precinct. We're watching officers and firefighters bring up a horde of gold, silver, and other precious metals from deep below the city's streets.

"Tell me, Lieutenant, are these the valuables that Stanley Cummings was hiding?"

"Mr. Larson, this is an ongoing investigation, so I cannot comment on that."

"Can you at least tell the people of New York if this is the lost gold?"

"Yes, it appears that these are the valuables that were thought to have been lost in the attack on the Twin Towers. Over the next few days, we will inventory everything we recovered."

"Where did you find it all?"

"The cache was in an abandoned subway tunnel. Now, if you'll excuse me, I need to get back to the station."

When Conrad walks away, Skip ends the segment. *"You heard it here, folks. The gold that was lost is now found. This is Skip Larson, reporting for PIX News 11."*

Among those listening to the news that day is a man with a particular interest in Skip Larson's report.

When Skippy's segment ends, Vito Lucchese points his remote at the TV and turns it off with a satisfied sigh. Tipping his glass to his mouth, he drains the last of his wine and summons an attentive waiter.

Bustling over, the waiter hands Vito an encrypted cell phone that Vito uses to dial a number he has committed to memory.

"Yeah," he says into the phone. "Get the boys together. We meet tomorrow."

"Jack, I need to talk to you," states Sergeant Burley after exiting Lieutenant Conrad's office.

"Yeah?" says Jack, looking up from his paperwork. "How's Hector?"

"Conrad sent him home. They pumped him full of antibiotics at the hospital and gave him a tetanus shot. He knows I.A. is gonna investigate the shoot, but he's still bummed that I had to take his gun. Conrad said it should be okay, though."

"That's good to hear. Now, what's with Grimes? What happened in the tunnel?"

"I guess he heard you guys coming and tried to escape. But he ran right into us. When he flashed the detonator, Gomez took a shot, and Grimes fell into the water. Gomez dove in after him, and while they were struggling, Grimes kept trying to activate the detonator. The water must have shorted it out because it never went off."

"Crap; that was a close one," declares Jack, rubbing a tired hand on the back of his neck.

"Tell me about it," replies John. "And get this. Grimes wants immunity in exchange for testifying. The D.A. said there would be no bail, but I guess he changed his mind when Grimes said he'd cooperate."

"Did you get him to say anything when you talked to him?"

"He claims he didn't kill Cummings."

"No shit. They all say that."

"I know, but he did say something else. He wants us to give him police protection. He's terrified that someone's gonna kill him."

"Aw, that's too bad."

"Yeah, but I wonder what could have him so scared. Hey, what did you guys find in the tunnel? I heard some rumors."

"There was a shitload of gold down there; more than we expected. Cummings and his crew must have been smuggling stuff out of the Tower for months. Cummings may have been hiding it for more than one person; we don't know yet. Only powerful people have that kind of money. That must be why Grimes is so scared." Jack runs his hand over his chin. "Fuck!" he exclaims. "There may be more than one player in this saga! Look, John, I gotta give Conrad my report before I go home. You got anything else?"

Burley shakes his head but then widens his eyes. "Hey, wait a minute," he says. "Before I gave my report to Conrad, I looked over the CSI report from New Jersey. It said they found fingerprints from Cummings and Grimes in the house, along with some other prints they couldn't identify. Those other prints were in the bathroom and on a laundry basket on top of the washing machine filled with dirty clothes. Some of the unidentified prints were also in the van. The report said they logged the laundry in as evidence, but I don't think they did anything else with it."

Jack stares at the floor while he considers what John said. "Looks like we should have sent our own CSI guys there," he mutters. "That's good thinking, John, but it's getting late; you may as well go home. Tomorrow, get your ass over to Cummings' place and bring that basket of laundry here. Oh, and get the van, too. I'll ask Conrad for a subpoena to get them released to us. I bet Lincoln, O'Toole, and Sarah Cummings are knee-deep in this hoopla."

"Okay, I can use the long drive to unwind. Today was a long one; I could use a little downtime," says John tiredly.

"Good. After my debriefing with Conrad, I'll tell Allison and Stone what you just told me. They should be back soon."

Burley's eyes light up at the mention of Sylvia Stone's name. "Um, you know," he says, "I got no one to go home to, so I think I'll hang around here until they show up."

"You dog!" smiles Jack. "Are you tapping Stone?"

"Ha! From your lips to God's ears," responds John wistfully.

Much later that evening, when the Big Apple winds down, Jack enjoys a quiet dinner at home. The meal is his favorite—meatloaf with mashed potatoes.

Chewing contentedly, Jack stares lovingly at his pregnant wife, and Didi smiles back. The Beemans gum seems to be working; Didi is enjoying the meal with no sign of the nausea that's been plaguing her these past months.

Happy that Didi is finally feeling well, Jack's thoughts turn to the baby. Bolting from his chair, he hurries over to Didi and drops to his knees to give her tiny baby bump a gentle kiss.

Loving Jack's attention, Didi places her hand on her husband's head. "I love you, Jack," she says softly.

As the couple embraces each other and their growing baby, their world comes to a stop, but life in the city goes on. In separate locations, Hector Gomez is fast asleep and snoring, Allison is trying to be patient while her kids do everything they can to stay up longer, and John Burley is eagerly carrying Sylvia Stone to the large bed in her hotel room.

At the same time, Vito Lucchese's evening is progressing splendidly. The mob boss is having dinner alone in the private room at the rear of his restaurant on Mulberry Street, one of the many establishments he owns in the city. Other businesses under his direct control are Republic Waste Removal and Vista Limousine Service, a newly-formed cab company. Those entities, including veiled control of numerous "gentlemen's clubs," local union chapters, and area construction companies, provide Vito with cover for his illegal gambling and prostitution rings, and his vast heroin distribution network.

Pouring himself a substantial amount of Lambrusco, the mobster raises his glass in a toast.

"So," he grunts happily to no one, "my gold has been found, and the city's cops are now keeping it safe for me! What could be better than that? Ha, ha, ha!"

CHAPTER NINETEEN

Morning comes too soon for Didi. When the shrill sound of the alarm clock dissolves the fog of sleep, she instinctively reaches out for the electronic assailant to silence it before Jack throws it across the room. However, his side of the bed is empty.

"Jack?" she calls out.

"In the kitchen, Babe," he replies distantly. "Getting an early start."

A minute later, Jack walks into the bedroom with a cup of hot Chai Tea.

"Here ya go," he says. "I called Sonia; she'll pick you up around 8:30." Bending over, he kisses Didi's forehead and then her belly. "Love you two. See ya later."

Didi places her tea on the bedside table as Jack makes his way to the large freight elevator at the far end of the loft. Rolling out of bed, she pokes her head out of the bedroom door just as Jack steps into the elevator. Before the doors close, Didi blows her husband a kiss and receives a wink in return.

Downstairs, Jack maneuvers his beloved Road Runner out of the underground garage and through the clogged city streets like a madman, confident that he won't get a ticket. Arriving at the First in a record twenty minutes, he climbs out of his ride to the appreciative stares of a rookie cop.

"Hey, Detective! You need some twenty-two-inch DUBs on that beast!" shouts the young cop admiringly.

"Nah!" answers Jack with a shake of his head. "Keepin' it old school!"

"Pretty cool!" nods the young man.

"Yeah! Sometimes the old stuff's the best!"

Moments later, Jack stands at the whiteboard next to his desk, adding Larry Grimes' name to the team's ever-evolving timeline.

At the Sheraton Hotel, Sergeant Burley awakens with a start. Rolling over, he grabs his watch and exclaims, "Oh, shit! It's almost eight!" Jumping out of bed, he gathers his clothes from the floor and starts dressing.

On the other side of the bed, Sylvia stretches and stares at her new beau's well-formed rear-end.

"Hey," John urges, "come on, get up! It's late and we gotta get going. Crap! I don't have time to go home and change."

"We can order breakfast in," suggests Sylvia.

John shakes his head. "No, I gotta go to Jersey today. I'll see you later."

John tucks his shirt into his pants and leans over the bed to kiss Sylvia goodbye, but Sylvia has other plans. Lowering John's zipper, she thwarts his attempt at a quick exit.

Over at Homicide, Jack is surprised to see Sergeant Gomez entering the department. Dressed in a Yankee jersey and jeans and wearing a ball cap on his head, he looks much too casual for work.

"What the hell are you doing here, Gomez? I thought they gave you a paid vacation!"

"Yeah, well, Conrad called last night and said I.A. wants to meet. He told me to come in early to get it over with, and then see the shrink about the shoot. You know, SOP shit. What's the latest on this mess?"

Jack takes a sip of his second cup of coffee. "Well," he says, "Grimes and his crew stashed away a whole lotta shit at that underground station. It took us over three hours to collect it all."

John gives a low whistle. "Seems excessive, don't ya think?"

Jack nods but doesn't comment. "Grimes claims he didn't kill Cummings. He'll be released from the hospital today, and then he's coming here with his lawyer. He wants a deal for immunity and police protection. I have a hunch he was hiding money that wasn't exactly clean."

"Mornin' guys," says a familiar voice. "How you doin', Gomez?"

"Considering that I took a bath in some nasty shit yesterday, not bad," Hector smiles at Allison. "I gotta speak with I.A. today and then head over to the shrink. Gotta air out my 'feelings' about the shooting. What B.S.! Hey, where's Burley?"

Jack looks at Gomez with a smirk. "Yeah, where is Burley? And where's Sylvia? It's after nine already."

"Hey, Gomez," notes Lieutenant Conrad, joining the group. "Rawlings wants to talk before you meet with I.A."

"Anything I need to be concerned about?"

"No, everything's fine," assures Conrad. "He wants to congratulate you on how you handled the situation, and personally walk you to the I.A. interview." Looking around at the small group, Conrad asks, "Why aren't Burley and Stone here yet? I thought Burley was going to Jersey today. I had a hard time getting that laundry basket released, and I'm kissing a lot of ass trying to get that van here, too."

"I bet Burley kissed a lot of ass, too," comments Jack with a fist pump.

Conrad shakes his head at his detective's crude gesture. "Let's go, Gomez," he says, crooking a finger at the sergeant.

As the men walk away, Jack turns to Allison, who has a puzzled look on her face. "I'm sending Burley back to Cummings' place in Jersey to pick up some evidence," he explains. "As soon as he decides to come to work, that is."

Sometime later, John finally arrives, and his colleagues note that he looks a little disheveled and that he's wearing the same clothes he wore the day before.

"I guess God heard me," says Jack with a laugh

and a gleeful pump of his fist. "How's it hangin', stud?"

Burley starts to comment, but Jack cuts him off with a wave of his hand. "Never mind, I really don't give a shit. Get down to Hammonton and ask for Chief Turner. He'll bring you to Cummings' place to get the laundry. Then get back here ASAP. Oh, and put on some cologne or something. You smell like sex and fruity perfume."

Burley tries to explain again, but Jack puts up his hand. "No, I don't want to hear it. Just go, Casanova. Besides, I'll have more fun when Stone gets here."

Knowing what Sylvia is in for, Burley turns abruptly and heads out of Homicide with his tail between his legs, and Jack and Allison's laughter in his ears.

"Hey, just to let you know," says Conrad, returning from escorting Gomez to his office, "I got a call from Grimes' attorney. He says the D.A. is prepared to offer immunity. They estimate that the stash we took in yesterday is worth over one hundred eighteen million dollars."

"Holy cow!" comments Allison.

"I also got a call from Liberty Casualty. They want to pursue legal action against Sarah Cummings. The shit is about to hit the fan, guys. Jealousy, greed, or revenge killed Cummings, and we need to find out who's responsible. Oh, and by the way, Rawlings called WPIX. Larson won't be hanging around the station anymore, but I'm sure you'll see him out there somewhere."

After the lieutenant leaves, Jack and Allison discuss their boss' comments until Sylvia Stone strolls into the room, dressed in a way that raises the officers' eyebrows. This morning, Sylvia's red hair is wound up in a bun, and she's wearing black slacks, flats, and a blouse buttoned almost up to her neck.

Anticipating a good show, Allison makes herself comfortable. Leaning back in her chair, she folds her arms over her chest and waits.

"Good morning, Ms. Stone," says Jack lightly, greeting the insurance investigator with uncharacteristic sweetness. "Did you have a good night's sleep? So glad you could make it in today. You know, we start work at eight. However, I'm sure you have a good excuse for being so late: Good movie, late dinner, or maybe a hot night with an NYPD officer? Coffee?"

Sylvia scowls but ignores the taunt. "Coffee would be fine, Jack. Black, two sugars. Are you jealous?"

"The coffee pot is over there," retorts Jack. "As police officers, we promise to protect and serve, but that doesn't include getting coffee or having personal therapy sessions. Oh, wait, I guess it does. The personal shit, anyway." Walking up to Sylvia, Jack takes a whiff of her hair. "Hmm, you smell like Old Spice and sex," he says. "I already talked to Burley this morning, so you don't have to explain." Grabbing his cell phone, he turns it toward her to display a photo of his wife. "This is my personal therapist," he says. "Like I said before, I've seen bigger and better. So, no. Not jealous. Not at all."

Jack looks over at Allison, who is now laughing

so loud, she's crying.

Looking at Sylvia, Allison shoots the redhead a look that says, "I-told-you-so," and laughs some more.

A few hours later, Sergeant Burley and Chief Turner are standing in front of Stanley Cummings' house.

"I never tire of the Barrens; it's so peaceful here," says Chief Turner.

In the quiet of the forest, a slight breeze makes leaves whisper and sway, while the songs of crickets and other small insects emphasize the solitude of their surroundings.

Breathing deeply of the cleansing pine scent, the men remove yellow crime scene tape from the entrance to the porch and step inside the house.

Burley is gratified to find the laundry basket still sitting on top of the washing machine. "Doesn't look like your CSI unit looked at this, but we will."

Exiting the house, the pair replaces the police tape and drives out of the forest, with the local bird population squawking their approval.

When the SUV re-enters the paved highway back to Hammonton, neither man notices a black Cadillac parked in the bushes behind a large sign on the side of the road. As they drive past, the car enters the roadway behind them.

At two o'clock that afternoon, Jack, Allison, and Sylvia are sitting around doing busy work while they wait for Larry Grimes. He and his attorney are expected to arrive at the First after his bail is taken care of.

Staring at the clock on the wall, Jack mumbles about the slow passage of time and wills the clock's hands to move. Knowing that it's useless to expect anything, he sets down his fourth cup of coffee and heads to the bathroom. "Where the hell is Burley?" he wonders on the way. "He should have been back by now. I'm gonna have to talk to that man about better ways to manage his time."

In New Jersey, Sergeant Burley slowly turns his head and looks out of the window of his police cruiser. Mystified, he notes that his car is sitting in a shallow embankment on the side of a lightly traveled road. Woozy and befuddled, he opens the car door and steps out on wobbly legs.

Checking himself over, he's relieved to find that he doesn't seem to be injured, save for a burning sensation on his right arm. The car looks okay, too. Gradually, he remembers being forced off the road after he left Chief Turner's office.

Back at the First, Jack's cell phone rings as he exits the bathroom. Glancing at the screen, he answers the call with a curt, "Where the hell are you, Burley?"

Still dazed, Burley answers in a slow drawl.

"Someone forced me off the road after I left Hammonton. They tasered me, and I just came to. I don't think they took anything. The clothes are strewn all over the back seat of my car."

"Holy shit, man! Are you okay?"

"Yeah, just shaken up."

"Do you know who did it?"

"Nah, I'm embarrassed to say I didn't see a thing. I was minding my own business, just driving back to the city."

"What the fuck?!" explodes Jack. "This case is getting real!"

"Look, it may take me a while to get back. I'm in a ditch, but it doesn't look too steep. I'll get back on the road after I get the cobwebs out of my head. I don't think there's damage to the car, but I'll call back if there's a problem."

"Hey, no rush! Take your time; just make sure you're okay to drive."

Jack ends the call and looks up to find Allison and Sylvia staring at him.

"What happened?" asks Sylvia. "Is John okay?"

Jack scratches his head. "Burley was forced off the road. He's okay, but someone's looking for something they didn't seem to find. Grimes better have some good shit to tell us! Whoever did that to a police cruiser wants something real bad." Jack sees Conrad motioning for them to enter the interrogation room, and says, "Guess it's time for us to go in and listen to a creep tell a story. Better be a good one, that's all I can say!"

CHAPTER TWENTY

Mafia chieftain Vito Lucchese is relaxing at a table in the dimly-lit back room of Little Italy's Ristorante di Cosenza. The Don sips contentedly from a glass of his favorite red wine while one of his many business associates squirms in a chair across the table. With his bald head and fireplug physique, the sixty-nine-year-old Don bears a strong resemblance to the late actor, Telly Savalas. However, unlike the actor, the crime boss is self-conscious about his lack of hair, so to compensate, he sports a thin mustache.

"Yesterday, I got a call from our guy down at the First Precinct," says Vito, placing his glass carefully on the table. "He said they have my gold, and I want it back. Get ahold of Tony Jancko; he owes me a favor. My little birdie told me that Tony helped the cops unload my gold. Invite him here for a late lunch."

Inside the police interrogation room, Larry Grimes turns to the one-way mirror and waves hello. Although Larry intends the move to let the cops know that he is not going to be intimidated, Jack is not impressed.

"Hey, Bud," Jack scoffs, "this isn't a birthday party where you wave at the camera. Just answer our questions so we can get out of here, okay?"

Larry shrugs and leans back indifferently.

Noting Larry's calmness, Jack wonders whether it's feigned or genuine, but decides to file that question away for another time. Looking down at the folder in front of him, he grabs a photo of Stanley Cummings. "Mr. Grimes, we'll start with something easy. Who is this?"

"That's Stan Cummings."

Without further comment, Jack successively displays photos of Sam Lincoln, Keith O'Toole, and Sarah Cummings, all of whom Grimes identifies correctly.

"Okay," says Jack, "you've confirmed that you know all the players in this charade, so tell me, when was the plan launched?"

Larry looks over at his lawyer, who nods slightly.

"It began at the annual Fireman's Ball, about seven months before 9/11. Stan had piled up some huge gambling debts from illegal poker games, so he started looking into ways he could get some money out of his company to pay back what he owed. Somehow, he found out about the abandoned subway line."

"His company was Precious Coins and Bullion, correct?" asks Allison.

"Yeah. Stan was laundering money for the Lucchese family and some Middle Eastern oil barons. He was converting their cash into gold coins and storing it in his vaults. He recruited me, Lincoln, and O'Toole to help him get some of the gold out of his vaults. He said he'd give each of us a cut."

"What did you have to do for your cut?"

"I was gonna set off an explosion. It was supposed to cover Cummings' fake death and destroy his store and the vaults. We were going to claim that it was a terrorist attack on his company, and it was supposed to happen on September 27, Yom Kippur. We started to take the gold out in August, so when 9/11 happened, well, it was perfect for us."

Shocked, Allison's eyes widen, and she emits an audible gasp.

"It was 'perfect' for you?" bellows an incredulous Jack. "You were 'happy' about the worst attack on American soil?!"

"No, no!" stammers Grimes. "But, well...yeah. It did fit into our plans, so..."

Quick as a flash, Larry's attorney leans over and covers his client's mouth with his hand to prevent him from saying anything else. Whispering intensely, he confers with Larry for several minutes until he finally permits him to continue.

No longer outwardly confident, Larry resumes his story in a voice trembling with emotion. "So that morning..." he begins.

"Which morning was that?" interrupts Stenhouse.

"It was 9/11. I went to the Tower...to help Stan... He was taking out the last of the gold, and the rest of the company's records...so everything would be ready for the 27th."

Stopping his narrative, Larry turns once again to his attorney, who looks back at him blankly. Sighing deeply, Larry stares down at the table, knowing he's in big trouble.

Continuing, he says, "We were at the Cortlandt Street station when the Tower started to come down, but I detonated the charges to cover our tracks. We headed to the lower level when the concrete and dust from the explosions filled the platform. We had just made it into the utility room when a cloud of debris from the collapsed Tower filled the tunnel. After the Towers were hit, we changed the plan and used the real attack to cover Stan's escape."

Allison glances quickly at Jack, and then turns to Grimes. "So what I'm hearing is, you guys decided to steal money from Vito Lucchese and some other powerful people, and you thought it would be an easy thing to do. What the hell were you thinking?"

"Hey!" complains Grimes, wincing at Allison's tone. "We knew that none of them would report it, and we thought Stan's faked death would end any questions!"

"What happened to fuck up this great plan of yours?" asks Jack with a sneer.

Larry sighs again. "I didn't know it at the time, but O'Toole was helping Stan funnel some of the money to Stan's wife and family. It's so ironic! Stan asked the guy who was fucking his wife to help him with his 'death'!"

"Yeah, ironic," mumbles Jack. "What happened after 9/11?"

"Stan 'disappeared' and then got tired of being alone and living a lie, so he decided to end his deception. He told us that he wanted his wife and family back and that he was going to turn himself in. I guess he thought he'd just serve some time and get out before he got too old. He also told Lucchese that he had his money."

"He did what?" asks Allison incredulously. "He thought it would be that easy?"

"Yeah, I guess so. But he didn't know that Sarah had already fallen for O'Toole."

While Jack jots down some notes, Larry stops to take a drink of water. Then he says, "I was at Stan's place the day before you found him at the Memorial. He said he was planning a special dinner that evening, so I went to the store to pick up some groceries he needed. When I got back to the house, he was beaten up pretty bad. He said Lucchese's men showed up and said he had to give them the gold within forty-eight hours. I don't know how they knew where he was. I left him there, and the next day, he was dead."

"A special dinner?" probes Jack. "Any idea who was invited?"

"No. He said he was going to have a special menu, but I had to get ingredients for some kind of fuckin' chili recipe! How special is that?"

"You said he wanted to turn himself in. How did you feel when you heard that? Now, before you answer,

I don't need any fucking side comments."

"Come on, Detective. How would you feel? I was angry! We were all angry! I gave up my life for that plan! I tried to talk him out of it, but he didn't want to hear anything I said."

"And what about the gold?" prods Jack. "Did he tell you how he was going to get it back to Lucchese?"

"I don't know how he was going to get the gold to Lucchese! I guess he was just gonna tell him where it was, and that SOB would have his goons pick it up!"

"Where do you live, Mr. Grimes?" asks Allison. "You couldn't have stayed in the tunnel full time."

"No, that was the easy part. I rented a room in a house on Staten Island, and I made all the rent payments in cash, which is how the owner wanted it, anyway."

"How did you all get down to the abandoned station without drawing attention to yourselves?"

"You know you can buy anything online, right? I bought transit worker uniforms and IDs. They looked real enough. Hell, I even got Stan a bogus birth certificate and a phony driver's license."

"What name was on Stan's phony ID?" asks Jack.

"Joe Stanley."

Larry takes another drink of water while Allison and Jack scribble notes.

"How did you get back and forth to Jersey?" asks Allison.

"Whenever we were going to work on the gold, I'd walk to the Staten Island Ferry terminal from my room. When the ferry docked in Manhattan, I walked to Cortlandt Street and went into the subway. I was dressed as a worker, so no one stopped me. After a while, the token vendors and transit cops recognized me—us. They thought we were going to work. Shit, we sure did go to work!"

"Why was there a bed and a hotplate setup down there if you had a room in Staten Island?"

"On days that the weather was bad, the others went home, and I stayed in the tunnel."

"Why didn't you go home, too?"

"I didn't have any reason to leave. The others have families."

"How did you move the gold if you were always walking to the station?" interjects Jack.

"I have a Chevy that I keep in Staten Island for personal use—you know, to get around town and run errands—and I drove it there when we needed to move the gold. Sometimes, after our shifts at the fire station, or whenever Sam, Keith, and I had time off, we'd pitch in and work together. The same went for Stan. And whenever we could, we worked nights and weekends. Hell, we treaded so much water down there that I thought we were gonna grow fins!"

"Buying phony IDs and stuff can get expensive," declares Allison. "How did you afford it all?"

"We were invisible to just about everyone when we dressed in our 'official' uniforms, so whenever I needed money, I'd go underground and get some coins. Damn, I must have frequented every pawn shop in Lower Manhattan!"

"Did you keep your cut in the old station?"

Before Larry responds, he leans over to whisper to his attorney.

"I kept some of my coins in Staten Island, and the rest is now in your evidence room. Like I said, when I needed money, I'd sell some of my coins for the value of the gold. Lincoln and O'Toole took their shares out. I have no idea if they converted their stash or where they put it."

"Okay, two more things," says Jack to end the questioning. "First, is there anyone else at Ladder Company 403 or anywhere else who knew about this or who was involved in the cover-up?"

"No, not that I know of," replies Grimes. "The only ones I know about are Sam Lincoln and Keith O'Toole. Stan wanted to get money to his family, and he did it through O'Toole, but I don't know if O'Toole told Sarah where the money was coming from. Sarah doesn't seem like the type to be naïve enough not to know something was up, but you'd have to ask them about that. Look, Detective, now that Lucchese knows where the gold is, he's not going to stop before he gets his money back. Stan was a fool to tell him where the gold was, so you better watch your collective asses."

As Jack is about to wrap things up, Allison leans over to him and whispers, "We need to talk."

"Yeah, definitely; after we get out of here," Jack

whispers back. Then he turns to Grimes. "This is the last question. We know that Cummings had other people helping him in Jersey and that one of them may have asthma. Is that person Salvatore Brusco?"

Grimes shakes his head. "No, Brusco's health prevents him from doing anything physical. Stan paid a few day laborers and some guys from Hammonton to help him out there from time to time. I remember that one of them did suck on an inhaler."

"Okay, that's it for today, Grimes."

When Jack and Allison open the interrogation room door, two armed guards and a representative from the District Attorney's office enter and escort Grimes out, followed by his attorney. The attorney brokered an agreement for the informant to be placed under twenty-four-hour guard in one of the department's safe houses until they need to question him further.

Allison grabs Jack's elbow and propels him into an empty room. With her back against the door to make sure no one comes in, she looks uncertainly at her friend and partner. "Jack," she stammers, "I never told this to anyone..." Swallowing nervously, she says, "I have a personal connection with the Lucchese family."

Jack stares at his partner. "What the hell?" he asks. "How?"

Allison doesn't answer right away. As Jack watches, she paces back and forth, trying to find the right words.

"Vito's my uncle; my late mother's maiden name

was Lucchese. She was the daughter of Vito's brother, and she didn't want any part of the family business." Allison uses finger quotation marks around the word 'business.' "She wanted out, so she married a plumber and left that life for the suburbs of New Rochelle. The mob kept tabs on her and our family, though. They knew everything about us. After Vito's brother—my grandfather—was killed by a mob hit, Vito took a special interest in my mom. I know he sent her money from time to time. If it would help, I think I could speak to him."

"You're a mafia chick?!" exclaims Jack, bowled over by the news. "Good to know, Giancarlo! Oops, I should probably stop ribbing you now. My knees are allergic to baseball bats!"

Allison gives Jack a nasty look, but he ignores it. "Look," he says, "if what you say is true—now, don't get me wrong, I don't doubt it, though I am a little surprised—I don't think Lucchese will do anything that would put you in jeopardy."

Allison shakes her head sadly. "Jack, don't take Vito lightly. He'd do anything to get his money, even storm this place, if he could. We need to be cautious, and we need to get Lincoln and the rest of the crew in here ASAP so we can question them before Vito gets to them."

"Okay. Those phony uniforms put O'Toole and Lincoln right in the middle of all this shit. Let's talk to them again. We also need a search warrant for Grimes' place so we can pick up the gold he stashed there. I'll talk to Conrad to get the legalities started." Jack tilts his head and narrows his eyes. "Hey, you know what?

Frank A. Ruffolo

Maybe that 'special guest' Stan invited for dinner poisoned him with arsenic-laced chili!"

"Now, there's a thought! You could be right!" exclaims Allison.

CHAPTER TWENTY-ONE

Across the city at Ladder 403, Captain Sam Lincoln makes an emergency phone call. He knows his subordinates in the rec room downstairs are talking about all the valuables they helped bring up from Grimes' hideout.

When the call connects, Sam hisses, "Keith! It already hit the fan! The cops found Grimes and the gold! We're next! What? No, I guess he didn't blow the place! I'm outta here! Do whatever you need to, but I'm gone!"

Slamming the phone down, Lincoln hurriedly stuffs some personal belongings into a duffel bag and leaves the station. Stopping first at the bank to empty his safe deposit box, he then heads home to pack.

Sam's call rattled Keith. The instant he hung up, he ran over to Sarah's house.

Using the house key Sarah gave him, he walks into her house unannounced and surprises her as she makes herself a sandwich in the kitchen. Sarah's smile at his unexpected appearance rapidly turns into a frown.

"Keith? You look upset. What's wrong, Honey?"

"I have something to tell you. Let's sit down."

Keith leads Sarah out of the kitchen and into the living room.

"Sarah," he begins, "you know that a lot of gold went missing when Stan disappeared after 9/11, right? Well, when Stan showed up again, the police and Liberty Insurance opened an investigation, and they found the gold. They're probably going to come after you, I mean us, for fraud. Stan's life and business policies were with Liberty, so I'm sure they're going to want you to return the money they gave you all those years ago. I talked to the attorney, and he advised me to come up with a story we both agree on. He's coming here tonight."

Sarah begins to cry, and Keith holds her tight.

"Don't worry, Honey. Everything will be fine," he says with a measure of self-assurance that he doesn't actually feel.

Melting into Keith's arms, Sarah assures Keith that she trusts him and is willing to do whatever he says.

However, as they sit huddled together, the brief smile that crosses Sarah's face when Keith doesn't notice seems highly inappropriate.

Outside of the interrogation room, Sylvia walks up to Jack and Allison.

"I want you both to know that we're pressing charges against Mrs. Cummings for insurance fraud. I spoke with the D.A.'s office and they've agreed to issue warrants for her, O'Toole, and Lincoln. I got a bad feeling that Lincoln suspects he's in trouble, though, because I tried to call him at the station, and they told me he left there suddenly."

Jack curses under his breath. "Fuck that bastard! He's gonna skip! We need to prevent him from leaving the city! Ally, tell the team to monitor all the airports and other points of exit, and get them to issue an APB on our other 'friends.' We don't want to lose them. Tell them to get some units over to their houses. Maybe we'll get lucky and catch them before they can do anything. And Ally," adds Jack with a concerned look at his partner, "after we catch them, I think you're gonna have to pay a visit to your uncle. You sure you're up to that?"

Giancarlo nods her head and walks away, mumbling, "I knew this was gonna happen eventually. This is one family outing I'm truly dreading."

"You busy at the moment?" Jack asks Stone.

"No."

"Okay, then come with me to Conrad's office."

With uncharacteristic restraint, Jack knocks lightly on the glass of the lieutenant's office door, prompting his boss to look up from his paperwork with a questioning expression. Jack allows Sylvia to enter first and then closes the door behind them.

"Lieutenant," Jack says, "in case you haven't

heard, Liberty Casualty is pressing charges against Sarah Cummings, Keith O'Toole, and Sam Lincoln."

"Yeah, I know," nods Conrad. "The D.A. is issuing warrants for their arrest."

"I just got off the phone with a guy at the Ladder Company 403 stationhouse," interjects Sylvia. "I wanted to talk to Sam Lincoln, but he wasn't there. The guy who answered the phone told me that Sam bolted out of there in a hurry."

"Aw, crap! He's on the run!" bellows Conrad. "I'll issue an APB for his arrest, and I'll have the guys send his photo to all the transportation outlets. Jack, as soon as Burley returns, be prepared to head out to join the search for that SOB."

"Okay, Boss."

"By the way," says Conrad, turning his attention to Sylvia, "your work here seems to be done now. I want to thank you and Liberty Casualty for all of your support. It's nearly noon, so have a seat, and I'll take you to lunch on the First's dime. Just give me a few minutes to get the ball rolling on Lincoln."

Sylvia makes herself comfortable as Jack exits the office.

"A little T and A goes a long way around here," he mumbles under his breath.

In Little Italy, Tony Jancko walks nervously into Ristorante di Cosenza. When he tells the hostess he has a meeting with Mr. Lucchese, she threads her way through the rows of tables and disappears into the kitchen.

Immediately, two imposing men dressed impeccably in black, Italian-made suits, exit the kitchen. Beckoning to Tony, they point him through tables full of hungry customers stuffing pasta and other delicacies into their mouths.

At the door to the secluded room, the men pat Tony down before they walk him to their boss. Sandwiched between the two goons, Tony removes a handkerchief from his slacks to wipe his sweating brow.

"Tony, *come va?*" smiles Vito, looking up from his meal. "Come and sit. How are Clara and the kids?" While the goons make their exit, Vito nods at a hovering waiter. "Get Tony an espresso with anisette. And a sfogliatelle."

Feeling the need to say something, Tony gives Vito a peck on each cheek and stammers, "Mr. Lucchese...it's an honor to be here."

"Yes, yes," replies Vito pleasantly. "You know, the food here is excellent, but you never stop by with your family."

"No... I don't... Sorry," splutters Tony.

"Hmm. So why are you here today?"

"Uh... I was told that you wanted to talk to me... sir."

Nodding, Vito offers Tony a seat while he takes a sip of wine and a forkful of eggplant parmigiana.

Tony is silent while he waits for the mafioso

to speak again, and he remains quiet when a rather large waiter serves him his coffee and pastry. Looking around, he notes that he's in a small room with lush carpeting and colorful scenes of Sicily dominating each wall.

When Vito finishes his meal, he wipes his mouth and clears his throat, all the while staring at the nervous man in front of him.

"Tony," he finally says, "when you were trying to buy your armored car business, you came to me with a problem. As I recall, the previous owner kept rejecting your proposals. I agreed to help with the negotiations and was able to convince him to accept your deal. Now at that time, I told you that in return for my help, you would owe me a favor and that I would ask for that favor at some time in the future."

"Yes, I remember, sir."

"Well, it has come to my attention that you recently helped the police transport some gold to the First Precinct. Is this true?"

Nearly choking on his sfogliatelle, Tony coughs loudly to clear his throat.

"Yes. Yes, sir," he replies hesitantly. "They found gold in an old subway tunnel. The TV reported that it was part of the gold from the Trade Towers."

Vito continues to stare at Tony. "Yes, I heard that, too," he responds calmly. "That's good, Tony. Now, you should know that some of that gold is mine. I thought it was lost forever, but now that it is found, I need your assistance to bring it back to me. I have some friends at the First who will make arrangements for you to pick it up. I'll be in contact with you again when everything's ready."

Sitting back in his chair, Vito takes another sip of wine.

"Well, now. Business is over," he says. "Would you like more espresso, or perhaps some of this delicious parmigiana?"

CHAPTER TWENTY-TWO

It is now mid-afternoon. The Big Apple lunch crowd has returned to work, so even though the traffic has ebbed slightly, in the city that never sleeps, there is always something going on—legally or illegally.

Sam Lincoln is one of many in the city whose intentions are not exactly on the up-and-up. He is currently driving to EZ Gold and Pawn Shop on the Lower West Side. The contents of his large safe deposit box are in a sturdy aluminum case on the car seat next to him. He needs to exchange his gold for cash, so he'll be able to pass through TSA screening.

Nervous as a blind cat in a room full of rocking chairs, Sam blows his horn impatiently at the slow-moving mass of busses, cabs, and other vehicles blocking his way, as if the sound of his horn will make them magically disappear.

A block away from his destination, he eases his car into a parking spot. Clutching the heavy case, he pushes and shoves through throngs of people lining the sidewalk, eventually arriving at the entrance to EZ Gold and Pawn.

Impatient, Sam rings the store's buzzer without letup, causing the owner to look up in irritation. When the proprietor recognizes the person at his door, his annoyance turns into a smile, and he reaches under the counter to hit a button that admits his longtime customer into his shop.

"Hey, Sam!" grins the owner. "Long time, no see. You got more gold for me?"

Out of breath, Sam lifts his heavy case with a grunt and places it on the table next to the cash register.

"Damn, Sam!" remarks Sid Geller at the weight of the container. "What the hell you got in there?"

Without comment, Sam opens the case just enough to let Sid see its contents. Inside are hundreds of gold and silver coins, along with numerous platinum bars.

Staring at the haul with widened eyes, Sid quips, "Looks like you firemen sure make good money! What do you want to do with it all?"

Nervous and in a hurry, Sam just wants to get on with this and leave. "No small talk, please," he says to his friend. "Just make me an offer. I'm late for a flight."

With a knowing nod, Sid switches into business mode. Reaching into the case, he brings out handfuls of valuables, separating it into small piles on the counter.

"Sam, this is a shitload of money," Sid declares. "I don't know if I have enough on hand. I mean, there are tens of thousands of dollars' worth here."

Now Sam is annoyed, as well as still being nervous as hell. "Bullshit!" he exclaims. "You got plenty of cash on hand; I've seen it before! Make me an offer, Sid, or I go somewhere else. You're not the only broker in

Manhattan. Get on with it, or I'm outta' here!"

Although puzzled by Sam's atypical attitude, Sid shrugs and grabs a calculator from where it sits on a shelf under the display case, next to a 12-gauge double barrel sawed-off shotgun. Looking over the piles of coins and bars he laid out on the counter, he punches numbers into the calculator and comes up with a figure.

"Okay, you have about $125,000 here. I don't have that much money on the premises, but I can give you $75,000 cash right now. I can wire you the rest after I go to the bank. That's the best I can do."

Sam pinches his nose with one hand and rubs the back of his neck with the other. Exhaling through his nose, he shouts, "You and I know that's still bullshit! I'll take $100k now, and I'll call you with instructions on where to send the rest!"

Sid sighs. "80k. That's all for now." Holding out his hand, he waits to see if Sam will shake on his terms.

Sam stares at Sid's hand and looks at his watch. "Okay," he agrees reluctantly. "Let's do this."

With a firm shake of Sam's hand, Sid starts writing up the paperwork. "I'll need the case, too," he tells Sam. "I'll get you the money after you sign the receipt. It'll be large bills."

Sam nods and signs the sales order while Sid places the hoard back into the case.

When the container is full again, Sid locks it and takes it off the table. "I'll be back in a minute," he tells Sam. "I gotta count out your money."

Carrying the heavy case into his office at the rear of the store, Sid makes sure the door is closed, and then picks up the phone. Earlier that day, he received a faxed bulletin from the First Precinct about Sam, and he is now about to use that information to his advantage. The call is patched through to Jack.

"This is Detective Stenhouse."

"Detective, this is EZ Gold and Pawn Shop on Beaver Street," says the store owner in a low voice. "You're looking for Sam Lincoln. He's here right now, and he's trying to cash in on hundreds of thousands of dollars' worth of gold and silver. I think he's heading out of town. I'll try to slow him down. Gotta' go."

Jack stares at the blank screen on his phone. He's unsure if he heard the hurried caller correctly but decides to check it out just in case.

"I got a lead!" he shouts into the room. "A guy says Lincoln is cashing out at EZ's on Beaver Street!"

"What's going on?" reacts a voice from the far end of the room. Sergeant Burley has just returned with the basket of laundry from New Jersey.

"John! Glad you're okay!" shouts Jack. "Come with me!"

Burley drops the basket and runs after Jack, who's already halfway to the elevator.

On the way, Jack sees Lieutenant Conrad and Sylvia Stone walking to the elevator for lunch.

"Lieutenant, I think we got Lincoln on the run! Can you get the guys in blue to EZ Gold and Pawn ASAP? Oh, and the laundry basket is in the squad room!"

Sam paces back and forth, staring at his watch. Fretting about the time, he yells, "Sid! What the fuck's takin' so long? I gotta' drive to Kennedy!"

"Hey, calm down!" replies Sid as he makes his way back to the front of the store with a canvas bag full of cash. I had to count it all out for you. How the hell do you plan to get this through TSA?"

"I'm prescreened. I'm gonna carry some of it on me, but most of it's goin' in my checked bag. I already paid some people off in Ho Chi Minh City, so I'm not worried about customs over there."

"Where?"

"Saigon, you idiot!" hollers Sam as he grabs the canvas bag and rushes out of the shop.

When the door closes behind him, he doesn't hear Sid ask, "You're going to Vietnam?"

Running back to his car, Sam opens the door in a hurry and tosses the bag onto the passenger seat. Then, he shoves his vehicle into the first break in traffic.

Jack and the cavalry—four patrol cars and a red '68 Road Runner with its blue lights flashing—miss Sam by a hair.

"He just left!" shouts Sid, meeting the cops outside his store. "He's heading to Kennedy for a flight to Vietnam! I got his shit here. Go get my money back!"

Shouting commands, Stenhouse and Burley direct the patrol officers to get a statement from Sid and to take charge of Lincoln's ill-gotten stash. Then, Jack calls Lieutenant Conrad to tell him where they're going. He also informs Conrad that they refused the patrol cops' offer of an escort to Kennedy. They don't want to call attention to themselves in case they catch up to Lincoln.

Jack drives south toward Brooklyn and the Hugh Carey Tunnel while Burley calls the First to get details on Lincoln's car.

"He has a white, 5 Series BMW," Burley soon declares. "License plate 403 BOSS."

Jack hears Burley's report but makes no reply. He is concentrating on weaving in and out of the heavy traffic toward the tunnel. When there's a break between cars, he says, "If we spot him, we'll follow him into Kennedy. That's where we'll nab him. Call Conrad to make sure he alerted TSA and Homeland Security. I want them at the terminal in case we miss him."

Zigzagging through the clogged thoroughfare, Jack concentrates on winding through traffic as if he were in a slalom ski race. But when he enters the tunnel, he remains in his lane—there is no longer any room to maneuver in the narrow tube.

Burley scans the roadway ahead for the suspect's vehicle. Suddenly, he calls out, "I got him! He's about seven cars up, right behind that Republic garbage truck!"

Keeping an eye on the BMW John identified, Jack

calls out instructions. "Contact Dispatch; tell them we spotted Lincoln. We'll be on Ocean Parkway soon, going south to the Belt Parkway. We should be at Kennedy in thirty minutes."

Burley gives Jack a thumbs-up, but he won't be able to place the call until they exit the tunnel.

Back at the First, Conrad postponed his lunch with Stone and hurriedly shoved the basket of laundry into his office. He is now also on his way to Kennedy Airport.

Left to fend for herself, Sylvia went back to her hotel and contacted Liberty Life and Casualty to update Corporate on the case. Then she turned on the TV and called room service for a solitary lunch.

CHAPTER TWENTY-THREE

On their way to the front porch of Sarah Cummings' brick Cape Cod home in West Hempstead, Detective Giancarlo and officers from the Nassau County Police Department take no notice of a pink dogwood tree and a mass of colorful azaleas, all in full bloom.

Single-minded in their mission, the officers focus on the task ahead and hope this stop, and the next one at Keith's house around the corner, will be uneventful.

As the troupe mounts the steps, Keith surprises them when he opens the main door.

"No need for trouble," he says from behind the outer screen door. "Sarah and I are prepared to turn ourselves in. Our attorney will meet us at Central Booking, so let's get this over with. We'll cooperate in any way we can."

Pleased by the ease of the arrests, Allison stands aside as her Nassau County colleagues cuff the suspects. Then she reads the charges and recites the Miranda Warning as the pair is led to a police cruiser.

Jack is still following Sam Lincoln's BMW. But when it turns into JFK Airport and enters a public parking garage, he stops following at the garage entrance.

Blissfully unaware that he was being followed, Sam continues up to the top floor and parks in a remote corner, near an outside wall. He takes a few minutes to scan his surroundings, and when he doesn't see anyone else around, opens the canvas bag and shoves as much money as he can into his pockets.

At ground level, Stenhouse and Burley wait for two airport police vehicles to pull up beside the Road Runner. Conferring with the airport cops, the officers decide on a plan. When they're ready, all three cars drive into the garage to locate Sam.

Still busy moving his cash around, Sam is oblivious to what is going on around him until two quick beeps of a car horn grab his attention. Glancing in his rear and side view mirrors, he is alarmed to catch sight of several officers approaching his car, and a red Road Runner blocking his exit.

"Shit!" he exclaims loudly and bolts out of the Beemer to the wall in front of his car. With his back to the barrier, he looks at the ground below while keeping a wary eye on the approaching detectives.

"I'll jump if I have to!" he yells.

Concealing himself behind Jack, Burley pulls out a Taser as Jack tries to keep Sam's attention away from his partner.

"Sam," says Jack calmly, "we're not going to leave, and you're not going to jump. But you know what? I don't give a shit if you do jump. If you take the coward's way out, the city will save a ton of money on your arrest and trial. So if you're going to jump, get it over with. I have better things to do than spend my time with an asshole at an airport."

Shocked by Jack's remarks, Sam stiffens and stares at him in disbelief, and this momentary pause provides Burley with the opening he needs. Extending his arm, he aims his Taser at Lincoln from his position behind Stenhouse and hits him squarely in the middle of his chest.

The weapon releases 50,000 volts that knock Sam to the pavement and make his body shudder and twitch. With Sam down and the Taser off, Burley unhooks the wires from the limp suspect and cuffs him.

Watching, Jack says sarcastically, "I'm disappointed, John. I really wanted to see him jump."

Looking up, John rolls his eyes at the crass comment and asks one of the airport cops for assistance. But when he moves to put Lincoln into the back seat of Jack's car, Jack yells, "Whoa!" and stops them in their tracks. "Hold on! I need to put a cover down! That jerk just pissed himself!"

While the cops support Lincoln under both of his arms, Jack retrieves an old blanket from the trunk and spreads it out on the back seat. When the seat is well covered, he steps away and allows the men to push and shove the cuffed and wet Lincoln into the Road Runner.

"Hey, John," calls Jack. "Empty Lincoln's pockets. I'll search his car."

"Your lieutenant is at the terminal with Homeland Security," declares one of the airport officers. "We'll tell them to let the lieutenant know that your suspect is secure."

"Great. Thanks for the backup," says Jack, shaking the man's hand. "Can you also let him know that we're on our way to Booking?"

"Yeah, sure," replies the cop.

Minutes later, Jack gives two quick beeps to the airport cops, and the Road Runner leaves the parking garage. The policemen will remain near Sam's car until it's picked up by an NYPD tow truck.

Vito Lucchese has a broad smile on his face. He has just gotten off a call from his mole at the First Precinct.

"Giovanni," he says to one of his soldiers, "that guy in the Evidence Room has the stuff we need. Get a hold of Jancko and tell him I want to see him tomorrow morning at eight a.m. sharp."

"Yes, sir, Don Vito."

It is now late afternoon, and Sarah, Keith, and Sam are being processed at Central Booking. While the attorneys try to get their clients released on bail, Jack and his team stand in front of the whiteboard at Jack's desk. Grabbing a black marker, Jack adds a large question mark next to the photos of Larry Grimes, Sarah Cummings, Keith O'Toole, Sam Lincoln, and Vito Lucchese.

"Okay," he says to his crew. "We got all the players except one: Vito Lucchese." Turning, he looks earnestly into Allison's eyes. "Tomorrow, you're gonna need to pay him a family visit. Take Hector with you. I.A. should be done with him by then, and he'll be back on duty. We'll talk to the rest of the players after you return."

"What do you mean by 'family'?" asks Burley, overhearing the conversation.

Ignoring John's question, Allison says, "No, Jack, I need to do it on my own. You know I'll get better access if I'm by myself."

"Not gonna happen," insists Jack. "If Gomez doesn't actually go in with you, then you'll wear a wire, and he'll stay outside in the car to listen and be close if you need help. Backup will also be on the street in unmarked cars in case things go south. You can't trust Lucchese, uncle or not. There's no doubt he's determined to get his gold one way or the other."

Jack turns back to study the whiteboard, giving Allison a moment to take John aside.

"It's a long story," she says with a sigh. "I'm Lucchese's niece."

That night, after the kids fall asleep, Allison snuggles up to her husband in their Westchester County apartment.

"Honey," she says, "the day I've been dreading is

going to happen in only twenty-four hours."

Mario Giancarlo, a purchasing manager for a local manufacturer, strokes Allison's hair.

"I know," he says soothingly. "But, Hon, you're not part of that family anymore. Just think of it as another day at the office. You'll be dealing with the bad guys like you always do. You'll do fine."

Allison sighs deeply. "It's my Uncle Vito's reaction that I'm worried about. As a cop, I knew this confrontation would come one day. I only hope I can keep my emotions from interfering with my job."

Sometime later, after a tender kiss and more reassurances from Mario, Allison slowly drifts off into dreamland.

Not everyone is able to sleep this night, however. Downtown, Jack remains wide awake as he lies beside Didi. With the Cummings case swirling around in his head, he watches his wife sleep and envies her peacefulness. Struggling to encourage his own sleep, he gives up the battle and stares into the darkness, listening gloomily to a lone siren that wails in the distance.

CHAPTER TWENTY-FOUR

When the alarm clock blasts out its obnoxious, mechanical ring at five thirty in the morning, Didi turns over and climbs out of bed, moving on still-drowsy feet to the bathroom. Although Didi's morning sickness has abated, her growing baby is relentlessly increasing pressure on her bladder.

With the alarm still shrieking, Jack shoots his hand out from under the covers and fumbles around the nightstand, searching for the offending object to silence its intrusion into the few hours' sleep he was finally able to get last night. Unable to find the off switch quickly enough, he grabs the entire clock and throws it across the room, smashing it against the wall, and leaving another mark on the drywall.

As intended, the clock falls to the floor in welcome silence.

Hearing the commotion from inside the bathroom, Didi knows what it means.

"Dammit, Jack!" she shouts from behind the door. "Not another clock! You're gonna have to fix that wall! It's a good thing I keep a spare clock around!"

Grimacing up at the ceiling he stared at for a good part of the night, Jack waits impatiently while Didi finishes her business.

Still inside the bathroom, Didi washes her hands and studies herself in the mirror, marveling at the slight baby bump on her naked body. Suddenly, Jack barges into the room and makes a beeline for the toilet.

"Sorry," he explains, "can't wait any longer."

While Jack does his thing, he looks over at Didi, who is still rubbing her belly. Sensing that Jack is looking, she turns to him with a frown.

"You know, Hon, we can't afford to keep replacing clocks," she says firmly. "If you can't control your reaction to their sounds, as annoying as they may be, you're going to have to do something about that wall—and soon. It looks hideous! However, on another note," she grins impishly, "I'm happy to know that you're still interested, even with all the changes I'm going through."

Jack grins back and adjusts his aim, trying not to pee all over the floor. After he flushes, he turns on the water in the shower, and Didi follows him in.

Tony Jancko is not happy to be back on Mulberry Street. He arrived early like he was told, but he's been alone in a small office at Ristorante di Cosenza for about an hour now. With his nerves on edge, the knowledge that he's going to have to do something that will probably be dangerous tugs at his soul. His legs shake uncontrollably, and he checks his watch repeatedly.

For the umpteenth time, Tony notes that it's still only 8:15 a.m. So, when he finally hears voices outside of the room, he instantly becomes alert. And when the door opens and Don Vito strolls in, Jancko's anxiety level hits the roof. Practically jumping out of his chair, he greets Lucchese with a kiss on each cheek.

"*Buongiorno*, Tony," responds the Don with a hand on Tony's shoulder. "Sorry for the delay. I had some urgent matters to attend to this morning. Sit; we have business to discuss."

Afraid of what the Don will ask him to do, the armored truck owner nervously reclaims his seat.

"Tony," begins the mobster, "I want my gold, so I need to borrow one of your trucks. After this meeting, four of my men will accompany you to your warehouse. You will give them uniforms and then you will drive them to the First Precinct in your truck. Your job will be to sit in the truck and wait. When they're done loading my goods, you will drive them and the truck here. Do this, and the favor you received from me will be paid in full. Do not fail me."

Nodding, Tony stands and thanks Don Vito. Then, he follows the kingpin's soldiers out of the restaurant.

While the men slide into the back seat of his sedan, Tony bows his head, takes a deep breath loaded with despair, and makes the sign of the cross. Oddly resigned to the job he has been assigned, he turns his car into heavy Mulberry Street traffic, and the Big Apple swallows him up like a well-chewed piece of fried calamari.

Blocked by a line of cars on East Houston Street almost three blocks long, Jack and a host of other irritated drivers wait impatiently for New York's Finest to clear an early morning traffic accident from the roadway. Jack's tossing and turning all night long has left him with little sleep and even less patience. Not a morning person by nature, he is now even more pissed off than usual. Glancing at the clock on the dashboard, he curses when he sees that it's almost nine o'clock.

"Didi's already at work, and here I am, stuck in this damn, damn traffic!" he growls, slapping at the wheel in frustration.

In the forty minutes since Jack entered Houston Street, he has traveled less than one block, and his patience is now non-existent. As his car creeps up to the corner of Norfolk Street, he decides that he can wait no longer. Grabbing his blue light, he places it on the dashboard, turns his wheel, and crosses the solid line. Barreling down the wrong side of the street amid a sea of middle fingers, he forces cars and trucks to slam on their brakes and swerve out of the way of what they consider to be an absolute madman.

When Jack arrives at the accident site on the wrong side of the street, the policemen working the scene rush to stop the reckless driver from proceeding any further. However, when they spy Jack's police badge waving at them from his outstretched hand, they permit him to pass.

Continuing to weave in and out of oncoming

traffic, Jack barely manages to avoid collisions of his own making until he finally turns back onto the westbound side of the street two harrowing blocks later, with more locals granting him angry, one-fingered salutes.

At almost 9:30, Allison, John, Hector, and Sylvia have been at the First for a couple of hours, but Jack is still nowhere to be found, and the crew is getting worried. He hasn't been answering his phone, either, which isn't like him.

Downstairs at the First Precinct, a Jancko armored truck has parked near the evidence area with its motor running. Four disguised mafia soldiers holding forged paperwork have exited the truck and are now standing at a locked gate, while Lester Smith, the officer in charge, goes through his paces.

Taking his time, Lester looks through their forms and finally grunts his approval. Thrusting his clipboard at one of the "guards," he asks for a signature to release the requested evidence.

"What's going on, Les?" inquires a passing officer.

"The D.A. wants to transfer some of the gold to the FBI. Something about an ongoing investigation —racketeering and money laundering," replies Officer Smith with bored indifference.

For a long minute, the curious officer seems to be unsure of Smith's explanation. He looks questioningly from Smith to the waiting guards, and then back again to Smith. But then something changes his mind. He takes a breath, scratches his head, and leaves the area without further comment.

In unspoken appreciation of the officers' lack of diligence, the soldiers return to the truck and motion for Tony to back it up to the loading platform in the evidence yard. With the truck in position, one of them tells Tony to be quiet and remain behind the wheel. Then, the four men begin to gather up their boss' bounty.

Still on his way to work, Jack's irritation hasn't abated, even though he's only a few blocks away from the building. He knows he's late, so when he finally arrives at HQ, he pulls up in front of the building with the intention of double-parking his car. However, when he sees the armored truck at the loading dock, alarm bells go off in his head. Dialing his boss from his car, he demands imperiously, "Why the hell is there a Jancko armored truck in the evidence yard?"

"I have no idea," answers Conrad, annoyed by Jack's tone. "Where the hell are you? It's 9:30!"

Suspecting that the worst may be happening, Jack snaps back, "Call the fucking Evidence Room! Something's going down right now!"

While Jack watches closely, one of the armored truck's guards exits the building with a heavy bag and loads it into the truck. Tapping his steering wheel restlessly, Jack waits impatiently for his boss to call back.

"It's bullshit!" shouts Conrad. "Try to stop them! I sent men out to help!"

Flying out of his car, Jack draws his weapon at two men who have just exited the building, however, a shotgun blast from a gun port on the side of the armored vehicle stops him cold. Buckshot hits him squarely on the left side of his chest and spins him backward about three feet, landing him flat on his back.

At the sound of gunfire, groups of plainclothes and uniformed officers converge on the street like marauding ants. Others, responding to Lieutenant Conrad's order, fire at the armored vehicle and the men around it, taking down three of the mafia soldiers in a brief firefight.

Caught in the middle of the gunfire, Tony Jancko ducks down low and tries to drive the truck away, but his retreat is blocked by police vehicles that rush in behind it.

It's a good thing that Jack paid attention this morning; something told him to wear his bulletproof vest. Doing its job well, the vest absorbed most of the buckshot, but a few pellets found his face, and his left arm is bleeding profusely.

When the firefight is over, the lieutenant and Jack's teammates rush into the street to assess Jack's condition. As soon as they see the amount of blood around his arm, Sergeant Gomez whips off his belt to use as a tourniquet.

Not realizing the extent of his injuries, Jack waves Gomez away and tries to stand, but when the pain in his face, arm, and chest threatens to overwhelm him, he quickly lays back down and waits for the pain and the ringing in his ears from the gun blasts to subside.

"Fucking Lucchese tried to get his gold!" he shouts hoarsely, until fresh pain stops him. Dripping with sweat, he moans, "Ohh, crap! I think my ribs broke!"

Kneeling next to Jack, Allison wraps a comforting arm around her partner. "Keep calm," she orders. "Don't move. Just lay there quietly. You lost a lot of blood. The EMTs will be here soon."

Against Allison's advice, Jack peels his vest away to check beneath it. Relieved when he doesn't see blood, he nevertheless suspects some type of damage in that vital region.

Giancarlo remains close to Jack until the EMTs arrive to attend to him and the others who were injured in the firefight. Sitting on the ground near him, she watches as her fellow officers arrest Tony Jancko, along with the connected guy who was shooting from inside the truck, and the three goons who were outside the vehicle.

When Lieutenant Conrad is satisfied that his officer is being taken care of and that the assailants are properly restrained, he begins to bark orders.

"Giancarlo! Go with Jack to Presbyterian Hospital! Gomez, talk to the guys in the truck and find out what the fuck just happened! Burley, check on the ones we hit, and find out if they survived! Get statements, if you can. I'll contact Jack's wife." Bending down, he retrieves Stenhouse's Glock from the pavement.

When EMTs arrive, they check Jack's wounds and wrap his arm tightly. When he's lifted into the back of the rescue vehicle, Giancarlo climbs in to accompany him to the hospital.

Burley's inspection finds that two of the fake guards have succumbed to their wounds, while another is in critical condition. An injured offender is transported to the same hospital as Jack in a separate ambulance, with a police officer on board.

Twenty minutes later, Lieutenant Conrad parks near Didi's boutique. This is the part of the job that is the hardest. Hesitating at the store's entrance, he stops and closes his eyes for a moment to summon up his courage. Then, he pushes the door open.

Standing at the counter, Didi instinctively knows that something is wrong when she sees Jack's boss. Trembling, she watches as Conrad walks toward her.

"Mrs. Stenhouse," says the lieutenant grimly, "there's been an incident. Jack is okay, but you should come with me. I'll take you to him."

Didi is shaking like a leaf. With her hormones going berserk, she screams, "Oh, God! Not my Jack! No, no, no, not my Jack!"

Lieutenant Conrad attempts to calm her, but she doesn't hear anything he says.

"Where is he?" she yells. "Oh, nooo…" she moans, holding onto the counter for support.

Conrad grabs Didi and hugs her tightly, still trying to get through to her.

"Mrs. Stenhouse!" he shouts. "Jack has been transported to Presbyterian Hospital! He was shot, but he'll be okay!"

When Didi looks him in the eye, he says more softly, "He's conscious, and I'm sure he'd like to see you. Come on; I'll take you down there. Don't worry; he'll be fine."

With his arm around Didi, Conrad escorts her out to his car while Sonia, Didi's assistant, rings up a customer and worries about her boss.

CHAPTER TWENTY-FIVE

Vito Lucchese is livid.

"*Fanculo tutto!* What the FUCK happened?" he shouts at his consigliere.

"The cops didn't fall for it," explains his trusted man. "One of the men was arrested with Jancko, and two others are dead. Another one is at the hospital."

Vito stares at his advisor with daggers in his eyes. "Get that fucking cop! Kill that Smith, that son of a bitch! Kill his family! Kill his pets! *Capeesh*?"

"Vito..." declares the consigliere in a soothing tone, "calm down. They'll be poking around here soon. We'll deal with Officer Smith soon enough. Right now, we need to talk."

Guiding the Don into the back room of the restaurant, the consigliere calls over his shoulder, "Bring us two Sambucas on the rocks! With coffee beans!"

While Jack is in surgery, Allison paces the ER waiting room, mouthing a silent prayer. When she sees Didi rush in with Lieutenant Conrad trying to keep up, she hurries over to the distraught woman.

"How is he?" shouts Didi. "I need to see him!"

"I know, but Jack will be okay. Let's sit down; I'll tell you what I know."

Allison points to a couch in the corner where the two women can talk privately. When they are seated, she says, "It's going to sound worse than it is, so try not to get upset." After pausing slightly to consider her words, she decides that honesty is best. "He took a shotgun blast to the chest, but his vest saved him! He does have a wound on his left arm, though, and there may be some rib damage. You can see him as soon as they finish patching him up."

"Oh, thank God!" exclaims Didi, exhaling the breath she was holding. "I was so worried! Are you sure he'll be okay?"

"Yes, that's what they tell me."

"Oh," breathes Didi, "I don't know what I'd do if I lost him! And he's going to be a father soon!"

Didi accepts a tissue from Allison to wipe her eyes and nose. "Heavens!" she gasps. "I don't want Jack to see me like this. I've been crying all the way over here." With a groan, she tries to smooth down her hair.

"Jack will be fine. He'll be sore, but he'll heal quickly. Come on; let's get you freshened up."

While the women head to the ladies' room, Conrad murmurs a silent prayer of thanks. Before long, a nurse walks up to him.

"Lieutenant, you can see Mr. Stenhouse before they take him to X-ray. They removed the buckshot from his arm and face, and now they want to take a look at his ribs. He's going to be here for at least forty-eight hours. He lost a lot of blood from the wounds in his arm. If he weren't wearing his vest, he'd be at the morgue."

Unfortunately, Didi returns from the restroom at that moment, and when she hears the word "morgue," she erupts into inconsolable tears. Talking to the nurse, Allison explains that Didi is Jack's wife.

"Oh, no, Mrs. Stenhouse, your husband is fine!" clarifies the nurse quickly. "Come with me! He's anxious to see you!"

Following the nurse, Didi and the officers pass a row of rooms until they come to an open curtain. Peering in, Didi gasps in shock when she sees Jack bandaged and lying in the hospital bed. But Jack, seeing his wife, cheerfully waves his uninjured arm.

"Hi, Babe!" he says. "I had a little accident!"

Sighing in relief, Didi rushes to her husband, and without thinking, leans over the bedrail and squeezes him in a fierce hug. Jack grimaces in pain but doesn't mind. When Didi pulls away to take a closer look, she realizes that Jack is uncomfortable, to say the least, so she pats Jack's hand.

"I'm going to be here a couple of days," he says with a wince. "Maybe you can stop by with your naughty nurse uniform and give me a sponge bath."

Looking on, Conrad laughs at Jack's cheekiness, but Allison rolls her eyes. Neither of them hears Didi's reply. Whispering in Jack's ear, she says, "I'll need to go home and change first. I'll come back later, if you feel you're up to it."

With a grin at Giancarlo and Conrad, Didi says happily, "Yeah, I'd say he's just fine. Can you drive me home, Allison? I need to freshen up and change for Jack."

Allison shakes her head in disbelief. "I can take you to the First; that's where Jack's car is. But, Jack, are you sure you're up to...that? You lost a lot of blood, you know."

With his free hand, Jack places his middle finger on the side of his nose and rubs it up and down. "I'm *up* for anything," he says wickedly.

The loud laughter that emanates from Jack's room prompts a stern nurse to burst in.

"We need to get Mr. Stenhouse to X-ray, and then upstairs to his room," the nurse states firmly. "Mrs. Stenhouse, you can go with him, and you can remain with him for a while, but not for too long. He should have some time to rest. You can return later with any personal items he may need. Visiting hours end at nine o'clock."

Didi leans down again to whisper something that Jack alone can hear. Then, she looks at Conrad.

"I want to stay a while, but I'll need someone to drive me to the station later to get his car."

"Well...neither of us can be here that long," says Conrad. "We don't know when he'll get to his room, and evildoers never take a rest. Call me when you're ready to leave, and I'll have a patrol unit take you to the car."

Motioning to Allison, Conrad nods toward the exit, and the pair says their goodbyes.

Just before they leave, Conrad quips, "Rest up for your bath, Jack!" But then, he becomes more serious. "Look, you got two weeks off. Your team will take care of the follow-up interrogations of your suspects, and I'll assist them with Lucchese's connection to the gold. Just concentrate on healing. I'll drop by again tomorrow to update you on our progress."

Jack nods at his boss but doesn't agree with his assessment. *Two weeks, hell!* he reflects. *I'll be back in twenty-four hours, even if I have to release myself!*

Soon, a nurse and an aide come into the room to transfer Jack to a gurney for the trip to X-ray. "Hey, I'm hungry," Jack declares to the aide. "What's for lunch?" Then, he reaches out and pinches Didi's shapely backside.

At the First, Tony Jancko is in the precinct's interrogation room, with Vice Squad Sergeant Jeffrey Turnbull conducting the interview, and Hector Gomez observing from behind the mirror.

"Mr. Jancko," states Sergeant Turnbull, "we feel pretty certain that it wasn't your idea to rob New York City police. So tell me, considering what you were after, and knowing the men who were with you, I need to ask you a question. When did Vito Lucchese put this plan together?"

"I can't say anything!" insists Jancko, shaking nervously and staring at his cuffed hands. "He'll kill me and my family!"

"Now, Tony..."

"Look!" interrupts Jancko. "I'll offer you just one thing, and don't ask me about anything else!"

"Okay..."

"They got an 'in' with the police!"

Turnbull offers police protection for more information, but Jancko stops him with a flick of his wrist.

"Don't tell me you can protect me if I talk to you! You couldn't even protect this station, so how the hell can you protect me? Sorry, but that's all I'm gonna say. I want a lawyer!"

"Why the hell are you involved in this crazy scheme?" persists Turnbull.

Tony shrugs. "I owed a favor, and he said all I had to do was drive one of my trucks to the First. That's it."

Before another question can be asked, the door to the interrogation room swings open and an impeccably dressed man walks in.

"Sergeant, I'm here to represent my client, Mr. Jancko," the man says dryly. "This interview is now over." Motioning to Tony, the attorney orders, "Let's get out of here."

"Not so fast," declares Turnbull, rising from his chair to stand between the lawyer and his suspect. "He'll go to Central Booking first. You can earn your retainer after that."

The black suit smiles. "Been there, done that, Sergeant," he grins, shoving release paperwork into the stunned sergeant's hand. "Now uncuff him so we can go have a nice lunch. Hey, you want to join us?" chuckles the attorney. "I know a good Italian restaurant on Mulberry Street!"

Turnbull stares in disbelief as the pair exits the room.

"He needs to be fingerprinted!" he calls after them. "How the hell?" In frustration, Turnbull turns to the mirror and shakes his head, while Hector Gomez does the same in the next room.

In the hallway, the attorney spies both sergeants exiting the rooms and watching him and Tony as they wait for the elevator. Unable to resist mocking police procedures, the attorney calls out, "In case you're wondering, his prints are already on file! I'm damn good, don't you agree? Good day, Sergeants!"

On the first floor, Allison is in front of the elevator, waiting for the car to arrive, when the door opens and Tony Jancko and his attorney walk out. Frowning, Allison stares after them and sighs with disappointment.

"How the hell did Jancko get out of here?" she queries Sergeants Turnbull and Gomez when she arrives on her floor.

With a weary shrug, Turnbull responds, "Lucchese's influence is everywhere."

CHAPTER TWENTY-SIX

"How's Jack?" asks Sylvia. "Is he okay?"

"He's fine," responds Allison, eliciting sighs of relief from Sylvia and John Burley. "His vest saved him. His arm got shot up pretty bad, but he'll be okay. Conrad gave him two weeks off, but knowing Jack, he'll probably be here way before then."

"How's his wife?" asks Gomez as he takes a seat nearby.

"Didi's all right…now. Jack wants her to give him a sponge bath."

Bursting into laughter, the crew shares off-color comments, and Sylvia uses the mirth to flirt with Burley when no one is looking.

Happy that the team is in good spirits, Allison permits the camaraderie to continue until she feels they've released enough of their built-up tension.

"Okay, guys," she says after a while, "let's get on with it."

When the crew settles down, she says, "A few minutes ago, I saw Tony Jancko leaving the department with a mob lawyer. Lucchese's got to be behind the attempted heist, so I'll pay him a visit tomorrow. John, what happened with the wounded guard?"

"Giancarlo," interrupts Gomez, "I gotta' tell ya that Turnbull left here fit to be tied! This place was full of Italian suits, and all the dirt bags from the armored truck buttoned up real fast. But what's this about Lucchese? You need help?"

"Oh, you were still with I.A. when we talked about that," says John knowingly.

Allison frowns at John and asks again, "What about that guard, John?"

"He's in bad shape. They took him into surgery as soon as he arrived at the hospital. The docs say he has a fifty-fifty chance of making it. They wouldn't let me talk to him."

Allison sighs and looks at Gomez, who is staring back at her with concern. "Hector," she says slowly, "I appreciate the offer, but I have to do this alone. It's personal, guys," she says, looking around at the others. "I'll explain more after I get back. Now let's get back to the case. Have any of our suspects arrived yet?"

"Allison, you know that Jack wants Gomez to help..." says John before Allison cuts him off with a stern look. Backing down, he answers Allison's question instead.

"Cummings and O'Toole are here with an attorney who's representing them both. Sam Lincoln should be here later this afternoon."

"Good. Make sure we interrogate each of them individually. We also need to get Grimes back. Sylvia, what's your company's position on all of this?"

"Liberty Casualty wants their money back,

period. We petitioned the D.A.'s office for our share of the captured gold, and if we get what we want, we'll drop the fraud charges. Then, we'll contact everyone on Stan Cummings' client list. We made reparations to them through his insurance policy according to the information we had at the time, but we didn't cover all the claims completely because much of the gold was missing. This fiasco is going to take some time to iron out."

"You know, with all this other bullshit, we're neglecting Stan's killer," says Allison. "We still don't know who murdered him. Burley, you picked up some laundry at Cummings' place in Jersey. Where is it?"

"I dropped it off with the Lieutenant," responds John. "The last time I saw it, he was carrying it into his office. I guess it's still in there."

"Good, get it and bring it to Forensics. Maybe there's a clue in there somewhere. Gomez, ask Conrad if the Cummings van was released, and see if he can get permission for our CSI guys to go to Hammonton."

Allison walks up to the whiteboard and points to photos of Lincoln, O'Toole, Sarah, and Lucchese. "One of these guys killed Cummings or had him killed. We have to keep digging." The detective pauses for a moment to search the files in her brain. Then, she turns toward the team. "Okay, slight change here. Burley, you get the laundry and talk to Conrad about the van, and about CSI going to Cummings' place. Gomez, you and I will interview Mrs. Cummings first, and then tackle O'Toole. Sylvia, I think you're done. You can observe our interrogations if you want, but you have a lot of your own work to do. People, let's put this puzzle together!"

As John walks away, Allison can't help but notice that Sylvia Stone is ogling his retreating back. With a scowl, she strides over to the insurance investigator.

"You break his heart," she hisses, "and I'll be all over you like white on rice."

Sylvia looks back at Allison in surprise. "That's not going to happen!" she insists. "John is...wonderful! I hope he doesn't break *my* heart."

"Okay," responds Allison, "that's good to hear. You know, if Burley screws things up with you, I'll be all over him just as fast. You're one of us now, and we take care of our own. "Look," she adds, "why don't you come out with us later? I'm sure most of us will be visiting Jack. Besides, you *really* need to meet his wife. Photographs don't do her justice!" Allison stops when a glint of mirth fills her eyes. "Maybe she can give you a lesson in the proper way to give a sponge bath!"

Chuckling heartily at her inside joke, she walks toward the hallway, leaving Sylvia looking at her with equal amounts of confusion and appreciation.

Seeing Giancarlo on the move, Hector follows her to the interrogation room, where Sarah Cummings and Keith O'Toole have been waiting for them with their lawyer. Sylvia enters the room next door, taking Allison up on her offer to observe.

"Okay," says Allison after taking a seat, "let's get started. I'm Detective Giancarlo," she says to the suspects' legal representative. "Sergeant Gomez and I will interview your clients; however, the interviews will be conducted separately. Officer Simpson will accompany Mr. O'Toole to another room where he can wait until we're ready for him."

Keith looks expectantly at his lawyer, who nods and whispers something. Keith nods back and leaves the room with the officer.

Sarah Cummings looks nervous after her lover leaves. Her breathing rate increases, she continuously winds a tissue around her fingers, and she compulsively wipes strands of hair from her face. It seems that she doesn't know where to look—at the video camera that will record her responses, or at the mirror, where she's sure someone is watching her.

Allison knows that Sarah is upset, so she pretends to write some notes to let her stew, all the while keeping a steady eye on her.

After a while, Gomez gives Allison a nudge, so she begins the interview.

"Mrs. Cummings, where were you the day before Stan was found at the South pool?"

"I was with Keith," Sarah replies. "We were discussing some of my investments. He took a job as a financial advisor after he retired from the Fire Department. I'm one of his clients."

Allison jumps on the opening that Sarah unwittingly presented.

"Mrs. Cummings, we all know you were more than just one of Mr. O'Toole's clients. You two have been having an affair for years, well before 9/11. Isn't that correct?"

Sarah is surprised but nods her head. "Yes, we became close. Stan had a gambling problem that took over his life and effectively ended our marriage a long time ago. Keith was a good listener, and well, we fell in love. So what?"

"So what? How's this? Stan faked his death to get rid of his debts to the mob, and he funneled money to you through O'Toole, not knowing that you two were doing each other. Years later, Stan decided that he wanted his old life back and he told you everything. However, you didn't want him back, so you poisoned him and thought it would be a fitting end if he actually did die at the Trade Towers like everyone thought he did."

Sarah's lawyer grabs her arm to prevent her from speaking.

"You have no proof that my client knew anything at all about where Stanley was all these years! You can't place her anywhere near him! She doesn't need to say anything else."

Allison disregards the lawyer's objections and looks directly at the suspect.

"Come on, Sarah," she chides, "are you going to tell me that you had no idea where all of your new-found wealth was coming from? Keith never told you what was going on?"

Sarah tears up and wipes her eyes with the crumpled tissue she had been twisting in her hands. Her attorney pats her back and whispers his permission to comment on Allison's question.

"Keith told me that his investments were paying off. He said he was taking care of the money I received from Stan's insurance company and the 9/11 fund that was set up for the victims' families."

"Really?" snickers Hector. "You believed that? I'm sure you knew that you'd lose all of that money if Stan suddenly came out of hiding. And you didn't want your husband back anyway, did you? You're in love with Keith now, so you actually had two motives to kill Stan—greed, and love."

"Look!" interrupts the attorney. "Unless you can provide a direct link that puts my client at the scene of Stanley's death, or even at Stanley's house, this conversation is over! We're working with the insurance company to return the funds they're requesting, and we may also file a suit against them! I'm ending Mrs. Cummings' interview now, but you can still talk to Mr. O'Toole. Just remember that I'll also cut that interview off if I feel you're infringing upon his rights."

Pleased with his speech, the attorney grabs Sarah's arm and guides her out of the room, leaving Giancarlo and Gomez alone.

Frustrated by the attorney's wrangling, Gomez slams a folder onto the table and jumps out of his chair.

"Sarah Cummings is some piece of work!" he shouts in disgust. "All of that hand-wringing and twisting of tissues! And that sobbing! Nice touch!"

Allison squeezes the bridge of her nose to try to avert a looming headache.

"We need at least one piece of evidence that connects our suspects to Stan's death. We found Grimes' prints at the house in Jersey, but his Staten Island landlord says he was in his room at the time we think Stan was poisoned. Oh," she groans, "I need some Ibuprofen. I think I'm going to get a doozy of a headache."

"Do you think Sarah did it?" asks Hector.

Allison rubs her neck. "Who knows? It's possible. I was just pushing buttons to see what might turn on. We still have to look over that van, and I hope our CSI team can do another search at Stan's place. And that dirty laundry, we need to test..."

Allison stops talking as Keith O'Toole reenters the room, trailed by the same attorney. The pair sit down opposite Giancarlo and Gomez.

"We're here for Mr. O'Toole's interrogation," says the lawyer frostily, "but be warned. I can cut things off just as quickly as I did before."

Allison frowns at the attorney and glares at O'Toole.

"Mr. O'Toole," she demands, "when did Stanley Cummings present his scheme to you, Larry Grimes, and Sam Lincoln?"

"It was at the Ball. Cummings had a bad gambling habit. He racked up a ton of debts and was taking gold from his business to pay his losses. Sarah and I both knew about his gambling, and I guess our affair was a result of Sarah's disgust with it. She wanted a divorce. She never got the chance to tell Stan, but I think he knew something was up."

"How did the plan evolve?"

"Somehow, Stan found out about an abandoned subway station, and he used that location to store the gold he was stealing from his business. He started moving the stuff out slowly, but it was taking too much time; he had to be careful not to be noticed as he went in and out of the subway tunnel. He needed help to move the rest of the gold more quickly, so he asked us to join him. That's when he came up with the plan."

"'Us' being Grimes, O'Toole, and Lincoln?"

"Yeah. Grimes provided the transit worker uniforms and IDs. With those uniforms, we passed unnoticed through the Cortlandt Street station."

"What else did Grimes contribute?" asks Hector.

"He was a munitions expert. We were going to blow up Stan's business on Yom Kippur, but the attack on 9/11 happened earlier and was perfect because it did the job for us."

Allison frowns and risks a direct question.

"Sarah knew where all of her newfound fortune was coming from, right?"

Keith leans back, hesitant about answering. But when his lawyer waves a hand to continue, he says, "No. Sarah knew about the gambling, but she had no idea that Stan was stealing gold to pay it off. She also didn't know that Stan was laundering money from Vito Lucchese and changing it into gold. I covered it all up by telling her that her investments were paying huge dividends. We all thought Stan Cummings' 'death' would become a dead-end for Lucchese so that Stan would be in the clear. It probably would have worked; however,

Stan wanted his life and wife back, so like an idiot, he contacted Lucchese. Soon after that, a couple of goons showed up and rearranged his face."

Allison stares hard at Keith to try to get a read on him.

"Mr. O'Toole, how do you know that Lucchese sent his men to Stan's place?"

Keith smirks. "When Sam Lincoln met with Grimes and Cummings, Cummings told them that he contacted Lucchese. Sam told me about it later."

Allison continues to monitor Keith intently, looking for any signs of cracks in his armor.

"Where were you when Cummings was poisoned?"

"Huh? He was poisoned?"

"Yeah. That's how he died. Didn't you know that?" asks Allison.

"No, um, I was home when I heard they found him downtown."

Surprised, Gomez chimes in with a question. "You weren't with Sarah, your main squeeze?"

Keith shakes his head. "We don't see each other every day. We had lunch the day before that, and then Sarah went shopping for a bridal gown. I didn't go with her; that's too much estrogen for me."

"So, you have no alibi for Stanley's death," summarizes Allison. "Stan wanted to stop running, and that would have meant no more money. He was your rival for Sarah's affection. Oh, and there's also the Lucchese family. Tell me again why you didn't kill Cummings."

"Okay, Detective," pipes up the attorney, "here we go again. You have no proof that my client was anywhere near Stan when he died. He confesses to helping Cummings get the gold, and that's it. Because that case is under investigation with pending litigation, my client won't answer any more questions. Again, show us proof of either of my clients' involvements or leave them both alone."

Rising from his seat, the attorney motions to Keith, and they both exit the room.

"We're missing something," says Allison as she and Hector gather up their files. "Someone must have made a mistake somewhere, and we're going to have to find it."

Suddenly, Lieutenant Conrad looms in the doorway.

"Sam Lincoln's release has been delayed until morning," he announces. "Because he's a flight risk, they're looking at him more closely. We'll talk to Grimes again tomorrow, and Burley's going to accompany our CSI team to Jersey to bring us the van. But now, Rawlings and I are going to the hospital to visit Stenhouse. Why don't you get the team to drop by as well? We can pick all of this up again tomorrow."

"I was planning on it," smiles Allison.

CHAPTER TWENTY-SEVEN

Jack is playing with his green Jell-O, pushing it between pieces of a partially-eaten brown object that he thinks is meatloaf. Although he's hungry, he can't bring himself to finish his hospital meal: a strange concoction drowned in an unappetizing liquid, surrounded by wrinkled peas.

"What's the matter," asks Inspector Rawlings with a snicker as he and Lieutenant Conrad peek through the doorway. "Not hungry?"

Jack is immensely relieved to see that Rawlings is holding out a paper bag with a familiar logo.

"Here," Rawlings says. "I thought you might need this."

Jack sighs and reaches eagerly for the bag.

"Oh, you guys are so good! You can finish this stuff if you want... Or if you dare," he says, pushing aside the hospital tray with a grimace, as he tries to find a comfortable position for his arm.

Fumbling with one hand, Jack pulls out a bacon cheeseburger and a bag of fries. "Hey, where's the beer?" he complains teasingly.

"You're welcome," laughs Rawlings. "How's the arm?"

Jack swallows a mouthful of burger before answering. "It's sore as hell. I hope you don't mind that one of your detectives has a beard. I didn't get a chance to shave this morning."

"Yeah, well," smirks Conrad, "you'll be here for a couple of days, so it doesn't matter if you shave or not. Jack, a quick FYI. The armored truck was driven by Tony Jancko, the owner of the transport service. He said Lucchese forced him to drive his truck to the heist, and he swore that Lucchese's men posed as guards and did the shooting. Lucchese already sent a lawyer to get Jancko out on bail, so I doubt he'll see any time behind bars."

"What about Lucchese's gorillas? Some of them were hit, right?"

"Yeah, two of them died, and one is in this hospital. The one who shot you from the truck is in jail with no bail."

Stenhouse readjusts his arm. "Did Giancarlo tell you her plan?"

Conrad nods. "Yeah, she met with us. We convinced her to wear a wire, but she insists on meeting Vito alone. So Gomez is going to stay outside with backup, just in case."

A sudden twinge of pain from Jack's arm causes him to inhale sharply, and that action creates even more pain from his bruised ribs. When the morphine takes over, he says, "That is one stubborn Italian chick."

"Oh, really? Now who would you be calling a stubborn Italian chick?" asks a semi-indignant voice from the doorway.

Looking toward the sound, Jack and his superiors laugh as Allison and several others enter the room.

John Burley and Sylvia Stone take turns greeting Jack and asking about his health, while Gomez places a large bag on the bed. Pulling out two ice-cold six-packs of Guinness, he hands a bottle to everyone present while Burley passes around a church key.

"Ahh," sighs Jack after taking a deep swig of his favorite brew. "This is almost better than sex. Thank you all, but don't get too comfortable with me not being around. I'll be back at the station tomorrow."

"Don't be stupid!" barks Rawlings. "The First Precinct existed way before you got there, and we'll do fine without you. Now... Hey! Slow down on that beer! It doesn't mix well with morphine!"

Jack glances sideways at the inspector. "Fuck the damn morphine! This is personal, sir! I'll be back there tomorrow, even if I have to crawl there!"

Just then, a familiar voice rings out from the hallway.

"Whoa, look at this crowd!" says Didi, dressed in a long trench coat buttoned tightly from her neck to her calves, with white heels and black fishnet stockings peeking out from under the hem. Allison and Sylvia roll their eyes at the sight, while all the men gawk—first in shock, and then in appreciation.

"You're right," whispers Sylvia to Giancarlo. "Pictures don't do her justice. No wonder Jack always says he's one lucky SOB."

Hearing the tail end of the whisper, Burley places a hand on Sylvia's backside. "So am I," he says to Sylvia quietly. Then, he leans over to Jack. "Beer is better than sex, huh? That's bullshit!"

Smiling, Jack mutters back, "Maybe Sylvia should stay and take notes."

Noting the goofy grins on Jack and Burley, Rawlings opts to cut things short.

"All right!" he orders. "It's time for us to leave so Jack can rest."

Pointing to the door, the inspector tries to usher everyone out, but most are still conversing with Jack. Spotting Didi in a corner, he walks over and gives her a peck on the cheek.

"Congratulations," he says warmly, "I hope it's a boy." Then, he turns back to the others, who are still talking. "Come on; let's go!" he insists.

Taking the hint, Gomez removes the unopened bottles of beer from Jack's bed. "I know they won't let you keep these in here, so I'll dispose of them properly, okay?"

On her way out, Allison stops near Didi. "Those heels must be at least six inches, am I right?" she asks her friend. "How in the world did you drive a stick shift?"

"My sneakers are in the car," confides Didi conspiratorially.

After everyone finally clears out, Jack raises the bed higher. "Wow," he says to his wife. "That's the first time I've seen you clear a room. Usually, they flock in when you show up."

Smiling wickedly, Didi checks the door to make sure it's closed and then slowly unbuttons her coat. As she does, she remarks, "So that's Sylvia, huh? She's not bad, Babe. A little skinny, but not bad. John must be having fun."

When all the buttons are undone, Didi removes the coat seductively to reveal a skimpy nurse's outfit that looks two sizes too small. Although he's seen all of this before, Jack's eyes still bulge out of their sockets and his blood pressure and heart rate skyrocket.

Didi knew that her teasing might cause an elevation in Jack's vital signs, so before she entered Jack's room, she stopped at the nurse's station to let the head nurse in on her plans.

When the alarms from Jack's room alert the nurse's colleagues, the woman says, "Don't mind the alarms from Room 207. That patient is receiving a late sponge bath."

CHAPTER TWENTY-EIGHT

For a city that professes to never sleep, Manhattan may have nodded off during the night.

Instead of being awakened at an early hour by the almost constant street noises outside of her apartment, Didi wakes up later today, and only because her cell phone is jangling on the nightstand. Focusing on the caller ID, she notes with alarm that it says Presbyterian Hospital.

"Oh, my God! Hello?" she answers, panicked that it may be bad news.

"Hey, Babe, I need another bath," says a muffled male voice.

"Jack, you bastard! What the hell?" hollers Didi, sitting up with a jolt. "You scared the shit out of me! Are you okay?"

"Fine as wine, Babe. Get yourself up and bring me some clothes. I'm checking myself out of this hellhole. I need to get back to work."

"Bullshit, Jack! You need to stay right where you are! You need to rest! I, or rather we, need you around for a long, long time!"

"I'm fine, Didi; I promise not to exert myself. Please get me out of here. If you don't, I'll catch a cab and go to the First in this lovely hospital gown."

Knowing that her husband would do precisely that, Didi exhales in resignation. "Dammit, Jack. I'll be there around eight."

"That's my girl. And wear your nurse's outfit again, would ya?"

"I will not wear that outfit today! You're incorrigible!" scolds Didi. "But that's why I love you. See ya later."

Laughing at his joke, Jack hangs up the phone while trying to ignore the sharp pain in his ribcage. After ringing for a nurse, he mumbles, "They're not gonna be happy when they find out I'm leaving."

Allison is the first one at work today. Sipping a latte, she stares thoughtfully at the whiteboard and nods when Sergeants Burley and Gomez join her.

"You want a coffee, John?" asks Hector.

"Yeah, thanks."

Hector leaves the group to fill two cups at the coffee station, prompting John to remark, "Seems odd without Jack here."

"Yeah," agrees Allison, "but if I know Jack, he'll be back sooner rather than later. When are you heading over to Jersey?"

"I'm waiting for CSI to contact me," answers John as he grabs a coffee from Gomez. "They said they'd be leaving around 8:30, so I have a few minutes. When are you going to Little Italy?"

Giancarlo sighs and finishes the last of her coffee. "Probably after Lincoln and his lawyer get here. Grimes is also coming in today; hopefully, before I leave. Vito always eats lunch at his restaurant at noon, so I want to get there around then. Too bad Stenhouse isn't here."

When a familiar figure walks up behind them, the trio turns around and stares in open-mouthed shock.

"What the hell?" erupts Allison. "I'm not surprised, but how did you get here? And *why* are you here?"

A bemused Jack responds with a wide grin, cheerful as a sunny day. "I checked myself out! Didi drove me in."

"How did your wife agree to you leaving the hospital?" asks a disbelieving Allison.

"I had to promise that I wouldn't exert myself," Jack responds slyly, adjusting his tan sports coat to hide the arm that's still in a sling. "But enough about me. What's going on today?" Jack lowers himself slowly into his seat as Giancarlo explains.

"Burley's going back to Jersey with our CSI team. They're gonna bring back the van from Cummings' place today, and Forensics has the basket of laundry. Grimes and Lincoln are due in with their lawyers, but we don't expect to get much out of Lincoln. And Gomez and I are gonna visit Lucchese."

"Stenhouse?!" barks Lieutenant Conrad. "I just got a call from the hospital! What the hell are you doing here?"

"Sorry I can't stand up, Lieutenant," says Jack from his chair. "I came here to help; I couldn't stay there any longer! The woman who's supposed to take care of me is older than dirt!"

Conrad glowers down at Jack. Although he's happy that his lead detective is back, he knows that it's way too soon. "Look," he orders, "If I think you're having any medical issues at all, I'll have a unit drag you back to the hospital. Forcibly, if need be. *Capeesh*?" Conrad waits for Jack to nod, and then continues. "Okay, now that my official response has been delivered, I'm happy you're here."

"Thanks, Boss," responds Jack.

"Yeah, yeah. You can help interrogate Lincoln and Grimes. You can remain seated for that."

"Okay," salutes Jack. "Anything else?"

"Let me get you all up to speed," says Conrad. "Grimes is here now, and Sam Lincoln will be here around eleven. The armored car guy and Lucchese's soldiers have lawyered up, but Gomez and Giancarlo are going to visit Lucchese. Vice always has an ongoing investigation into Vito's prostitution and illegal gambling rackets, so he's probably expecting us, anyway. O'Toole said Lucchese was laundering money through Cummings and that Cummings owed Lucchese a shitload for his gambling debts, so the theory that Stan stole some of Lucchese's money to pay the mobster back, works. But he ended up changing his mind. He regretted his greedy plan to fake his own death."

"Do we have any hard evidence to back that up?" asks Jack.

"No. Let's hope CSI and Forensics can come up with something. And we still need to figure out who Stan's killer is. Oh. Stop by my office later. I have your weapon and badge."

"Okay, will do." With a grunt, Jack struggles to rise from his chair. "Thank God for OxyContin," he says. "I'm gonna go have another chat with Grimes."

From a nearby desk, Burley announces, "Hey, guys, CSI is heading out now, so I'm gonna meet them downstairs. See you all later."

As Allison and Jack settle into their seats opposite Larry Grimes and his attorney, Allison notices that Larry is looking at Jack with a puzzled expression.

"I heard you were involved in that shooting yesterday," Grimes says to Stenhouse. "Guess you heal fast."

"Yeah, fast enough," replies Jack, wincing at the throbbing pain that's beating like a kettle drum from his arm to his ear. "You, ah, said Cummings wanted to end the charade, which is what made the house of cards come crashing down on all of your heads."

"Yeah, that's what I said."

"We confirmed your alibi for the night Cummings was poisoned. Your landlord said you were home that night. Did any of the others ever visit Cummings in Jersey?"

Larry shrugs. "Sure, they all did at one time or another."

"Including his wife?"

"I don't know about her."

Jack attempts to find a comfortable position. "Okay," he says after squirming in his seat, "who do you think was most upset about Stan's new plan? You?"

Larry stares at the ceiling as if he were looking for divine guidance. "No, man. That would be Keith. He wigged out when he heard Stan wanted out. Said he was gonna kill the prick; that he and Sarah had a good thing going. Hell, we all had a good thing going! I guess you could say we all wanted to stop Stan from turning himself in!"

When both detectives' eyes go wide at Larry's comment, he quickly adds, "Look, I don't know who did it! But if I was gonna kill someone, I would have dumped him in the middle of the Pine Barrens. I wouldn't have brought him to a public place!"

"When was the last time your group got together?" asks Allison.

"It was the weekend before Stan was killed. We met at a small restaurant in Chinatown, and we all tried to talk him out of it. That was when we realized he wasn't gonna change his mind. Keith blew up and stormed out of the place. Lincoln told Stan that he'd try to calm Keith down, but after the meeting, Stan called me and said he wasn't gonna stick around. He was making plans to leave the country; he wanted to get out before it all hit the fan. That's when I set up the charges to blow the station."

Jack's pain is getting worse, so he stands and paces to try to ease it. "I have a couple more questions before we end this interview," he says between gritted teeth. "You said you bought transit worker uniforms. Are you the only one who supplied them? And how did you get the explosives and that new ID for Stan?"

"I got everything online."

"How did you get the gold down there?"

"The uniforms made us 'invisible,' so over the course of a few weeks, we carried the gold to the station in our toolboxes. Keith and I worked there every day. Well, I did, anyway. Keith sometimes took time off to sniff around Sarah. Sam worked there at night, or when he was off duty from the fire station, and Stan worked whenever he could."

"Didn't Stan think he'd be recognized? He owned a pretty exclusive depository."

"Nah."

"How did you pay for all the stuff you needed?"

"You can buy anything if you got enough money. Gold opens a heck of a lot of doors, you know," replies Grimes with a sneer.

"Did O'Toole or Lincoln ever say how they hid their newfound fortunes from friends and family? Especially after the 9/11 tragedy?" interjects Allison.

Scratching his head, Larry thinks for a minute. "No, not really. I guess they used safe deposit boxes or offshore accounts. I mean, that's how I would have done it if I had to hide it from someone who might find it."

Uncomfortable and out of sorts, Jack leans against the one-way mirror for relief. "Mr. Grimes, how did Cummings hook up with the Lucchese family and end up laundering their money?"

Larry shakes his head. "Stan was a regular at one of their illegal poker games; he was a big-time gambler. He won a lot, but lost a lot more. From time to time, Vito and his son would join in on the games, and they started talking about the vaults at Stan's company. Stan told them he could sanitize their money and hold it all in gold. He was such a fool! When he lost his shirt in their poker games, he used the gold they stored in his vaults to pay them back. I guess he thought they'd never figure out he was paying them back with their own money. What an idiot!"

Jack glares down at Grimes. "Okay, that's it for today. I'm sure we'll talk again. Unless Lucchese finds you first."

Crooking his finger at Allison, the officers leave Grimes staring at their backs with a worried look on his face.

When Jack enters the room next door, he finds Hector still observing Larry seated at the interrogation table.

"Looks a little scared now, don't he?" remarks Hector.

Jack joins the sergeant at the mirror. "I'm gonna check with the D.A. to see if they got the warrants for bank records. I'm sure the suspects' houses have been searched already, but I need that extra piece of the puzzle. That will keep me busy here while Burley is in Jersey and you guys are having brunch with Ally's favorite uncle."

When Stenhouse returns to his desk, he notices that Lieutenant Conrad is talking to Allison and Hector in his office and that the door is closed.

"Giancarlo, I have a wire for you," instructs Conrad behind the closed door. "You're gonna wear it so Gomez can hear what's going on. We'll have backup outside, so if Gomez thinks it's going south, we'll respond immediately."

"Lieutenant, when they pat me down, they're gonna find that transmitter!" objects Giancarlo. "I'm not gonna wear it!"

To emphasize his point, Conrad pokes his finger into Giancarlo's shoulder. "This is not a request, Detective! It's an *order*! You are *not* walking in there with no way for us to know what's going on! The transmitter is small; it's the size of a button. You'll clip it to your undergarments, a place I'm sure they won't check. A female tech officer will show you how to put it on."

"It's a crotch radio?" smirks Allison. "Hope I don't short it out."

"Oh, God. Thanks for that image, Detective," groans Conrad as he walks to his desk. Leaning down, he removes a button transmitter from a drawer. "This thing is only 3/8 of an inch in diameter, but it has a two-hundred-foot range. It broadcasts on Line Three." Tossing the object to Giancarlo, he says lightly, "Here ya go. Now, get outta here."

Outside of Conrad's door, a tech officer motions for Allison to accompany her to the ladies' room.

As she enters the bathroom, Gomez shouts, "If it takes more than ten minutes to put that thing on, you're having too much fun!" prompting Allison to flash him the bird with both hands.

Resigned to the limitations of his injured body, Jack sits gingerly down at his desk to make a phone call.

"Yeah, is this the 9/11 Memorial security office? I'm calling from the First Precinct. I need to review the videos from the morning Stanley Cummings was found. Twenty minutes? Okay, thanks."

Using the time the 9/11 Memorial cop needs to pull the videos, Jack walks slowly to Lieutenant Conrad's office, where he finds the lieutenant sitting at his desk, staring absently into the squad room through his glass wall. When the lieutenant spots Jack, he waves him in.

"Everything okay?" asks Conrad. "You feeling all right?"

"Yeah, I'm fine," says Jack, turning his head to the side to click the vertebrae in his neck. "I thought my arm would bother me the most, but it's my damn ribs. Lieutenant, I need a driver to bring me down to the

9/11 Memorial. I got security down there to pull the videos from their cameras the day Cummings showed up. I want to look at them again to see if I can figure out how he got there."

Conrad scrutinizes Jack's arm to see if there is any blood showing through the bandages and is happy when he sees none. "Okay," he says. "I'll flag down a uniformed officer to drive you there. But you should know that I've asked the officers on duty that morning to come up here to tell us what they saw." Conrad looks at his watch. "Lincoln will be here about noon, so you got two hours to view the tapes. The officers in question should be here this afternoon."

Opening a drawer, Conrad removes Jack's Glock and his concealment holster and badge. He begins to push them across the desk but stops when he remembers that Jack is going to need assistance. Walking around the desk, he hands his subordinate his badge and helps him secure his weapon.

"Thanks, Boss," says Stenhouse. "Now, I don't feel naked anymore."

CHAPTER TWENTY-NINE

Across town, Giancarlo and Gomez have pulled up in front of Ristorante di Cosenza, and unmarked backup have parked down the street. It's unusual for convenient parking spots to be found in this busy city, so the officers consider it to be a good sign.

When Giancarlo leaves the car, Gomez turns his radio to Channel Three. Listening intently, all he hears at this point are background noises and rustling fabric. Straining to hear more, he mumbles, "Hope she remembers to give the mic some room to pick up dialogue when she sits down. Good thing she's wearing a pant-suit."

Allison hasn't entered the restaurant yet. She has stopped in front of the door, a little hesitant to walk in.

Vito's restaurant is well-known in the city. The original owner opened it in the twenties—before Prohibition took hold—and since then, numerous crime bosses, from Lucky Luciano to Carlo Gambino to John Gotti, have filled its rooms with blood, honor, and bullet holes.

Inhaling deeply, Allison pushes on the door and remembers that she was here once before—when she was a small child. It was for a birthday party, she thinks. Shaking her head, she tries to clear that memory from her mind.

The history of the store and Allison's memories from long ago refuse to leave her completely, however. Once inside, she is startled by an oppressive feeling that many of the mobsters' unfortunate victims are all around her, staring at her morosely. So, when a voice calls out from behind the bar, she jumps in nervous tension.

"Little Ally, is that you?"

With a tentative smile, Allison turns to the voice. "Hey, Vinnie. Is Uncle Vito in?"

Vinnie Giacomo, an older soldier who now tends the restaurant's bar, walks around the long counter to kiss both of Allison's cheeks. "Come on," he says, grabbing Allison's arm, "he'll be happy to see you. But you're gonna get patted down, you know. SOP, right?"

Ally follows Vinnie as he leads her through a maze of wooden tables, chairs, and checkered tablecloths filled with diners who ignore them as best they can.

In the private back area, Allison spies two goons standing at either side of a closed door. Vinnie explains who she is, and when he turns back to her, she hands him her gun.

Understanding the process, Allison extends her arms to the side while one of the guards checks her for a wire or other weapons, without getting too personal. Satisfied that she's clean, the goon turns around and enters the room. Seconds later, he waves Allison in.

At the far end of the dining area, Vito is standing beside his table, waiting for his niece with out-stretched arms and a wide grin. "Ally! It has been too long!" he says enthusiastically. "You look good! Come and sit! Have some espresso and talk to your Uncle Vito."

Feeling a little more at ease, Allison kisses Vito on each cheek and then sits down, pulling her chair close to the table. She remembers not to cross her pant-suited legs in order to give the transmitter room to do its work.

"Uncle Vito, I'm not here to visit," she says. "I'm here on police business. I thought it would be better if I talked to you personally, before things went any further."

Feigning innocence, Vito sits back in his chair and asks, "Police business? I have done something? I work as a legitimate businessman, Ally. Tell me, how are your family, your children? Are they doing well? You need to bring them here for a nice meal. On the house."

"Uncle Vito," says Allison firmly but respect-fully, "we should really stop the charade. You don't care about my family. I'm here because your men attacked the First Precinct. We know Stanley Cummings stole your gold and that he was laundering money for you. He owed you bigtime for his gambling debts, and now he's dead. I know you didn't kill him because if you did, we would have never found his body. So please tell me what you do know about his death."

Vito looks hard at his niece but says nothing.

"Look," declares Allison into the uncomfortable

silence. "Vice is coming after you, but you already know that. I guess they're always after you, so that's nothing new. But today, I'm here to see if you can tell me anything that could help us find Stanley Cummings' killer."

Vito's expression softens slightly. As Gomez listens in, he says, "Ally, I am hurt that you do not think I care about you. *Tu sei la mia famiglia.* You are family." When Ally begins to protest, Vito waves a hand, and his tone becomes hard. "I know you are wired, my little niece, and I know that you have backup outside. *Io non sono stupido.* I am not stupid. I also know that Vice is investigating me. But this thing at your precinct was not mine. I think some loyal people have an interest in helping me."

Allison listens quietly while her uncle tells his tale.

"It is true that Stanley stole my money and that I wanted him dead. Everyone thought he was dead, including me, and I believed my money was lost. Then he called me and said he wanted to give my money back. He told me where he was, and I sent my people to make sure he would do as he said. The next day he was dead. I had no reason to kill him. I still want my money."

"Then do you have any idea who did it?"

"Look to his partners, *cara mia.* It is probably one of them who bumped him off. Allison, with all of these questions, you have hurt my feelings. Your mama was very special to our family. She was the first to go out on her own, away from the family business, but we have kept all of you in our hearts. You are special to us. If you weren't, you wouldn't be sitting here now."

Allison sighs but presses on. "So, you know nothing about any of this? Come on, Uncle Vito, I know you, and I know that you sent someone to trail Sergeant Burley while he was driving back from Jersey."

Vito smiles. "I lost money, little Ally. Cummings is dead, and you are questioning the others. They will pay for what they have done. As I said before, I am a legitimate businessman. I do not know anything about your Sergeant Burley. I have many loyal employees who look out for my interests and my safety. As you know, we are a very close-knit family." Vito waves his hand. "Now, let's stop all of this police talk. I ordered your favorite—fried eggs with red peppers. We will put these matters away and speak about your family. By the way," he says, grinning at Allison, "Sergeant Gomez, we are bringing you and your friends some espressos, and if you're nice, some cannolis. We support our local police, you know. Say hello to each of them for me, will you?"

Listening to the conversation in the car outside the restaurant, Gomez stares at the radio in surprise when he hears his name. A minute later, he hears a deep laugh followed by a tap on his window.

Standing beside his vehicle is a waiter with a tray of espressos and cannolis for him and the other undercover officers parked down the street.

Favoring his injured arm and ribs, Jack makes his way slowly through the ever-present crowd of tourists at the 9/11 site. His destination is the small media room adjacent to the entrance of the Trade Tower Museum.

Ignoring the 'No Admittance' sign, he pushes the door open and stops as his eyes rove over the bank of monitors that keep a vigilant watch over Memorial Park and the surrounding area.

"Excuse me, sir!" snaps a Homeland Security officer. "This is a restricted area! No one is allowed in here!"

Due to his injuries, Jack is more short-tempered than usual, so instead of identifying himself respectfully, he throws his badge down on the counter in front of the officer. "There's my approval. I'm Detective Jack Stenhouse from the First Precinct," he declares icily. "I called to review the tapes from last week's incident at the South Pool."

In response to Jack's churlish behavior, the officer retorts with his own measure of disdain. "Good morning to you, too, Detective," he states dourly. "It's nice to see how professional the city's cops are. Take a seat over there. I'll put the video on monitor four."

Jack's first impulse is to keep the veiled insults going, but because he's short on time, he tamps down on his irritation. Walking over to the designated monitor, he eases himself into the chair.

A few minutes later, he is watching two police officers peering at something on the ground next to the 9/11 retaining wall. The wall blocks the view of what they are looking at, but he knows that Stanley is lying there on the ground because that's where he was found. The next frames show the two cops backing off and talking to each other animatedly. Without sound on the tape, Jack doesn't know what they are saying, but he knows that Conrad will be asking them a lot of questions when he interviews them later that day. As the tape plays, he sees the officers talking into their shoulder mics. The cops remain in view for at least ten minutes, until EMTs arrive and take over.

"Can you show me a different view of the area before this happened?" Jack calls out. "Like maybe from a camera on Greenwich Street a few hours earlier?"

The Homeland officer hits a few keys at his computer station and does a quick search of the stored footage. "We have an overhead camera that faces Greenwich," he announces. "Our cameras are offline from 10 p.m. to 6 a.m., but NYPD has officers on overnight duty. They were the ones who reported the incident."

"Yeah, I read their report; we're gonna talk to them later. I want to see how Cummings got to the pool unnoticed."

A few clicks later, a new video starts rolling on Jack's monitor. When the time stamp registers two a.m., Jack makes a request.

"Hey, can you put it on fast forward?"

When the officer complies, Jack watches images race by with nothing happening onscreen until a black vehicle pulls up and a man falls out. Before Jack can ask for the tape to be stopped, the vehicle moves out of view.

"Okay!" he shouts, "stop the tape here and rewind it a few minutes. Then, go forward in slo-mo."

After a few keystrokes, the officer joins Jack, and they both watch as a black van parks at the Memorial and Stan falls out of the side door. When the van pulls away, Stan pushes himself to his feet and stumbles toward the South Pool, all the while gripping his stomach as if he were in pain. At the side of the screen, they see the two officers trying to roust a homeless man, neither of them noticing the new arrival. When Stan reaches the pool, he sits on the wall for a few minutes and then collapses onto the ground. At that point, the camera no longer sees him.

Jack stares at the screen, deep in thought. "Can you rewind this until just before the van appears? Then pause it when it comes into view."

"Yeah," says the officer, walking back to his computer.

When the image returns, Jack leans closer to the monitor with a wince and a groan to get a better view of the van. Noticing Jack's pain, the officer calls out, "Hey! Were you involved in that shootout at the First?"

"Yeah," responds Jack. "Can you burn me a copy of this video? I need to get it over to Forensics."

Jack's arm is now throbbing; he can feel his blood rushing through damaged blood vessels. As he waits for the officer to burn a DVD, he rises from his seat and leans against the wall for support.

"Damn, Detective," says the Homeland Security officer when he hands Jack the DVD, "you look like shit. You need some water or something?"

"I'll be fine; I just need to take my meds. Thanks

for your time."

Jack places the DVD into his coat pocket and heads back to the police cruiser. On the way, he spies a vending machine and stops to buy a Coke. Popping a pain pill into his mouth, he takes a sip and then continues on his way at a slow and steady pace. Although there is a throng of tourists all around him, none of them seem to notice a man in obvious pain in their midst.

Eventually, Jack reenters the back of the waiting police cruiser. Sighing in relief, he adjusts his sling and says to the driver, "Hey, do me a favor, will ya? Try not to hit so many potholes on the way back."

"Yeah, right," mocks the officer. "From your lips to God's ears. This is Manhattan, Bub."

With blue lights flashing, the driver reenters traffic as Jack twists slowly and carefully in his seat to look back at the place where Cummings' body was found.

Sergeant Burley is now in New Jersey. He expects to spend a good part of the day in the Pine Barrens with the New York CSI team as they go through Stanley's cabin. Standing on the sidelines, he watches them work for a while and then steps outside to soak up some fresh air.

As the screen door slams closed behind him, he hears blue jays squawking while the tow truck operator hooks up his rig to the Cummings van. Soon, his eyes are drawn to something shiny, partially obscured by gravel and pine needles.

Donning a pair of Nitrile gloves, Burley steps off the porch and bends down. Picking up the object, he examines it closely and finds that it's a small brass plate engraved with the words, "Genuine Snakeskin." Retracing his steps, he climbs back up to the porch and re-enters the house.

Grabbing an evidence bag from a CSI team member, he places the brass plate into the bag and stows it in his pocket, rather than into the general evidence container.

"Hey," Burley says to the team leader. "You can handle this here, right? I'm gonna accompany the van back to the First. When do you think you'll be done?"

"We should be finished in an hour or two."

Nodding, Burley walks back outside. Standing quietly at the porch railing, he looks out into the ever-encroaching forest, amazed by the intense quiet. *This place is so different from the city. It's nice, but I don't know if I could take it full time.*

Breathing deeply, he inhales the strong scent of pine and forest funk and sneezes. The irritation, a sharp reminder of his continual battle with allergies, sends him straight into the filtered, air-conditioned shelter of his cruiser to wait for the tow truck driver to head out with the van.

CHAPTER THIRTY

Jack is back at his desk after his visit to the 9/11 Memorial, feeling more relaxed after taking only a half dose of OxyContin. *I don't need to get addicted to this shit*, he reminded himself at the time.

When Allison and Hector return to the station, he immediately inquires, "How was the loving family reunion?"

Instead of replying, Giancarlo purses her lips and Gomez chuckles.

"Looks like you're feeling better," Allison mutters as she drops into the nearest chair. But when Gomez continues chortling behind her, she whips around and stares daggers at him, forcing him to stop.

Noticing the exchange, Jack fakes a tone of mock severity. "Ya better not piss her off or she'll break your kneecaps," he says, wagging his finger at Hector. Then, he turns to Allison. "Seriously, how'd it go with Uncle Vito?"

Still not replying, Allison takes a quick look around the squad room and notes that the three of them are the only ones there. So she swivels her chair toward the wall and reaches inside her slacks. Removing the transmitter, she flicks it quickly into the nearest wastebasket.

"Don't say it, bro," Gomez warns Jack with a cautionary glance.

Swiveling back toward her colleagues, Allison's face reveals a deep scowl that dares either of them to make a comment. Looking from one to the other, Allison waits a beat for one of them to say something snide, and when silence reigns, she nods gratefully.

"Back to the job, men," she declares. "So here's how it went. Lucchese said nothing; he claims he's a legitimate businessman. He did admit that Stan stole his gold, but he insists that he didn't order his killing. Lucchese does *not* like to lose money, so we should expect that some of Vito's 'friends' will probably visit our suspects."

"That all?" asks Jack.

"Yeah."

"Okay. Guess that's to be expected."

Moving slowly, Jack reaches across his desk and picks up the DVD. "I got this from a Homeland Security guard at the Trade Tower museum. It's a copy of what the surveillance cameras captured the night Stan showed up."

"Did you find anything useful on it?" asks Hector.

"Yeah. It shows Stan being dumped there just after three a.m. and it looks like whoever drove him there used Stan's van."

"What about the two cops who were on duty that night?"

"They're gonna be here later to tell us what they

saw. Oh, and Burley is on his way back with the van."

"Okay, that's good," comments Allison. "Anything else new?"

"No, not really," says Jack. "CSI is still working at the house, and Forensics is still studying the laundry." Turning his head, he looks at the whiteboard. "We got suspects, but no firm leads. Can one of you take this DVD to the techs downstairs?"

"I'll do it," offers Allison.

"What do you think about Mrs. Cummings?" asks Gomez. "She has a motive."

"Yeah, she could have done it," says Allison, "and she has no alibi for that night. But we have nothing that shows she was ever at the scene, or that she even knew where Stanley was hiding. Moreover, we have nothing that connects her to Stan's house, the van, or anything else."

Rising from his desk, Jack adds a question mark next to Sarah's name. Then he sits back down and removes his jacket with slow and deliberate movements. When his arms are free, he drapes the jacket over his desk and slides his left arm out of its sling. "Wow, that feels better," he says with a sigh. "Okay, let's work hard on getting some meaningful info out of Lincoln or O'Toole. We need something that will link these people to Stan's murder. Ally, talk to the CSI team when they get back. Find out if they got any evidence that our suspects were in the house or the van. Until we get something solid, all we have are suspicions and theories."

"Jack," calls Conrad from his office doorway, "the officers from the Memorial have arrived."

With a grunt, Jack slips his arm back into the sling, rises from his chair like an old man, and walks into Conrad's office.

"Use my desk," says Conrad. "I'll stand here and listen."

Jack takes a seat at his boss' desk and settles his arm into a position where it hurts the least. Then, he glares at each of the officers seated across from him.

"No eyes on the area?" he begins undiplomatically. "Looks like you two are in deep shit. Maybe parking enforcement duty for a while?"

Cringing at Jack's approach, Conrad clears his throat and interrupts his detective before he can say anything else.

"Jack, these are Officers Stevens and Egan. Internal Affairs will talk to them about that night, so let's move on."

Complying with his commander's reprimand, Jack directs his next comment to Officer Egan, the older of the two men. "I looked at the tapes today," he says, "but I want you to tell me what happened."

Stung by Jack's initial criticism, Egan doesn't answer right away. Instead, he deliberately wastes time. Turning his head from side to side, ostensibly to relieve a crick in his neck, he replies only after a few moments of jerky movements.

"We were near Greenwich when we spotted a vagrant sitting in the middle of the South Pool Promenade," he begins. "We recognized him because we removed him from that same place several times before; we've arrested him for vagrancy more than once. We usually try to get him to leave peacefully—he's an old Vietnam Vet—so we didn't want to arrest him again. But he was drunk and uncooperative. We didn't see or hear the van pull up because we were busy with that guy, so our best guess is that Cummings walked in alone and fell behind the wall, out of our sight. We got the vagrant out and things were quiet until the shift change. That's when Cummings woke up. He was moaning and vomiting, so we called for EMTs."

Jack looks over at Conrad. "That agrees with the video," he tells his boss. Then, Jack transfers his gaze to the second officer. "Can you add anything?"

"Everything went down just like he said," replies Officer Stevens. "We didn't want to arrest the Vet, but looking back, maybe we should have. We might have seen Cummings come in if the Vet wasn't taking up so much of our time."

Jack rises from behind Conrad's desk. "That's all I need, Lieutenant. The ball is now with you and I.A."

When Sam Lincoln arrives in the squad room with his lawyer, Allison is on the phone with the D.A.'s office, so she follows them with her eyes as they walk toward Conrad's office.

Seated at his desk nearby, Jack also watches the arrivals. Removing his arm from the sling, he relaxes into the back of his chair and waits. Minutes later, the men exit the office with Conrad, who motions for Stenhouse and Hector to join them. Wondering why she's not included, Allison raises her brows at Stenhouse in a wordless question while she continues her telephone conversation.

When the group arrives at Interrogation Room Two, Jack makes himself as comfortable as possible. Seated in a hard plastic chair, he slowly and carefully places his arm back into the sling.

"How are you feeling?" asks Sam, eyeing Jack's arm. "I heard you got hit pretty bad. The news said there was an attempt to steal evidence from the station."

"A little buckshot won't stop me," replies Jack. "Now, let's get down to business. We know that you and O'Toole visited Stan at his place in Jersey. Did Stan's wife ever go there?"

Sam looks at Jack for a minute. "Not that I know of," he replies with a shake of his head, "but you should probably ask Keith that question. Those two are inseparable."

Feeling a twinge, Jack looks down at his arm and continues talking without looking up. "Did Keith ever tell Sarah that Stan wasn't dead?"

"You're asking the wrong guy," glares Sam.

Ignoring Sam's objection, Hector presses the point. "Do you think Keith told Sarah where all of her wealth was coming from?"

"As I said, Detectives," frowns Sam, "I don't know what Keith and Sarah talked about. I do know that he was pretty agitated when Stan said he wanted to end the scheme. I heard him say that he'd see Stan dead before he'd let him blow it all away."

Now, Jack glares at Sam. "And you?" he asks. "Did you like the idea of Stan coming clean and spilling the beans?"

"Hell no! But I figured the charade wouldn't last forever, so I had Plan B."

Jack settles into the back of his chair, cradling his injured arm with his free hand. "Sam, you're an accomplice to grand larceny and insurance fraud, and you're also a suspect in the murder of Stan Cummings. What was your Plan B? Why the hell shouldn't we charge you with Cummings' murder right now?"

Sam matches Jack's relaxed demeanor but adds a lopsided grin for effect. "I was on duty at the station that entire night. There were no calls, so I never left the building. I couldn't have poisoned Stan."

"We arrested you at the airport. Where were you going?"

"I planned to get out of Dodge. I was headed for Vietnam."

"Vietnam, huh?"

"Yeah. I thought it would be a good place to hide out. But hey, I spoke to a representative from Stan's insurance company, and we reached an agreement that satisfies them. They're going to get their money back, and I'm going to go free, no charges. So although Plan B didn't work, Plan C will. Now, it looks like everything that concerns me has been resolved, so I'll be leaving, if you don't mind."

"I do mind," says Jack curtly, boring a hole into Sam's eyes. "Until this case is closed, you better stay right here in town. And by the way, Vito Lucchese also wants his money back, so if I were you, I'd lay low until your Plan C, whatever that is, actually goes into effect. Have a nice day, Mr. Lincoln. I'll be in touch."

At the mention of Vito Lucchese, Sam's face goes pale, and he freezes in his chair. When he makes no move to leave, his attorney gives him a nudge.

As the suspect's and attorney's chairs scrape away from the table, Jack nods slightly at the mirror, and also rises from his chair.

"Oh, I forgot one thing," he says apologetically. "Can you hold on a sec?"

On cue, a technician from the Forensic Department enters the room.

"Mr. Lincoln, we need to collect some of your DNA," explains Jack. "This young lady will take a swab of your mouth."

Backing up a step, Sam shouts, "Central Booking did that when they took my fingerprints! Why do you need to do it again?"

"Oh, it's just a convenience for all of us if we take another sample here," says Jack before a stabbing pain stops him from talking.

Sam's lawyer urges his client to cooperate, so Sam gives in. Standing quietly, he opens his mouth wide to allow the tech to swipe a cotton-tipped stick along the inside of his mouth. Frowning deeply, he watches as she places the stick into a glass tube.

While the tech gathers up her tools, Sam snorts his disapproval and hurries out of the room, his attorney rushing to catch up.

Still in pain, Jack sits back down at the table. The pain pill is wearing off, and he's feeling pretty bad.

"You need help?" asks Gomez.

Nodding reluctantly, Jack leans on Hector, and they walk slowly down the hallway.

"Well," snarls Jack, "aside from collecting the DNA, that was a fucking waste of time."

"Not really," declares Gomez confidently. "Did you see the expression on Sam's face when you reminded him that Lucchese still wants his money? I thought he was going to shit himself!"

Jack begins to laugh at the image but stops suddenly and groans. Wincing in pain, he says, "Man, don't ever try to laugh with busted ribs."

When the pain fades to a tolerable level, he continues walking. "We need to keep an eye on Lincoln," he says. "I think he's going to bail. Besides, even though I dislike the guy, we still need to protect him from Lucchese."

A couple of hours later, Jack looks down at his wrist to catch the time but remembers that his watch is not there. "Dammit," he mutters and turns to the clock on the wall instead.

"Hey, Gomez," he says. "Burley isn't here yet, and I'm starved. Let's go to Bubby's—I need a burger and a beer. Or maybe two beers and a burger." Spotting Giancarlo at her desk, he shouts, "Ally, you're driving! I'll treat you to lunch, and you can fill us in on the status of the warrants."

CHAPTER THIRTY-ONE

Although today's commotion outside of Ristorante di Cosenza is by now a familiar sight, nearby business owners, residents, and ogling tourists still raise their cell phones high to record the actions of the men and women of New York City's Vice Squad.

With Sergeant Vincent Spinelli leading the way, the Vice SWAT team streams out of their MRAP vehicles with military precision. Like a swarm of bees, the fifteen-person team storms the restaurant, taking customers and mafia soldiers by surprise.

Minutes later, the eatery's diners and workers file out as Vice Squad members enter, weaving their way through the dining and kitchen areas.

Outside of Vito Lucchese's private room, a short gunfight erupts as the men who pledged their blood attempt to protect their Don. They are out-gunned, however, and are swiftly overtaken by officers in blue.

When the Don's protectors are out of commission, Spinelli follows his team into Lucchese's inner sanctum, where they find Vito calmly eating at his favorite table.

Seemingly oblivious to the commotion outside his door, the Don looks up from his plate of antipasto only when Spinelli stops directly in front of his table.

Smiling cordially, Vito holds up a glass of Lambrusco.

"What can I do for you gentlemen?" he asks. "If I knew you were coming, I would have had a meal prepared."

Without saying a word, two SWAT officers force Lucchese to his feet and handcuff him while Spinelli recites the familiar verses of the Miranda warning. "Mr. Lucchese," the sergeant adds, "you are being arrested for money laundering and attacking a New York City police facility. Federal authorities will also charge you with tax evasion."

Vito is not worried. "I'll be out in an hour," he smiles. "I'm a legitimate businessman. You're making a big mistake."

Spinelli gestures toward the door, and the officers lead the mobster away. As the sergeant watches them go, he turns to the nearest officer and mutters, "Legitimate, my ass."

Jack has been waiting eagerly for his bacon cheeseburger. When it arrives, he takes a big bite, chews quickly, and washes it down with a deep gulp of Guinness. Setting the glass down, he wipes his mouth with a satisfying sigh and catches Allison's disapproving eye. The detective is drinking an Arnold Palmer and makes sure Jack knows it.

"Yeah, I see it," Jack quips. "I'm on duty and shouldn't drink, but fuck it! I think I deserve some extra goodness today."

After another bite of his burger and another deep draught, he says, "Okay. Now, we can get down to business. What's the latest on the warrants?"

"The D.A. is working on them," says Allison, putting down her BLT and wiping her fingers on a napkin. "They should be finalized tomorrow. They'll permit us to search the houses."

"Good," says Jack as he finishes his Guinness and adjusts his position to make himself more comfortable. "Grimes and Lincoln have alibis, so we need to concentrate on the two lovebirds."

"What about Lucchese or his men? Do you think they murdered Cummings?" asks Gomez. "I know it doesn't fit Lucchese's M.O., but we shouldn't rule him out yet."

"You have a point, Hector," says Allison, turning to the sergeant sitting next to her in the burger joint booth. "There's a chance that one of his men did it. But if my uncle wanted him dead, he'd be part of some construction project by now, or buried in some other inaccessible place. Neither Mrs. Cummings nor Keith O'Toole has an alibi, so it could have been one of them, or even both of them."

Jack finishes his burger and starts on his second beer. "Tomorrow, we'll go out to the Island to visit the loving couple," he says. "Meanwhile, Burley should be back at the station after lunch, so I'll talk to him and then go home. I'm so damn sore," he moans. "I need to rest."

"You should rest," agrees Allison. "If it weren't for your vest, you'd be dead," she reminds him. "The doc said you lost a substantial amount of blood."

"Yeah, I know. I'm in pain right now, but I don't want to take any more drugs. It's about time to change my dressings anyway. The doc said I need to spread a silver-based antiseptic salve over my stitches twice a day. I also need to take one of those huge antibiotic pills. Are you ready to go? I want to be sure to talk to Burley before I call Didi to pick me up."

"No need to call Didi, bro. I'll give you a lift," offers Gomez. "I've been meaning to get over to the boutique to pick up something special for my girl," he says with a wink.

Jack begins to laugh but quickly stops. "You dog!" he manages to mutter while he waits for the pain in his ribcage to subside. When it returns to a dull ache, he adds, "Thanks for the ride."

While Jack asks for the check, Gomez finishes the last bits of his burger and Allison heads to the ladies' room. When the bill is paid and Allison is still nowhere in sight, the men step outside to wait for her.

Standing in the noonday sun, Jack dons his mirrored sunglasses and looks out at the hordes of scurrying people on the sidewalk.

"In our line of work," remarks Hector, "I often wonder how many of these people have wanted to kill someone at one time or another."

"Yeah," agrees Jack, "and I wonder how many of them have tried and succeeded."

A short time later, they return to the station. When they walk into the squad room, Sergeant Burley lifts his brows in surprise.

"What the hell?" he asks. "What are you doing out of the hospital?"

"Couldn't keep myself from seeing your smiling face," replies Jack. "Anything new in Jersey? Oh...and how's Sylvia?"

Burley rolls his eyes at Jack's insinuation. "I found this on the ground outside the cabin," he says, handing Jack an evidence bag. When Jack looks at him questioningly, he adds, "It says, 'Genuine Snakeskin.' CSI checked it. It's clean, no prints."

Jack turns the bag over in his hand. "Snakeskin? It's probably from a pair of boots. We're going to search the Cummings and O'Toole houses tomorrow, so I'll look for a match. For now, I'll put it into the file for safekeeping."

"Forensics is going to start checking Stan's van tomorrow," declares Burley. "They also said they'll have some info on that bundle of laundry by morning. I'm going to go down there now to see how they're doing. Maybe I can get them to start on the van today."

"Okay," says Jack absentmindedly. While Burley was talking, Jack was studying the photos of Sarah Cummings and Keith O'Toole on the evidence board. "Everything seems to point to these two," he says. "I believe one or both of them is the killer or killers. Let's hope the specialists can give us something definitive." Then Jack sighs, drops the marker, and jerks his head in the direction of the door. "You ready to go, Gomez?"

On the way to the elevator, Jack and Hector pass John, who is looking at some messages placed near his desk phone. "You want to come with us to pick out something for Sylvia?" Jack asks John with a mischievous grin.

Without looking up from his reading, Burley flashes Jack half a peace sign.

It's now early afternoon. The homebound traffic hasn't started to build yet, but the city's streets are clogged, nonetheless. It takes thirty minutes for Gomez to reach Didi's store on the Lower East Side; a drive that should only take fifteen minutes, if traffic ever ran smoothly. Gomez drops Jack off in front of the store and then parks in an empty spot about a block away.

Didi is surprised to see her husband at this time of day.

"Hi, Hon. Closing time isn't for another couple of hours. What's wrong?" With an arm around Jack's waist, Didi guides him toward the counter.

"Just a little tired," sighs Jack. "Things are slow, so I'm taking a couple of hours off."

"I'm so glad to hear that," states Didi. "You do look tired." Pulling out a stool, she instructs Jack to sit.

Sinking onto the backless chair, Jack lets out another sigh and runs his fingers through his hair.

"Hector drove me over. He's parking the car. He wants to get his girlfriend a special outfit."

"Oh, I can sure help him with that," smiles Didi.

A minute later, the door chime rings, and Sergeant Gomez walks into the boutique. Spying Didi, he greets her with a kiss on the forehead.

"Deidre, you're going to make a wonderful mother," he says, patting her swollen belly. Then, thinking better of it, he retracts his hand swiftly. "Oops," he says. "I hope you don't mind. I can't resist baby bellies."

"That's okay, Hector," chuckles Didi, dismissing his apology. "Jack told me you're looking for something special."

"Yeah, it's for Olivia, my new girlfriend," says Gomez. "It's our one-month anniversary. I thought maybe something red and sexy?"

"Hmm, I have a few things I think you'll like," winks Didi. "Come over here while I get them," she commands with a crook of her finger. "You can also look through this catalog. The lingerie is shown on models, so you can get an idea of how they'll look on your girlfriend."

"*Oye*, Hector!" calls Jack. "Remember, that catalog's just for lookin', not for takin' home!"

At eight o'clock that evening, a phone rings in

West Hempstead.

"Keith, you and Sarah better watch your combined asses," stresses a voice. "Lucchese wants his money, and he doesn't care where he gets it."

CHAPTER THIRTY-TWO

Jack feels a little better the next morning. Although his arm is still bandaged tightly, it's no longer in the sling.

Since driving four on the floor is still not possible, Didi will drive him to work and pick him up later for a doctor appointment.

When they arrive at the First Precinct, Jack pauses before leaving the car. Knowing that his wife is forced to sit farther away from the steering wheel because of her growing belly, he hesitates to leave the two loves of his life. Knowing that he must, however, he finally steps out and closes the car door behind him. He remains at the curb until the car melts into Manhattan traffic. When he can no longer see it, he turns around and heads into the building.

As Jack walks toward the entrance, his mood improves as greetings from coworkers come his way. Comments such as, "Hey, man!" and "Good to have ya back!" accompanied by high fives and smiles, make Jack walk a little taller, and when he arrives in the Homicide squad room, Hector's chipper mood intensifies his good feelings.

"Hey! No sling today?" hails Hector. "Looks like you're doing better! How d'ya feel?"

As usual, Jack is ready with a quick retort. "With my hands, man," he says cheerfully. Sitting down, he asks, "How'd it go last night? Did Olivia like her gift?"

Hector smiles at the memory. "I know *I* did," he says.

A few minutes later, when John and Allison saunter in, Hector declares, "Hey, John, you really need to check out Didi's place. You know, for Sylvia."

Overhearing the guys' conversation, Allison knows where it will soon head, and she doesn't want to hear it this early in the morning. "Okaaay!" she commands with a clap of her hands. "Let's get to work! John, call Forensics to see if they have any updates. I'll check with Conrad about the warrants."

Not one to let good banter end without comment, Jack shouts, "Hey, Allison, why don't you give your hubby a treat and go shopping at Didi's, too?"

Turning toward the whiteboard, Allison claims, "Who says I haven't done that already?"

Mid-gulp, Burley coughs up some of his coffee. "Dammit, Giancarlo!" he sputters. "Now, there's an image burned into my head for all eternity!"

Turning, Allison stares daggers at Burley while everyone laughs except Jack. He had begun to join in the merriment, but the pain from his ribs shut that down quickly.

Burley, however, is on a roll. Unable to stop the teasing, he says, "Uh oh! I pissed off a Mafia chick! I'mma inna bigga trouble now!"

Annoyed by John's comment, Allison gets ready

to return the jab, but before she can say anything, she's called into Conrad's office. Walking past her colleague, she points two fingers at her eyes and then aims them at John's face.

With a wide grin at Allison's gesture, Burley returns to business. "Well," he says to the remaining team members, "about Forensics. They got a hit on one of the laundry items. They found dried sputum and powdered arsenic on a Buffalo Bills jersey. Stanley must have been wearing it when he was poisoned. The killer may have thrown it into the laundry basket with the intention of washing it later. They're re-checking it and the other clothing for more evidence."

"Or," ponders Jack, "Stan could have been wearing it when he was using the arsenic to kill the raccoons that were eating his blueberries."

As that thought trails off, Jack looks off into the distance to consider a new thought that pops into his head. "But you know, you may be right," he admits. "Maybe the killer wanted to wash it. Go down to Forensics. Ask them to concentrate on the jersey, and stay there while they go over the van."

After Allison leaves Conrad, she returns to the group waving the search warrants for the Cummings and O'Toole homes. "We're good to go!" she announces.

Jack sucks in a deep breath but quickly regrets it. "Damn ribs," he mutters, wincing at the pain. "Okay," he says after a minute. "John will remain in Forensics while the rest of us go out to West Hempstead to check the houses." Reaching into the file, he grabs the bag containing the metal plate Burley found. "Maybe we'll get lucky," he adds. "Let's roll."

As the sun plays peekaboo with the clouds, Allison drives an unmarked sedan north on Long Island's Woodfield Road, followed by a Nassau County police cruiser. Because she and her companions are out of their jurisdiction, two of Nassau's cops will accompany them as they serve the warrants.

Trailed by the Long Island officers, Allison drives past Sarah Cummings' house to check it out before they commit to their mission. Sitting in the passenger seat, Jack notes, "The SUV is in the driveway, so I guess she's home."

Nodding, Allison turns left at the next corner and parks on the swale in front of Keith O'Toole's house on Bedell Terrace, with the Nassau escort right behind her.

Notified of the warrants, the couple's lawyer steps out of O'Toole's house to meet Stenhouse, Giancarlo, and Gomez amid a neat arrangement of juniper bushes and blue spruce trees. Backed by the two patrol officers, Jack hands the warrant to the attorney, who scans it and then motions them toward the house.

Watching from the door, Keith steps aside to allow the group to enter the house through the small foyer that leads to a hallway.

Sergeant Gomez notices an office nearby and calls out, "I'm going to take a look at O'Toole's computer!"

Bristling, Keith's lawyer asserts, "The stipulations of this warrant do not allow you to remove any property or possessions from the premises!"

"Oh?" replies Jack coolly. "We have the right to search anything and everything. I suggest you advise your client to give us his password so we can review the computer's contents here. If you don't, we'll confiscate the whole thing and search it elsewhere. *Capeesh*?"

For a tense minute, Keith and his lawyer have a hushed but animated conversation. Then, Keith reluctantly gives Sergeant Gomez his password: Aureus911.

While Gomez reviews computer folders and documents in the office, Jack and Allison head for Keith's bedroom, where Allison begins her search by looking through drawers, and Jack makes a beeline for the walk-in closet.

Glancing about, Jack immediately spots a pair of black snakeskin boots on a shoe rack. Reaching down, he turns them over to inspect the soles and then walks over to the bed, where he takes the small brass plate from his pocket. "Hey, I got a match!" he declares. "This is a snakeskin boot that's missing a tag like the one Burley found in Jersey!"

Detective Giancarlo walks over to take a look. "Well, that definitely puts Keith at Stan's place," she states.

"Hey, guys!" calls Gomez from the office. "Come and see this!"

Hearing the excitement in Hector's voice, the pair hurries down the short hallway to find Hector beaming in triumph at Keith's computer. "I looked through the history file and found the searches that Keith did on arsenic and other poisons!"

"Look, I..." begins Keith from the doorway until his attorney stops him with a warning glare.

"We have nothing to say at this time," intones the lawyer. "That is circumstantial evidence."

"Stan was killed by arsenic poisoning," reacts Jack with bitterness. "Your client has no alibi for the murder, and we now have evidence that he was at the scene of the crime. We know he threatened Cummings and that he has a motive because he's boinking his wife, so... Mr. Keith O'Toole, you are under arrest for the murder of Stanley Cummings. You have the right to remain silent. Anything you say can and will be held against you in a court of law. Since you already know your rights about hiring an attorney, I don't need to say anything else."

Turning to the Nassau County cops, Jack instructs them to take O'Toole into custody.

"You can't arrest me! I didn't kill Cummings!" objects Keith as he's being cuffed. "What the hell am I paying you for?" he shouts at his lawyer. "Do something! Say something, for God's sake!"

"We'll take the computer and the boots," Jack informs the cops. "Gomez, call the D.A. and accompany Nassau's finest to the jail. Giancarlo and I will now visit Mrs. Cummings. We'll meet you later at the First."

Calmly and coolly, Keith's lawyer places a hand on Keith's shoulder. "You have nothing to worry about," he murmurs. "I'll go with them to Sarah's house, and I'll have one of my colleagues meet you at the jail to arrange bail. Don't worry; this is nothing. You'll be out by tomorrow."

But Keith isn't mollified by his attorney's assurance. As he's being led away, he shouts over his shoulder, "This is bullshit! And as a lawyer, you suck!"

After Sergeant Gomez and the Nassau County police officers march O'Toole out of the house, Jack and Allison climb back into Allison's car for the quick drive around the corner to Sarah's house. Following closely is the ever-present attorney.

In the car, the pair discusses their next move.

"Let's not serve the warrant to search Sarah's house today, unless we have to," says Jack.

"Okay," agrees Allison. "We should interview Sarah about Keith first."

Within minutes, they are sitting at Sarah's dining room table, and Jack is beginning the questioning.

"Mrs. Cummings, did your fiancé give you any indication of what his plans were? We just arrested Mr. O'Toole for the murder of your husband."

Shocked, Sarah blanches but leans over to talk privately with the attorney.

"Keith was upset about something for a while," she says, "but he never told me what was bothering him. When Stan showed up at the Memorial, he told me where all of the money was coming from. He also said the police found out where Stan was hiding all these years, and that Stan wanted to come back home. But my marriage with Stan was over long before 9/11. His gambling drove a large wedge between us, and I couldn't take it anymore."

"Is that why you turned to Mr. O'Toole for comfort?" asks Giancarlo.

A small smile appears on Sarah's face. "I already told you. He became a close friend, and we eventually fell in love. I was planning to divorce Stanley, but 9/11 happened, and I thought I became a widow." Then, the smile disappears. "He...he couldn't have done it, could he? I mean, yes, Keith was really angry, but to kill Stan?"

"Mrs. Cummings, we'll be in touch," says Jack. "I'm sure we'll talk again. Thank you for your time."

On the way out, Jack slows down to look at some framed family photos displayed on a table near the door. When one picture in particular piques his interest, he leans over to study it more closely.

On the drive back to Southern State Parkway, Jack is silent while suburbia passes by. As Allison merges into highway traffic, he says, "Something isn't right."

"What do you mean?" inquires Giancarlo, checking her rearview mirror.

"My bullshit meter is off the charts. I can't shake an uneasy feeling about this whole case. Didn't it seem like Sarah threw her fiancé under the bus?"

CHAPTER THIRTY-THREE

Keith's day is not going well. The Nassau County cops have delivered him to their Mineola headquarters to fill out the paperwork for his transfer to Manhattan Central. Hector waited for him at the station for a while, but he is now on his way back to Manhattan.

He should have stayed longer, though.

While Hector was driving back to the city, he received a call from one of the Nassau cops. It seems that an error was made, and instead of sending O'Toole to Manhattan's First Precinct, he was now on his way to Rikers Island. The cop apologized for the mix-up, but the deed was done.

"Guys, there was a screw-up with O'Toole," announces Burley when he arrives back in New York City.

"Sounds like I'm back in Florida," says Jack, shaking his head as he munches on a snack of corn chips and Coke. "What happened?"

"The paperwork came through to transfer O'Toole here, but the officers who showed up are bringing him to Rikers instead."

Dismayed, the fizz in Jack's soda makes him

cough, which in turn, causes him to grimace from pain.

"Oh, damn, that hurt," he mutters. "But how the hell is O'Toole going to Rikers? He'll be in deep shit if they put him in there! We need to fix this!"

"Why are you so concerned about O'Toole?" asks Allison. "Didn't you say you thought he killed Cummings?"

"I do think he's our best suspect, but that's not relevant. Lucchese is now at Rikers, and if he finds out that O'Toole is there, too, he's a dead man."

"What the hell are you saying, Jack? Now you think O'Toole didn't do it?" stares Gomez quizzically.

"That's not what I'm saying," Jack says after taking another sip of Coke and rising from his chair. "I'm gonna talk to Conrad. We have to try to get O'Toole out of Rikers. Call Forensics and get Burley back up here."

Jack waves at Conrad from his boss' doorway. Although the lieutenant is on the phone and seems to be involved in a serious conversation, he ends the call and gestures for Jack to enter.

"You look grim, Detective. What's up?"

"Somebody fucked up, and O'Toole is on his way to Rikers instead of Central Booking! We gotta get him out of there, Boss. Lucchese will have him killed for sure!"

"Geez. Doesn't anything go right? All right, I'll look into it, Stenhouse, but I don't think I'm gonna get anywhere. He's locked up now, and I don't think anyone cares where. I was just talking to the D.A. He convened a grand jury for an indictment on O'Toole, so as far as he's concerned, the case is closed. I'm also pulling Forensics off the case because they're backed up with a lot of work. It's over now, Jack. Your team did good work. Go home and take a breather. The city will drop another dead body at your feet real soon."

Although Jack heard what his boss said, he continues to press his case.

"Lieutenant, we need to keep this one open for a while. I have a new theory about what happened, so until I check it out, I need the techs to keep looking for clues."

Conrad stares into Jack's steel gray eyes. Deep down, he knows Stenhouse is right to be cautious, but he also knows the city keeps throwing shit their way, so he has to push things along.

"Jack, it's done," he replies firmly. "The case is officially closed. If you think there's more to it, look into it on your own time. Just don't let me find out that you used police resources and personnel to help you. Understand? Now gather up your team and go celebrate."

Frustrated by the system and the lieutenant's shuffling of priorities, Jack's bulldog comes out.

"Dammit, Lieutenant!" he shouts. "Why all this bullshit? The case is not settled! Why can't we just..."

"That's enough, Detective!" barks Conrad, cutting him off. "The D.A. wants it closed and so does the mayor! I repeat, it's officially over, and that's an order! I'll do what I can to get O'Toole out, but now, go home!"

Seething with anger, Jack replies through gritted teeth. "Yes, sir. But we...*you*, are making a huge mistake!" Turning on his heels, he storms out of the office and slams the door behind him, breaking the door's upper glass panel. "Send me the fuckin' bill!" he shouts at Conrad, who is stunned by his departing detective's anger and the shards of glass covering his office floor.

As Jack storms back to his desk, Giancarlo, Burley, and Gomez stare at him in disbelief. They know Jack is impulsive, but the behavior they just witnessed was more volatile than usual. None of them wants to ask Jack to explain, so they wait for him to volunteer the information.

Predictably, they don't wait long.

"The fuckin' D.A. decided on his own that O'Toole is the murderer, and the mayor agrees!" Jack shouts, waving his hand wildly. "Conrad got overruled, so he kissed ass and went along with it! He shut the whole thing down! This is total crap!"

Jack sighs and collapses into his chair. "I saw a photo at Sarah's house today," he says a little more calmly. "She was wearing a Buffalo Bills jersey—the same team's jersey we found at Stan's place. We're officially off the case, but Conrad gave me the okay to continue to work on it on my own time. At least he gave me that!" he hisses, slamming his hand on his desk.

The team is also upset by the new developments and they each try to outdo each other as they shout their complaints. They can't believe that after all the effort they put into the case, the loose ends will remain loose.

"Guys!" yells Jack to get their attention. "Go home! If you want to help me, meet me here tomorrow at six, and pray that Lucchese doesn't bump O'Toole off before we can get him out!"

With loud sighs and mutters about unappreciated work and management incompetence, the officers prepare to leave the station.

As Allison packs up to head home, she says, "You broke his damn door, Stenhouse! Do you know how many times I've wanted to do that exact same thing?"

"Yeah, I broke it," mutters Jack, "but I'm gonna have to pay to fix it. I'm glad Didi's making good money at her place. Go on home now; the case is over. I'll let you know if I discover anything new."

CHAPTER THIRTY-FOUR

At 4:30 the next morning, Jack's cell phone rings and jolts him awake. With a low groan, he swings his legs over the edge of the bed and sits upright on the mattress.

Naked except for his mummy-wrapped arm, he wearily lifts the phone from the night table and mumbles gruffly, "Yeah? This better be good." After listening silently for a few minutes, he replies, "Okay, Boss. I'll be there as soon as I do my three S's."

Looking over at his naked wife, Jack smiles at the curves that never fail to remind him of the front bumper of a '58 Caddy. Reaching down, he slaps Didi on the ass to wake her up. When she turns over, half asleep, she asks, "What the hell, Jack?"

"Work calls," he says. "Gotta go."

"Oh, no," Didi moans. "Sonia's off today. If you take the car, how am I gonna get to work?"

Jack walks over to a pair of pants draped over a chair. Pulling out forty dollars, he tosses the money on the bed.

"Get a cab or call Uber. I'll pick you up for dinner."

Now, Didi is wide awake. "Um, how are you

going to drive a stick, Jack?"

"Oh, damn, I forgot." Dialing Conrad back, he announces, "I'm going to need a ride, Boss. Can you have someone here in fifteen?"

With a sheepish grin, Jack retrieves his forty bucks and walks into the bathroom.

Later, when Jack enters the squad room, Conrad is already there, waiting.

"Since it's only 5:20 and I'm here early, like you asked, do you at least have coffee and donuts for me?" asks Jack.

Ignoring the remark, Conrad lowers himself wearily into the nearest chair.

"What is it, Boss? You look green."

Conrad sighs and runs his fingers through his sparse hair. "I got bad news. You were right. O'Toole was killed last night."

"What?!" sputters Jack. "I told you! That's..."

Conrad holds up his hand to stop Jack from speaking.

"They got the guy who stabbed him. I know it's bad, but now it's really over, so we have to move on. I also called the rest of your crew in this morning, 'cause we got another body. A jogger was found under a tree in St. John's Park."

Jack rolls his eyes and gears up for an outburst,

disregarding the pain that he knows will follow. "FUCK IT, LIEUTENANT!" he shouts. "We're the ones responsible for killing him!"

Raising both hands in a gesture of helplessness, Conrad tries to smooth things over while conceding that Jack's instinct was correct.

"Look, I said you were right, but it's completely out of our hands!" he asserts. "The D.A. is going to have to handle the O'Toole mess now. We're out of it!" Then Conrad sees Jack's expression and changes tactics, suspecting that nothing will mollify his subordinate.

"Last time I checked, Stenhouse, you are one of several detectives on this police force," Conrad states firmly. "There are plenty of other problems in this city, Officer. We got another victim to worry about, so here's your new assignment."

Conrad pulls a piece of paper from his pocket and lays down the law. "Get over to the park. Your team should already be there with CSI. You got work to do." Then he softens a bit and adds, "Let me know if you find out anything else about the Cummings murder."

Frowning, Jack takes the paper and turns away. "You bet I have work to do," he mumbles behind gritted teeth. "O'Toole was innocent."

The area commonly known as St. John's Park is across the street from the First Precinct. Because it's early, the Big Apple hasn't greeted the new day yet, and its roads are somewhat empty.

Jack decides to walk to the park under the blanket of pre-dawn darkness to try to clear his head. Watching for a break in traffic, he crosses the busy thoroughfare to reach the park and the sea of blue lights around it.

As the morning progresses, the tall buildings in the area become more and more evident as their occupants wake up and turn on their lights.

Seeing Giancarlo up ahead, Jack nods at her and walks over. Although neither of them says anything, their silence speaks volumes.

Together, the pair walks across the center of the park to a bank of trees, where they find Sergeants Gomez and Burley. Gomez, always the thoughtful one, has brought coffee for the crew, so he hands each of them a cup.

Jack accepts the coffee without comment. He's still pissed about O'Toole, his arm, his ribs, and leaving his wife too early in the morning. His arm is no longer in a sling, but it is still almost useless and hangs limply at his side.

Noticing Jack's foul mood, Gomez tries to ease the tension by offering some cheer.

"Mornin' guys," he chirps. "You're looking better today, Jack. Did you drive the Road Runner in?"

Thanking Gomez for the coffee with a salute of his cup, Jack says, "No, I still can't drive a fuck'n stick. Had to leave my ride with Didi. Do we know what's going on here?"

"Not yet. All Conrad said is we got a dead body.

CSI is working the scene, so I guess we'll find out soon."

When silence once again descends upon the group, Burley looks at each of his friends. He knows they are all upset and that they're trying to avoid asking the questions they desperately want answers to, so he plunges forward and queries Jack directly.

"What are you going to do about the Cummings case?" he blurts out boldly. "We heard about O'Toole."

Jack stares at each member of his team. "I know you're just as upset as I am. Joe down in Forensics owes me a favor, so I'm going to ask him to do some extra-curricular activities on that Bills jersey. I have a theory about what happened, but I'm not going to play my hand until I get all my ducks in a row."

Burley is pleased to see that Jack isn't giving up easily. "By the way," he adds, "do you need help payin' for Conrad's door? I've wanted to slam that thing many times!"

"That door is mine," Jack says firmly. "Thanks for the offer, but I'll take care of the cost. Didi's been taking in a shitload of money at her boutique, so I'm good. Let's get started on our new case."

The group finds the medical examiner kneeling on the ground near a tall oak tree, looking over the body in question. Jack attempts to squat down next to him, but his injured body betrays him and almost puts him on his ass. With a grimace, he rocks back onto his heels.

"What do we have here, Doc?" he asks.

"We got a black female, possibly in her twenties.

She's been decapitated." Pointing nearby, he says, "Her head is at the base of that tree over there. 'Allah is great' was written on her forehead in Arabic. It looks like it was done with a black marker. I believe she died about two hours ago. As you can see, her blouse is ripped open, and she's not wearing undergarments. Either she was sexually assaulted, or she had consensual sex before she was killed. There's blood over there," he points to an area about fifteen feet away that has been cordoned off. "It appears that she was dragged from there and placed under this tree. There's plenty of blood, and I'm sure the attacker was covered with it. There's no ID on the body, but she's wearing gold jewelry and a diamond watch."

Looking at the watch, Allison remarks, "Well, she wasn't mugged. That watch is worth about ten G's."

"Excuse me, Detectives," says a patrolman, approaching the group. "A homeless man just handed me this purse. He says he found it in the bushes about a hundred feet away."

With a gloved hand, the M.E. takes the purse and opens it. Inside is a wallet containing a driver's license and some credit cards. "Well, Detectives, looks like we have a name."

Donning a glove offered by the M.E., Jack takes hold of the license. "Her name is Cherille Jacobs. Her address is on the Upper East Side: 22 East 88th Street. That's near the Guggenheim. No wonder she's wearing a Rolex."

With a wince and a grunt, Jack tries to stand up on his own but gives up and reaches for Burley's offered hand.

"Thanks, bro. I can't wait 'till this shit is healed."

Brushing off his slacks, Jack hands out his first orders for the new case. "Bring that homeless guy over here so Detective Giancarlo can interrogate him," he says to the patrol officer. "Ally, when the M.E. is finished, take Gomez with you to observe the autopsy. John, you and I will go back to the station to find out what we can on Ms. Jacobs. I need to speak to my pal, Joe, anyway. And since I can't drive, you can be my chauffeur for the rest of the day."

As the crew disbands to complete their assignments, Stenhouse lets John in on the personal mission he's assigned to himself.

"I've been thinking about the Cummings case a lot," he says on the way back to the station, "and I've changed my mind. I don't think O'Toole killed Cummings. I want Forensics to continue to check that jersey."

"Really?" says John. "What's so special about the jersey?"

"Stan's a city boy. He grew up in Queens Village and met his wife at NYU. She's from Tonawanda, so I bet that jersey's hers."

"Tonawanda?"

"Yeah, it's near Buffalo. You know...Buffalo Bills...the jersey from Stan's house?"

"Okay..." replies John, still unsure about the jersey's significance.

"When we were at Sarah's house yesterday, I saw a photo of her wearing a Bill's jersey."

"Oh. Now, I see where you're going with this."

"After you get background information on Cherille Jacobs, give Larry Grimes a call. See if you can get more info on Stan and Sarah, like how they met, and anything relating to the Buffalo Bills. I'm gonna contact Forensics. Before O'Toole and Sarah were booked, CSI found unidentified fingerprints at the house. We have O'Toole's fingerprints from his official records, and now we have Sarah's DNA from her booking."

Burley stares at Jack with his brows knitted together in a frown. "What the hell are you saying, Jack? *Sarah* killed her husband?"

As the elevator door opens to the third floor, Jack replies, "I'm not saying anything yet."

CHAPTER THIRTY-FIVE

Joe Ellison has worked as a forensic scientist for NYPD for the past ten years. Known for his meticulous and unrelenting search for answers, he's considered to be the go-to person in his department.

At the moment, Joe's attention is focused on blood samples from a recent crime scene, so he is unaware that Jack is standing behind him.

As Joe adjusts the eyepiece of his microscope, Jack tries to fake a cough, but his broken ribs only allow him to clear his throat. Startled by the sound, Joe flinches.

"Jack!" he cries. "You snuck up on me! How's the arm?"

"Hurts like hell, but it's not as bad as my ribs. Hey, I'm cashing in my chips today. I need you to do something on the QT."

"You got it, Jack. What do you need?"

"It's the Cummings case. I need you to cross-reference those unknown fingerprints from the van and Stan's house with Sarah Cummings. I also need you to continue to look at that jersey."

Joe cocks his head. "That case is closed, Stenhouse. All the evidence has been stored away."

"Here's what I'm thinkin'," says Jack. "O'Toole didn't do it, but because he's no longer around, the D.A. took the easy way out and put the blame on him so he could get this thing out of his hair. I need good, hard evidence on Mrs. Cummings before I can ask Conrad and the D.A. to reopen the case."

Joe stares at the floor while he thinks. "Okay," he says. "You get me the jersey, and I'll work on it tonight."

Upstairs in Homicide, Burley is on the phone with Larry Grimes.

"Good morning, Mr. Grimes," he says politely. "This is Sergeant Burley."

Surprised by the call, Grimes asks, "What do you want? I thought the case was wrapped up. Didn't you guys charge Keith with Stan's murder?"

"Yes, well, Keith was killed last night, and we think Lucchese was behind it."

When there is nothing but silence on the phone, Burley asks, "Mr. Grimes, are you still there?"

"Holy good God!" exclaims Grimes. "I spoke to my lawyer early this morning! He said my new identity and witness relocation papers were sped up, and that everything should be ready this afternoon! You think Lucchese will target all of us?

"Do bears shit in the woods?" replies Burley. "But that's not why I called. I have a couple more questions about Mr. and Mrs. Cummings. You said they were frequent visitors at Ladder 403. You said Stan made donations to your station and the Fireman's Fund long before he was married, and that he continued to do so afterward. Can you tell me how Stan and Sarah met?"

"Geez, Sergeant, I have no idea how they met. All I know is that they went to NYU together."

"I need you to think, Larry. Can you remember anything they may have told you about themselves?"

"Well, Stan was a big football fan, and they went to a lot of games at Giant Stadium. He proposed to Sarah at a Jets game—one of those Fireman and Policeman Appreciation Days. That's the only thing I remember. You know, if you guys did your job right, you'd already have seen the pictures that were taken at the games. Ladder 403 always has a photographer around to record company events."

"That will do just fine, Grimes," Burley says with a smile. "Thanks."

When John ends the call, he makes a beeline for the men's room to evacuate the three cups of coffee he drank this morning. When he exits, he bumps into Jack, who's returning from Forensics.

"What did you find on Cherille Jacobs?" asks Jack.

"She was a financial advisor at Fidelity Investing and Trust Company, a major firm on Park Avenue. I arranged for a meeting there later this morning. Maybe an investor lost money or something, or maybe there's a boyfriend or an ex with a grudge."

"Okay, that's good."

"I also talked to Grimes," says John. "He said Stan

and Sarah went to NYU at the same time and that he proposed to her at a Jets game on Fireman Appreciation Day. He said Ladder Company 403's photographer was there, so I bet that flash drive Giancarlo brought back has pictures from the game. Seems Cummings was a big spender. He hired a bus for the firehouse crew that day, with drinks and everything."

Jack nods and clicks on Giancarlo's contact number on his cell phone. "Allison, where's that flash drive you got from the firehouse with all the photos on it?"

Allison thinks for a while. "It's in the case file, but it must be in lockup by now."

"Oh, yeah, the case file that's locked up in my desk?" smirks Jack. "Thanks."

Back at his desk, Jack unlocks the bottom drawer and pulls out an oversized accordion file. Trying his best to reduce the amount of pain these actions cause, he unclasps the organizer and searches inside for the flash drive.

As he slides the object out, he catches sight of Conrad walking by, so he quickly transfers the drive to the inside pocket of his sports coat and replaces the large organizer in the drawer, locking it away from curious eyes.

Noticing his detective's surreptitious movements, Conrad asks, "Anything you'd like to tell me, Stenhouse?"

"Yeah," says Jack. "Burley got a lead on our victim at the park. Did you know she was decapitated and that the killer wrote, 'Allah is great,' on her forehead?"

Conrad opens his mouth to question Jack again, but Jack silences him by continuing his narration.

"We ID'd her as Cherille Jacobs. She lived near the Guggenheim and worked on Park Avenue as a financial advisor. Giancarlo and Gomez are observing the autopsy, and Burley and I are going to check out Park Avenue and her apartment."

"The press is going to have a field day with this one," sighs Conrad. "I'll try to contain as much of it as I can." Distracted by Jack's description of the new case, Conrad starts to turn away, but then stops and looks squarely at Jack. "Is there anything else you want to tell me?"

"Nope," responds Jack with a blank expression. "Maybe later, Boss. After we get back." Rising from his chair, he motions to Burley.

Conrad waits until the two detectives leave the floor, and then bends down to open Jack's drawer. When the drawer won't open, he hears a jangling noise behind him and turns around to see Stenhouse smiling and waving a set of keys at him from inside the elevator.

Rolling his eyes, Conrad gives up and heads for his office.

CHAPTER THIRTY-SIX

Manhattan's clogged arteries are now pulsing with rush-hour traffic, and the blue light on Burley's NYPD sedan does little to help. As Jack maneuvers around the blockages with his good arm, Burley huffs, "You look uncomfortable. Didn't you say you wanted me to drive today?"

"Yeah, but I'm okay right now," answers Jack as he cruises past their destination, looking for a parking spot.

Not finding a spot nearby, Jack abandons the search and pulls onto the sidewalk instead, three feet from the door to Fidelity Investing and Trust Company.

Shutting down the engine, he says to Burley, "Hand me the mic, will ya?" Keying the buttons, he calls Dispatch to notify them of his unique parking spot and then grabs his cell phone to place another call.

"This is Detective Stenhouse with NYPD's First Precinct. Badge number 157," he says into his phone. "This is a Code Orange. I need you to review your tapes of the Verrazzano toll booths after 4 a.m. on the tenth. I'm looking for a newer model silver Porsche Cayenne, plate number AG123LT."

Catching the eye of the puzzled Sergeant, he states, "Just tying a pretty bow across Sarah's ass."

As the men walk toward the building, Jack spies a traffic cop heading their way and flashes his badge. With a nod of her head, she passes them by and continues walking down the street.

Freed from the likelihood of a citation, the pair navigates through a revolving door into a marble foyer with a large mahogany reception desk at the center, an immense crystal chandelier high above, and a marble staircase with a mahogany and gold handrail circling up to offices on the second floor.

"Good morning, gentlemen," announces an attractive, green-eyed blonde from behind the desk. "You seem lost. May I help you?"

Jack's mirrored sunglasses mask his cheating eyes as they wander over all of the woman's good parts. Moving his eyes to her face, he displays his badge and ID and states, "I'm Detective Stenhouse, and this is my partner, Sergeant Burley. We're from the First Precinct. Do you know Cherille Jacobs?"

"Yes, I know Cherille. She didn't come in today. Is everything okay?"

When there is no response from either officer, the blonde asks, "Is there something I can do for you?"

"We need to speak with your manager," says John.

"Okay. I'll get Mr. Leone for you. Please have a seat," replies the woman, pointing to a grouping of leather chairs on one side of the foyer.

Pocketing his sunglasses, Jack leads the way, and the men make themselves comfortable. While they wait, Jack being Jack, uses the time to satisfy his curiosity. Gazing hard at Burley, he blurts out, "So, Johnny boy, how's our new friend, Sylvia?"

John tries to appear nonchalant as he says, "She's doing fine. She's in Boston on another case. Why?"

With a sly smile, Jack replies, "I know you two are doing the horizontal bop, so I thought I'd catch up. Going to Boston, are we?"

John rolls his eyes. "From your lips to God's ears. I hope to go up next weekend, though."

When a silk-suited man walks down the stairs, the detectives turn at his approach.

"Good morning," says the man. "I'm Stephan Leone. How may I help you?"

Jack rises slowly from the thick cushion of his chair. His arm is still stiff, and the stitches tug and pull, restricting his movements.

"We need to talk to the manager about Cherille Jacobs. What is your position here?"

Upset that the officers don't know who he is, Stephan Leone turns to the receptionist with a hard look and then returns his gaze to Stenhouse and Burley. "I'm sorry my receptionist didn't introduce me properly," he says. "I'm the owner and CEO of Fidelity Investing and Trust Company." Puffing out his chest, he purses his lips and tugs at his shirt cuffs to expose expensive diamond and platinum cufflinks. "Please follow me. We can talk in my office."

On the way up the spiral staircase, the officers notice that Stephan Leone repeatedly gazes down at the receptionist in a decidedly unfriendly manner.

At the top of the stairs, they enter Leone's private office, which is larger than the entire Homicide Division squad room at the First. Trying not to let their lack of refinement show, the detectives gape at the striking marble and shale flooring, the custom furniture, and the curved, 65-inch 4K Ultra HD TV hanging above an ornate marble fireplace near a tasteful grouping of plush chairs and elegant tables.

With an attitude that his shit don't stink, the CEO motions to the chairs and bids the men to sit. "I see that you've noticed my furniture," Leone declares with a note of triumph. "Do you recognize it?"

Puzzled, the detectives answer, "No."

Disappointed for the second time, Leone recovers and states proudly, "It's from Casaragi Furniture Company. I'm sure you've heard of them."

Again, they answer, "No."

Still wanting to impress his clearly unsophisticated guests, Stephan adopts an even more superior attitude. "Would you gentlemen like a cup of freshly ground coffee imported from Europe? It's absolutely heavenly. Or perhaps some refreshing sparkling water? I have it bottled specially for me."

Jack clears his throat. "No. Thank you," he says. "We're here to talk about one of your employees. Cherille Jacobs."

"Oh?" responds Leone. "We're wondering what happened to Ms. Jacobs. She didn't report for work this morning. We called her, but there was no answer. Is she all right?"

"She was murdered this morning," replies Jack bluntly. "Actually, she was decapitated. So, no, she is not all right."

Shaken, Stephan Leone closes his eyes and exclaims, "Oh, no! What are our clients going to think?"

"Your clients?!" explodes Jack. "One of your employees has just been killed in a horrific manner, and all you can think about are your clients?!"

Flushed with embarrassment, Leone tries to explain. "No, no, not at all!" he stammers. "Cherille was one of our best advisors! This is tragic! With all the terrorism going on in the world, I'm worried about our clients, that's all. Do you think we're being targeted for some reason?"

Jack is still upset but manages to hold it in this time. "Mr. Leone, I have no idea about your clients," he replies icily. "I'm sure Homeland Security will contact you if there's a problem. Do you know if any of your customers had an issue with Ms. Jacobs, or if she had problems with a family member or a boyfriend?"

"No, I don't know. Come with me to HR," declares Leone, rising from his chair. "Mrs. Wesley can help you with that. I do recall hearing about an incident with Cherille's ex-boyfriend, but I don't know the details. Follow me, please."

Exiting the large office, Stenhouse and Burley once more follow Stephan Leone, who leads them this time down an elegantly decorated hallway to a door marked, 'Human Resources.' Inside the office, he introduces the detectives, explains why they're there, and makes a hasty retreat.

When the human resources manager and her assistant heard about Cherille, they both began to cry, forcing Jack and John to wait while the women attempt to compose themselves.

As they wait, Jack sizes up the manager and guesses that she's in her mid-thirties. However, when he spots a family photo on her desk, he's surprised to see that she's much older. The woman finally speaks when her assistant excuses herself for the ladies' room.

"I'm sorry," Mrs. Wesley says, dabbing at her eyes, "Cherille was a lovely person and a friend to all of us. This is terrible!"

At least someone here gives a shit, muses Jack. "Mrs. Wesley, Mr. Leone said that there was an incident with Ms. Jacobs' boyfriend. Can you elaborate?"

With a deep sigh, the woman looks down at her computer. Several keystrokes later, she says, "Here it is. About two weeks ago, Cherille's ex-boyfriend showed up here, and we had to call the police to have him removed from the premises. Cherille said he changed his religion and that she broke up with him because of it. He said he didn't want her to work in a place like this anymore."

"What did he mean by, 'a place like this'?" asks Burley.

"I don't know," responds Mrs. Wesley with a pained expression. "I never found out."

"Do you have a name for her ex?" asks John.

"Yes, his name is James Booker, but Cherille said he changed his name when he became a Muslim, and I don't know his new name. Cherille took out a restraining order on him because he became violent."

Jack turns to Burley. "Check with the 19th Precinct on that restraining order, and get an address on Booker, or whatever his new name is. Mrs. Wesley, is there anything else you can tell us about Cherille Jacobs or James Booker?"

"Nothing besides standard HR information on Cherille. This is all too terrible! Cherille was a wonderful person! You probably want her parents' address. She talked about them a lot and listed them as her emergency contacts and beneficiaries. They live in Ridgewood, New Jersey. Her father is chief oncologist at Sloan Kettering Cancer Center in Montvale, and she was very proud of him. I'll print their address out for you."

Stenhouse and Burley thank the woman for her cooperation. As they walk back down the hallway, they overhear Stephan Leone chastising his receptionist behind his ornate mahogany office door.

"What an ass," mutters Jack.

On the way to Cherille's apartment on East 88th Street, Burley contacts the 19th Precinct about the restraining order she placed on her boyfriend, and at a stop light, Jack calls Detective Giancarlo.

"Here's the number for Cherille's parents," Jack says to Allison, hanging up quickly so she won't have a chance to object. Jack is more than happy to pass the task of informing the next of kin onto someone else. It's one part of the job that he absolutely hates.

Not surprisingly, there is no place to park on the street in front of Cherille's apartment building, so Jack double-parks and calls for a patrol car to cover him.

In the building's small lobby, John presses the buzzer next to the manager's name and identifies himself and Jack through the intercom. Once they're buzzed in, they wait for the manager to join them.

CHAPTER THIRTY-SEVEN

Jack opens the door to Cherille's apartment with the key supplied by the manager and pushes past Burley, wincing as his ribs register their protest.

Sweeping through the apartment, the pair looks at and in everything.

In the bedroom, Burley opens drawers and moves clothing around. "Hey, I think I found something," he says. "It's a tee shirt from Greenwich Street Tavern. That's the one near the park. Maybe she was there last night."

Jack grunts his agreement and grabs a photo frame from Cherille's nightstand. Turning it over, he removes the picture and places it into his jacket pocket.

"Come on," he announces. "I don't see anything here. Let's head down to that tavern to ask some questions."

In the lobby, Jack hands the apartment key back to the building manager and thanks him for his cooperation.

When they arrive at the tavern, Jack unexpectedly slides into a vacant parking spot directly in front of the establishment. "Whoa," he says appreciatively. "It's about 'effin' time I found a good parking spot that I don't have to make myself!"

Greenwich Street Tavern is a sports bar stylized like a classic English pub. Wooden floors creak under the detectives' feet as they move past tables and chairs under framed sports memorabilia and photographs of London. The cops take in the typical tavern scents of beer and cleaning agents as they head toward the back of the establishment.

"Sorry guys, we don't open till noon," calls the bartender.

Approaching the bar, the men see a tall Adonis with blonde hair and green eyes looking back at them. Jack reflects, *This guy looks like a typical bartender. Wonder if he even knows how to make a drink.* Flashing his ID, he asks, "Hey, how ya doin'? I'm Detective Stenhouse, and my associate here is Sergeant Burley," he nods to John. "We want to ask you a few questions."

"Sure, whaddya need?" the Adonis replies, putting down the rag he was using to clean the bar.

Jack reaches into his pocket and removes the photo he took from Cherille's bedroom. "Was this woman here last night?"

"Yeah, that's Cherille," says the barkeep after a quick glance. "She's one of our regulars. She was here, got stinkin' drunk, and left with a guy who offered her a ride."

"Do you know her well?"

"Well enough. She comes in a lot."

"So, is it normal for her to leave with a stranger?"

"No, but she's been getting drunk a lot lately. Another guy was in that booth in the corner, and he was watching her all night. Seemed odd. When she left, he got up and followed the two of them out."

"Can you give us descriptions of both men?"

"Well, the one who followed them out was average height, about five-nine. He was black and had a beard."

"What was he wearing?"

"I think it was one of those colorful shirts; those traditional African prints. He didn't drink anything but club soda all night."

"What about the guy who gave her a lift?"

"Neat clothes, average build, also black. What's this about?"

"Cherille was murdered last night," responds Burley. "She was found in Saint John's Park, decapitated."

The bartender's eyes open wide and he leans back on the edge of the rear counter in shock.

"Holy crap!" he exclaims. "You mean the guy who picked her up, killed her?"

"Could be," answers Jack. "Or it could have been the one who followed them out. Do you know the guy who picked her up?"

Frowning, the bartender thinks for a while, and then a lightbulb goes off in his head. "I don't think he's been here before, but I got a credit card from him. Hold on; I'll get it from the office."

Jack looks around, scanning the empty tavern.

"Why haven't I ever tried this place before?" he mutters.

"If you like fish and chips, theirs are the best," states Burley.

Minutes later, the bartender returns with a name and credit card number. Jack tips the man an imaginary hat and smiles his thanks.

Back in the police cruiser, Jack issues a new order to Burley. "When we get back to the First, find out what you can on the guy who picked up Cherille." Then, with his foot on the brake, he steps on the gas, revs the engine, and releases the brake, causing the police-issued sedan to lurch away from the curb with its tires squealing so loudly that they drown out the sound of the horn's two quick beeps, Jack's signature move.

Jack looks over at Burley. Missing his beloved Road Runner, he says sadly, "It's not the same in this thing, bro. It's not the same at all."

Back at the station, Jack receives a call from Allison. "We talked to Cherille Jacobs' father," she says. "You owe us big time."

Detective Giancarlo and Sergeant Gomez are on their way out of Sloan Kettering after breaking the news of Cherille's death to her father, Dr. Sam Jacobs.

"Thanks," says Jack. "I'll buy you guys steak dinners."

"You know I'm going to hold you to that, don't you?" responds Allison.

"No prob."

"Where are you now?"

"We're at the station. When you get back into the city, I need you to stop at the 19th Precinct to request a copy of a restraining order Cherille placed on her ex-boyfriend, James Booker. He changed his name and his religion and is now a Muslim, but we don't know what he calls himself now. Also, do an online check on this guy, you know, Facebook, Twitter, and the rest. And get his address. Call me back when you know where he lives; we'll meet you there. Also try to find out which mosque he attends."

When the call ends, Jack turns to Burley. "Looks like I'm buyin' steak dinners. You want in? You can bring your main squeeze."

John raises his brows in surprise. "Steak for everyone? Did you win the lottery or something?"

Later, Burley checks leads and tries to get an address on the guy who hooked up with Ms. Jacobs at the bar, while Giancarlo and Gomez analyze the information they've compiled so far.

Deep in thought, Jack stands in front of the whiteboard from the Cummings case, trying to make sense of the data. He doesn't hear Giancarlo walking up behind him, so when he doesn't react to Giancarlo's presence, she taps him on the shoulder. "Earth to Stenhouse. Are you there?"

Startled, Jack turns sharply and is rewarded by a wave of pain from his damaged ribcage. "Yeah?" he asks gruffly. "Whaddya want?"

Seeing Jack's grimace, Allison is concerned that her partner may not be able to keep up if he's still hurting. Staring into his deep gray eyes, she asks, "You okay, Jack? We need to concentrate on the Jacobs case now. Conrad wants to know when you're going to clean that board off."

"Gotta wrap this case up properly before I do that. Don't worry; I'll handle the boss. What's the skinny on Booker?"

Referring to her notes, she says, "Booker's new name is Amiz Shabaz. His Facebook page is full of ISIS crap, and Homeland Security already has a file on him. He lives a couple of blocks away from Cherille. He was working in an ad agency on Park Avenue, but he quit about six months ago. That was about the time he started to get into Islam. Homeland Security says Shabaz is a member of a mosque on East 78th that's headed by the Imam who wanted to build a minaret for his group near the Twin Towers. When the Imam was denied the Twin Towers location, he took over an old warehouse near the East River instead."

"Good job. Let's get over to that mosque for afternoon prayers. Then, we can go…"

"Hold off, Jack," orders Conrad firmly. "I need to see all of you in my office."

Surprised by Conrad's stiff demeanor and the

four gray suits accompanying him, the officers follow their boss and his companions.

When everyone is inside Conrad's office, he closes the door with a scowl that rises unbidden every time he sees the temporary wooden panel replacing its busted glass. Resisting the urge to berate Jack once again for his temper tantrum, he orders Sergeant Gomez to close all the blinds, citing a need for privacy.

Gomez taps Burley on the shoulder to ask for his assistance, and within seconds, the group is shielded from outside view.

"All right," begins the Lieutenant, "I called you guys in here at the request of these men from Homeland Security and the FBI. Both agencies have been monitoring your guy, Amiz Shabaz, and the Manhattan Islamic Center he's been attending for a while now. Imam Khobani, the center's leader, is also under investigation. They think he's radicalizing some of his members, and they're preparing to raid the mosque today."

Conrad stops and gestures toward one of the gray suits. With an almost imperceptible nod, the suit picks up the narration. "I'm Agent Ken Watts from Homeland Security. We've been monitoring Mr. Shabaz's phone calls and discovered that he's in contact with local radicals and overseas agents of ISIS that both we and the FBI have been tracking." Reaching into a pocket, he produces a photograph of Amiz. "This is Shabaz, and he's currently at his condo. If you go there now, you can arrest him on any charge you like, but we'll take control of him after he's booked. We have a man on the inside who says he's a key witness to what's going on in that mosque. We plan to file federal charges against Amiz, and he'll be prosecuted to the full extent of the law. But we need to get access to him first."

Knowing full well what could happen if the federal government gets its claws on the suspect in their latest case, Stenhouse blows his top. "Bullshit!" he yells. "We have good reason to believe that this guy decapitated a young woman! If he cooperates with you, he won't be held accountable for a heinous murder! You'll let him plead out on the murder charge because you want him for something else! This is FUBAR!"

Conrad stares at Stenhouse angrily in a silent order to get himself under control. Then, in no-nonsense terms, he declares, "NYPD *will* work together with our federal partners on this case, Jack. After this meeting, go to Shabaz's condo. If you find hard evidence that he's responsible for Jacobs' death, arrest him. The FBI will take over after that. These gentlemen will go with you to back your team up." Conrad knows that Jack isn't going to take this order without protest, so he adds hastily, "Go now, Jack. No more talk, and no more resistance. We're all on the same side here. Just get it done. Understand?"

Jack peers at Conrad like a sniper zeroing in on his target but he dutifully grabs the photo of Shabaz. "Yes, SIR!" he growls, "But it's still bullshit!"

Before Jack can storm out of the office, Conrad stops him. "I have something for you." Holding out a folded piece of paper, he explains, "It's the bill for the glass panel. Cash only; no checks, please."

Jack takes the invoice and snarls, "Just be thankful your damn door is already broken." Then, he stomps out of the door.

When Jack is about ten feet down the hallway, he turns around and shouts loud enough to be heard back in Conrad's office.

"What the fuck you all waiting for, a formal invitation? I'm getting this asshole, and if he resists, I'll kill the bastard! If you want this guy alive, you better come along!"

While the others in Conrad's office confer on last-minute instructions, Jack marches to the elevator and enters the car alone. Turning around, he gives them all the bird as they try to catch up to the closing doors.

Not wanting to waste time with the elevator, Giancarlo heads toward the stairs, followed by the agents.

"He wouldn't kill him, would he?" asks one of them as they race down the steps.

"Well, if he doesn't, I will," she responds.

Rushing to catch up, the group takes the stairs two at a time. When they finally emerge onto East 67th Street, they find Jack leaning casually against the front of an unmarked police sedan.

"Took you long enough," he complains. "Let's roll."

CHAPTER THIRTY-EIGHT

Accompanied by officers from the 19th Precinct, a convoy of unmarked police sedans heads across town to the apartment building where Amiz Shabaz has been living a quiet and so far unremarkable life.

The tight convoy arrives on one-way street, East 80th Street, looking like something the White House or a high-ranking diplomat would dispatch. With help from the 19th Precinct, Jack, Gomez, and two Homeland Security officers block the street off at Second Avenue, while Allison, Burley, and the FBI do the same at the other end of the block.

When the road is sealed off from further vehicular traffic, Jack and his team thread their way toward Shabaz's apartment building through a crowd of curious onlookers. Held at bay across the street, the bystanders use their cell phones to record what they're seeing, effectively becoming unofficial paparazzi for this operation.

As they walk through the crowd, Jack spies a young woman snapping his photo. Grabbing Gomez by the shoulder, he whispers, "Follow my lead." Unsure of what Jack is up to, Gomez trails him as he strolls over to the woman.

Placing his uninjured arm around the woman's

back, Jack motions for Gomez to do the same on her other side. "Take a selfie, Babe," Jack smiles to the woman. When the shutter clicks, Jack gives the woman a wink and walks away.

As luck would have it, just as the pair reaches the building's entrance, Amiz emerges into the sunlight in jeans, a black dashiki, and a black skullcap. Jack walks up to him, displaying his badge in an outstretched hand.

Spooked by the two officers and the rest of the scene around him, Amiz pushes Jack aside, causing him to crumple to the pavement. When Jack falls, Amiz capitalizes on his challenger's immobility. Turning quickly, he runs down a nearby alley toward 81st Street, with Giancarlo right behind him, yelling for him to stop. Spurred into action, Gomez and Burley separate and sprint toward patrol cars parked at both ends of the block, hoping to cut Amiz off when he exits the alleyway on the next street.

In front of the building, Jack remains on the pavement clutching his side, waiting for the pain to subside.

Racing toward the suspect in the narrow concrete passageway between neighboring buildings, Allison expertly dodges parked cars and dumpsters as she closes in on her prey.

Fearful that he'll be caught, Amiz unwisely focuses his attention on the officer behind him, noticing too late that Sergeant Burley and several FBI agents are approaching him from the other end of the alley. Unable to stop, he runs directly into Burley, who grabs him and knocks him to the ground. When Aziz can't get away, Burley picks him up from the asphalt and slams him against the concrete canyon wall to cuff him.

"Going out for a morning jog?" asks Burley. "Come on; let's go have a nice chat about Cherille Jacobs."

With Amid laughing carelessly, Burley escorts him back to his apartment building.

On his feet again and sore as hell, Jack stares angrily at the cuffed man.

"Well, now," he says menacingly, "it looks like you assaulted a police officer. Let's go upstairs to your place where we can talk in private."

Joined by a couple of FBI agents, Jack and his team escort Amiz up to his small, three-room apartment.

Inside the unit, the officers shudder at the disgusting living conditions they see in every room: roaches crawling over dirty dishes filled with decaying food, dozens of empty fast food bags, and dirt and grime everywhere. Moreover, as if to confirm their suspicions, tacked onto every available wall space are propaganda flyers and computer-printed images of past ISIS acts of terrorism.

Trying not to inhale the awful stench from the rotting food and who knows what else, Burley pushes Amiz onto a small sofa while Jack, still smarting from his brush with the suspect, ducks into the apartment's single bedroom.

Scowling at a large black ISIS flag tacked above

the bed, Jack marches toward a closet and pokes his head inside. Spotting a duffel bag partially obscured by a pile of clothes, he drags it out into the living room and opens it in front of Amiz. Inside are a large, blood-stained carving knife and some blood-stained clothing. Jack looks up at Amiz for an explanation.

"She was a Nazarene whore who deserved death!" Amiz boasts proudly. "*Allahu Akbar!*"

Disgusted, Giancarlo recites the Miranda warning. When she's finished, an FBI agent declares, "Looks like you got your killer, Detectives. We'll follow you to Central Booking and take over from there. Homeland Security will search the rest of the apartment. Thanks for your help."

"That's it?" exclaims Jack, troubled by the lack of inter-agency cooperation. "You take our killer, and we just walk away? Like I said before, this is Fubar!"

Not one to back down without a fight, Jack turns his attention to Shabaz, still seated on the sofa. Placing his thumb under the man's lower jaw, he pushes upward, forcing Shabaz to rise to ease the pain from Jack's thumb on his pressure point.

With Shabaz' face contorting in pain, Jack stands eyeball to eyeball with the bearded radical. "Make no mistake," he growls. "there will be no virgins waiting for you when you die, but as long as you're still on this planet, I'll be around," he sneers, pushing hard against Shabaz' chest and forcing him to fall back onto the sofa. Turning around, Jack stomps out of the apartment, ignoring critical looks from the FBI agents.

Understanding how Jack's mind works, the team

knows that he probably won't be coming back, so Gomez scrambles to follow him while Giancarlo grabs the duffel bag, and Burley directs the arrestee toward the door.

Behind them, the FBI agents lock the apartment and rush to catch up, again.

Alone with Gomez in the elevator, Jack mutters, "If I were in better shape, I'd have beat the shit out of him."

"You must be mellowing in your old age," smirks Gomez as Jack rotates his arm and shoulder. "I figured you'd just shoot his ass."

Jack balls his fists in frustration. "Fuck it all!" he shouts. "I need a beer! Giancarlo and Burley can take care of the paperwork bullshit!"

In the lobby, Jack and Hector wait impatiently for the rest of the group to emerge from the elevator. When Jack sees Amiz, he stares at him with his famous sniper squint.

"Ally," Jack orders, "bring this guy to the station and handle the paperwork with Booking and the Feds, okay? Gomez and I will write our fucking reports later. I'm getting a burger and a beer—or two."

As he passes Amiz, Jack leans in close. "Watch your back, prick," he hisses. "If the Feds let you go, I'll be right there around every corner, waiting to end this properly."

Amiz stares at Jack uneasily as he walks away. Out of view of the agents, Jack turns around and points his hand back at Amiz, mimicking a gun.

Outside, in the sunlight of the Big Apple, Jack slips into the patrol car he arrived in and starts her up. Not waiting for Gomez to fasten his seatbelt, Jack gives his trademark two quick beeps and squeals down Second Avenue.

"It's not the same," he says wistfully. "Not the same at all. This thing is slow as shit."

CHAPTER THIRTY-NINE

"How are you doing?" asks Hector.

Before answering, Jack takes a sip of Guinness to wash down a large chunk of bacon cheeseburger. "Still sore. And that asshole didn't help," he replies. "Gotta go for therapy for my arm. How are the fish and chips?"

"Damn good. Why can't all of our cases be this easy? And speaking of that, what the hell is going on with you and the Cummings murder?"

With a sly grin, Jack pops the final piece of burger into his mouth. "My pal Joe is checking on a couple of things for me."

"Yeah? Like what?"

"It's that Bills jersey. It just keeps bugging me. Stan grew up in Queens Village, so it's doubtful that he was a Bill's fan, but Sarah was wearing one in that photograph. I want to check the photos on the flash drive that Giancarlo got from Ladder 403. I hope there's proof on it that O'Toole didn't do it."

Gomez shoves the rest of his fries into his mouth and grabs the check. "My treat," he declares. "You still have to buy me a large steak, though." While he lays some cash onto the table, he adds, "It's getting late, and we got a shitload of paperwork to do. Oh, by the way, if you need a couple of bucks to pay for Conrad's door, I'll help you out."

"I got it," says Jack. "It was totally worth it."

As they exit the tavern, the Adonis behind the bar waves in their direction.

Across town, Sam Lincoln grabs the bags he packed in preparation for fleeing the city on an "extended" vacation, and exhales to calm his racing heart. Opening the front door for a quick getaway, his way is blocked by two large men in tailored silk suits. Staring at the closest of the two, a man with a broad, square jaw and a broken nose, Lincoln gasps as the man discloses his destiny.

"Mr. Lucchese wants to speak with you."

Instantly, an enormous hand grabs Lincoln by the throat and squeezes tightly. The last things Sam remembers seeing are the broken nose and a fist heading for his face.

Although Giancarlo and Burley finalized their reports on the Shabaz arrest an hour ago, they are still at the station when Stenhouse and Gomez return.

"What happened at Booking?" Jack asks.

"Reps from the D.A. were there," replies Allison, "but the FBI and Homeland Security were scurrying around the place like roaches in Amiz's kitchen. They took hold of Amiz as soon as we got there and whisked him away." Glancing down at her watch, Allison says, "Right about now, they should be all over that mosque like flies on shit. I bet it'll be on tonight's news." Spinning her chair around, Allison faces her partner. "You looked like death warmed over earlier today."

"I'll live," Jack says. "Just a little sore."

Bending down, Jack unlocks his lower desk drawer and pulls out the large organizer on the Cummings case. Fishing around inside, he finds the flash drive containing the firehouse photos, and with a well-aimed throw, tosses it at Giancarlo, who catches it in both hands.

"Can you plug that thing into your laptop?" Jack asks. "I gotta check some photos."

Giancarlo opens the drive with a few clicks of her mouse. "Here it is," she calls. "Wanna see?"

When Jack joins her, Allison vacates her chair so Jack can sit in front of the computer.

Scrolling slowly, Jack reads through the directories list until he comes to one labeled "Jet's Game." Opening it, he finds what he's looking for and points at the screen. "Do me a favor and print these two photos, then put them into the Cummings file with the drive and lock it all up again in my desk. Here's an extra key; give it back to me in the morning. I'm late for my physical therapy appointment."

"Is that appointment with your therapist, or with Didi?" asks Burley with a puckish grin from a few desks away. "And how the hell are you going to get there, anyway?"

Jack chuckles. "I have an appointment with both of them today, if you must know. I'm gonna take one of those official POS sedans again. Oh, say hello to Stone for me, okay?" he tosses over his shoulder on his way out.

Giancarlo turns back to her screen and grins as she looks at the two photos Jack pointed out. "Jack's got a new suspect," she singsongs to a popular childhood taunt. "This is getting interesting!"

At Ristorante di Cosenza, Michael Lucchese, Vito's son and heir to his father's empire, glares at two of his father's soldiers.

"Take that piece of shit's body to the runway expansion at LaGuardia and dump it there," he orders, dismissing the soldiers with a wave of his hand.

As the men depart, Michael lifts a sheet of paper from the table. "This is a bank account in the Cayman Islands," he says to his father's consigliere, who has been waiting patiently in a nearby chair. "Get our fucking money back and put it in there."

When the advisor leaves to carry out his boss's command, a waiter inches over to the table.

"I'll have the lamb shank and a Peroni," the young mobster states casually.

Seated in her office at the boutique, Didi is counting the receipts for the day while Sonia is in a room at the rear of the store, instructing a pole dancing class. The boutique closes at five, but the popular class ends at seven.

Even though the front door is locked and there are people in the rear studio, Didi doesn't like being alone in the office when the store is closed. Jack was supposed to be there at five, so when the clock shows six, she begins to get anxious.

At the sound of the front door rattling, Didi jerks her head up and tenses. When the noise continues, she reaches in a drawer for her .380 semi-automatic handgun and rises from her chair. Holding the gun at her side, she places her forefinger above the trigger guard and pokes her head around the office door. Seeing no one in the short hallway, she inches her way slowly down the corridor to the front of the store. When the rattling becomes louder, she stops and takes a deep breath. With her heart beating wildly in her chest, she peers around the corner.

Standing outside the door is Jack, looking down at his cell phone.

Breathing a sigh of relief, Didi drops the arm holding her gun and walks toward Jack as she listens to her cell phone ringing at her desk.

Watching Didi come toward him, Jack stares with surprise at the .380 in her hand. When she unlocks the door, he enters with his hands raised.

"Damn, woman! I know I'm late, but what the hell? Ya gonna frisk me, Doll?"

With equal amounts of exasperation and reassurance, Didi locks the door again and shouts, "You scared the SHIT out of me, Jack!"

Reaching out, Jack hugs his wife with his unimpaired arm and kisses her on the cheek.

"Sorry, Babe; I was running late. Guess I should have called first." Glancing down at her large abdomen, he asks, "How are we feeling today?"

"Bloated, Jack. Just look at my stomach! I can barely button my slacks!"

"To me, you're as beautiful as ever, and you'll become even more dazzling with every pregnant day. Oh, by the way, I need two hundred bucks. I sorta busted a window."

Folding her arms in front of her chest, Didi knits her brows together in a scowl.

"Slammed another glass door?" she asks disapprovingly. Shaking her head with irritation, she walks back to her office, with Jack following. At her desk, she grabs the night deposit bag and gives him his money.

"I hope you enjoyed it, Jack, but you really need to ease up on that temper! We need to hang onto all the money we can get. We're going to have a baby!"

"Yeah, I know," replies Jack, properly chastened.

Sighing, Didi asks, "How did the therapy go?"

"Not bad, Dee. Not as much pain today. They called the surgeon and recommended that my stitches be removed sooner than planned. They say I'm healing well. The doc wants to see me tomorrow, so maybe he'll take the stitches out. It's just my damn ribs now;

they're still really sore. But that's enough about me." Hugging Didi, he says, "You'll always be my beauty, you know."

"Yeah? We'll see if you still think I'm beautiful six months from now," retorts Jack's tired wife. Grabbing the night deposit bag, she says, "There's a fried chicken place next to the bank. We can stop there for dinner."

"No pickles and ice cream, or any other weird cravings?"

Didi leans in and murmurs in Jack's ear, making his eyes go wide.

"Damn, woman!" he exclaims. "We'll have to stop and get us some whipped cream, then!"

With a sly smile, Didi heads for the door as Jack smacks her on the ass.

The class is just ending in the workout room, so Didi asks Sonia to lock up for the night. The couple leaves the boutique with Didi driving the Road Runner, and Jack following in the police cruiser.

Back at the First, Joe Ellison is still hard at work, even though it's well past quitting time. He has checked the fingerprints and DNA specimens found in Cummings' place, the van, and the dirty laundry.

After analyzing the data, he reaches a conclusion and sits back in his chair.

"Jack was right," he mumbles. "This is sure to hit

the fan!"

As Joe begins to prepare a report on his findings for Stenhouse, he glances at the clock on the wall and grimaces when he sees that it's already nine-thirty.

"Shit," he grouses, "time flies when you're having fun."

Most of the construction to lengthen LaGuardia's runway number 04/22 is scheduled to occur at night and in the wee morning hours. The work is progressing smoothly. The new section now extends past Rikers Island in New York's East River, the site of the famous prison.

In the course of the new construction, workers dump giant granite boulders into the river from a dredging barge to provide a firm foundation for the expanded airstrip.

Just after 1 a.m., a black Cadillac DTS enters the construction site and heads toward the end of the new strip. When it reaches the farthest point it can safely travel, the president of the construction company exits the vehicle with the union rep, and both men walk to the edge of the river.

Noticing the visitors, the site manager hurries over.

"Good evening, Mr. Donnati. What brings you way out here?" he asks warily.

Shivering from the cold, the executive states, "We got complaints from the union about working conditions on the runway and the barge. Get your men out of here while we inspect the area. Give them a twenty-minute break and get me the motorboat."

The site manager is surprised by allegations that he is not running a solid operation, but he quickly snaps to.

"Yes, sir. Right away, Mr. Donnati." Turning around, he runs to his pickup to grab a bullhorn from the truck's bed. Then he runs over to a small hut and hits a siren.

"Break off, break off!" he yells into the megaphone. "Twenty minutes all clear! We got visitors!"

At the sounds, all work stops, and the crewmen walk away from the job site without comment. Stoppages have happened before, so they are accustomed to being interrupted.

A few minutes later, a motorized boat pulls up to the temporary dock constructed at the tip of the runway extension.

"Go out to the barge and bring the men back," Donnati orders the boat's pilot. "After you dock, take a walk."

Without hesitation, the pilot points the boat in the direction of the barge, leaving the company exec, the union rep, and the site manager staring across the water at the lights of Manhattan. The night is cold, the air is sharp, and the men are silent as they watch the city's lights shimmer and dance in the distance.

Ten minutes later, the president and the union rep are alone with the empty boat bobbing up and down at its moorings.

Turning around, Donnati motions to two men who have been sitting in the back of the Caddy. Obeying their boss' prior orders, they exit the vehicle, walk to the rear, and open the trunk. Reaching in, they work together to lift out an oversized leather bag. Grunting, they carry the heavy load between them to the temporary dock, where they drop it into the waiting boat and climb in after it. Soon, the boat disappears into blackness.

Maneuvering around the barge, they tie up alongside the section containing the boulders that will be dumped into the river. Out of sight of land, they struggle to send their bag over the boat's side, adding their gift to the runway's foundation.

When Donnati sees them returning to the dock, he dials a number on his cell phone. Across the city, another phone rings at Ristorante di Cosenza.

"It's done," says the company man. "Your package has been delivered."

CHAPTER FORTY

"Good God, look how much bigger they are! Guess I'll have to change my name to Didi-di." Wearing only a bra and panties, Didi stares with unbelief at her profile in the mirror of the master bathroom.

Laughing at Didi's comment, Jack tries to protect his bandages with a plastic bag while he rinses off in the shower. "Whoever said that more than a mouthful is wasteful?" he chuckles through the shower door.

When he's finished rinsing off, he wraps a towel around his waist and exits the stall to see his pregnant wife still contemplating the changes in her body. "You look great!" he says to his extra-buxom wife.

Didi is secretly pleased by Jack's compliment but she still smacks his ass in mock irritation as she leaves the bathroom. "I'll start breakfast," she calls out. "One egg or two?"

"Two, Babe, and lots of bacon."

In the bedroom, Jack notices the time when he picks up his watch.

"Hey, Dee! Hold off on that breakfast! It's getting late, and we need to go! Help me wrap my ribcage, will ya? We'll have to grab something at the donut shop on the way." Jack isn't happy when he can't care for himself, but he doesn't mind occasionally asking his wife for help.

After getting the bandages on, Didi helps Jack don a pair of black slacks and a black pullover, then assists him with his shoulder holster. When he's fully dressed, he grabs his Glock and holsters it.

While Didi is in the bathroom putting on her makeup, Jack removes his compact Kel-Tec firearm from the night table and attempts to wrap it around his ankle. He is dismayed when he realizes that he needs help with that, too.

With a sigh, he takes his tan blazer out of the closet and walks into the living room with the Kel-Tec to wait for Didi.

Just as he's about to switch on the TV, Didi enters the room dressed in slacks and a white blouse that's straining to stay closed.

"I need some new clothes," she groans. "I'm already busting out of these."

"Anything for my little mommy," Jack says as he watches Didi lower herself as best she can to help her hubby with his ankle holster.

Jack's left arm is pretty loose today; the therapy seems to be working. Although the stitches tug a bit, he can steer well with his left hand.

Jack is happy to be back in his beloved Road Runner. As he pulls out of the apartment's parking garage, he sets the car's tires on fire, and oh, yeah, gives two quick beeps of the horn, a tradition that goes back to his days with the Fort Lauderdale Police Department.

After he drops Didi off at the boutique, he sets off on his drive across town to the station. Although he knows that rush-hour traffic will be bad at this time of day, he still can't get used to how it clogs the city's streets like unhealthy arteries after years of chicken-fried bacon.

One frustrating hour later, Jack finally arrives at his desk with donut crumbs on his slacks and a cold cup of coffee in his hand. When Lieutenant Conrad catches sight of him, he yells, "Stenhouse! My office!"

Jack knows he's late—again. Throwing out the remainder of his coffee, he checks in with his boss.

"Sorry, Lieutenant. Bad traffic," he explains, hoping to stave off a rebuke. "Here are the keys to the police sedan. It's parked at my place."

"Okay," says Conrad, taking the keys and dismissing Jack's explanation. "Have a seat. I got some news on the Jacobs case."

Conrad closes the door and sits behind his desk. "Burley talked to the sleazebag who picked the victim up at the bar. His name is Cliff Hunt. He confessed to slipping a roofie into her drink and leading her outta there, propped up on his arm. He said he drove near the park and parked in a dark spot. He forced himself on her in the car and pushed her out when he was done. He said he didn't see her after that and figures that she must have stumbled her way into the park. I don't know how she made it through the traffic that whizzes around there."

"So this Hunt guy didn't kill her?" Jack asks.

"No. Turns out that Shabaz was also pretty talkative. He said he followed the two of them and watched her enter the park. It seems he had been following Cherille around for days. Said he was waiting for the right time to get back at her for dissing him. Shabaz caught up with her in the park and killed her. We confirmed that the blood on his clothing belongs to Cherille. And if that isn't bad enough, he boasted that he had sex with her headless body."

"Holy crap!" mutters Jack.

"Yeah, he's a real peach. The Feds raided the mosque yesterday and got a cache of weapons and ISIS propaganda stuff. Good job on that one, Jack."

"Thanks. I'm still not happy about the Feds taking over, though."

"I know. So, how's Didi doing with her morning sickness?"

"Fine, I guess. I'm keeping the Beeman's gum company afloat."

Conrad smiles at the reminder of when his own wife was pregnant. "Look," he says. "I need you to do whatever you have to so you can get here on time every day. It's not good that you saunter in after everyone else. Now get out of my office and finish some of that paperwork that's piling up on your desk. Oh, and don't forget; you owe me money for the door."

"Oh, yeah," says Jack. Reaching into his jacket, he takes out a sealed envelope. "Here. This is for the glass, and I have to say, it was worth every penny." Rising hastily, he rushes out of the office before Conrad can lay into him.

Delighted that he got in another jibe at his boss, Jack is in a good mood as he strolls past Giancarlo. Tapping on her desk to get her attention, he says, "Going downstairs to see Joe. Be right back."

In the Forensics department, Jack greets the tech as he peers into a microscope.

"Hey, Ellison. Got anything for me?"

Rising from the lab table, Joe stretches and yawns, then motions Jack to his desk.

"You look awful," says Jack with characteristic brusqueness. "What's up with you?"

Joe peers steadily at Jack over his wire-rimmed glasses. "Didn't get much sleep last night, courtesy of you," he replies. Then, he tosses Jack a folder. "Here ya go," he proclaims with a flourish. "You were right-on. I found fingerprints on the laundry basket and the radio knobs of the van, and I cross-checked them with our systems. They all belong to Sarah Cummings. I found hair inside that Bill's jersey, too. It belongs to a blonde female, and my guess is that Sarah Cummings is that female. More complete tests will take a while, but it looks like she was there, Jack."

Jack smiles widely. "Thanks a bunch! I owe you a nice steak dinner!"

Rushing back up to Homicide with the file clutched tightly in his hand, Jack ponders the shitload of steak dinners he's promised to a lot of people lately.

Grabbing the Cummings file from his desk, he

shouts to Giancarlo, Burley, and Gomez, "I got her! Sarah killed her husband! I'm gonna go talk to the boss!"

Waving both files, Jack barges into Conrad's office without knocking.

"I got some info that you need to share with the D.A., ASAP!" he declares brightly.

Caught on the phone again, Conrad holds his hand over the mouthpiece.

"Dammit, Stenhouse!" he growls quietly. Turning back to the phone, he says, "Sorry about that, Commissioner. Thank you. Yes, I'll call you back."

Frowning, Conrad hangs up the phone and scowls at his subordinate. "That was the Commissioner, Detective! You better have a good reason for interrupting that call!"

"Yeah, I do!" Jack insists. "You know I had a gut feeling that O'Toole didn't kill Cummings, right? Well, I did some checking after I saw a photo of Sarah Cummings wearing a Buffalo Bills jersey. Sarah was from Tonawanda, a suburb of Buffalo, and she was a Bills fan. She met Stanley at NYU, but he liked the Jets and wouldn't be caught dead wearing the Bills." Conrad exhales wearily and motions for Jack to get to the point. "I had Forensics check the Bills jersey we found at Stan's house. They found strands of hair from a blonde female, and they're trying to match them to Sarah as we speak. Also, Sarah's fingerprints were found on the laundry basket and inside the van."

"Okay, sounds good so far," says Conrad hesitantly.

"That's not all," says Jack. "They also studied the CCTV tapes from the Memorial the night Cummings showed up. They identified the plate from the black van that pulled up to the area and were able to get a partial image of the driver. It was a blonde female. I had the Port Authority check the videos from the Verrazzano toll booths that same night, and they show Sarah's car crossing over from Staten Island. She would have had to use the bridge if she was driving home from Hammonton."

Lieutenant Conrad seems surprised by the amount of evidence Jack turned up after he pulled his team off the case. "This is great work, Jack," he admits begrudgingly. "I'm glad I let you have extra time."

Excited by his discoveries, Jack disregards the backhanded compliment and keeps talking. "You need to get the D.A. to re-open the case. Sarah Cummings poisoned her husband and dumped him off at the Memorial."

Handing the Forensics file to his boss, Jack watches as he leafs through the new evidence. "Okay," Conrad says. "I'll call him and get back to you. Be prepared to make another trip out to the Island."

When Jack steps out of the office, Sergeants Burley and Gomez surround him and steer him toward Giancarlo's desk.

"Okay, spill it!" they demand.

"I had Ellison in Forensics do more checking. It turns out that Sarah killed her husband, not O'Toole. Blonde hairs are on the Bills jersey we found at Stan's hideaway, and her prints are inside the van. A blond was driving the van that dumped Cummings off at the Memorial, and Sarah's car is on Transportation Department footage heading toward Long Island on the Verrazzano-Narrows Bridge." He looks at Giancarlo. "The pictures you got from the firehouse nailed it. Stan's wearing a Jet's Jersey, and he's standing next to Sarah, who's wearing a Bill's jersey. It's the same one that was in the laundry basket."

Giancarlo's brows knit together in a frown. "So, what the hell is the D.A. gonna do now?"

"I don't know," says Jack as he walks over to the whiteboard and draws an arrow pointing to Sarah's photo. "Conrad's going to call him."

When Hector hears the phone ringing at his desk, he leaves the group to answer it. A short time later, he returns, waving a piece of paper to get his colleagues' attention.

"Hey, I just got a call. We got another dead body. This one's in front of Goldman Sachs. It looks like a guy either jumped off the roof or was pushed."

"You and Burley handle it," orders Jack. "I have a feeling that Giancarlo and I will be busy this morning."

A short time later, Lieutenant Conrad opens his office door and calls to Jack. "The warrant will be ready in an hour!" he says. "I also contacted Nassau County Police!"

CHAPTER FORTY-ONE

At 9:20 that morning, Jack is on his third cup of coffee when he's joined at his desk by Lieutenant Conrad and an older woman. When Allison sees the lieutenant, she walks over to hear what he has to say.

"The Nassau County guys picked up Mrs. Cummings," Conrad states. "She's in their lockup facility in Mineola." Nodding to the woman at his side, he introduces her as Alice Harden from the D.A.'s office. "Alice has all the transfer paperwork, and she'll accompany you and Giancarlo to pick Sarah up. Good work, Jack," he adds grudgingly. "Don't fuck up this transfer."

Jack rises from his chair with a half-smile that masks his ire at the suggestion that he had anything to do with O'Toole's botched transfer.

"Let's go get our bad guy...uh...gal."

"Yes, let's go!" agrees Alice Harden excitedly. "I heard that you drive a '68 Road Runner! It's been a long time since I was in a muscle car. My high school boyfriend had a blue Road Runner, and I've loved them ever since. Not the boyfriend; the car," she adds with a twinkle in her eye.

Turning on her heel, Harden leads Jack and Allison in exiting the squad room. Jack whispers behind Alice's back as they try to stay close.

"She's in pretty good shape for an older lady. Reminds me of my mother."

Sensing a great opportunity to get a dig in, Allison feigns shock at Jack's comment. Gasping softly, she asks, "You got a sick Oedipus thing, Jack?"

Uncharacteristically embarrassed by Allison's insinuation, Jack feels his face flushing crimson and is mortified by this rare reaction.

"Huh?" he stammers quietly. "No, you... Wait, you got that all wrong! No way! FUCK! Not on your life!"

Powerless to control her extreme delight at Jack's distress, Allison bursts into sidesplitting laughter.

When the awkward pair joins Alice Harden in the elevator, Alice quips, "Hey, I like a good joke. What's so funny?"

Now, it's Allison's turn to flush red. Shaking her head, she mutters, "Oh, it's nothing, just a private joke."

When the doors close, Jack catches Allison's eye and makes sure she sees him rubbing his own eye with his middle finger. Hearing Allison's responding chuckle, Alice wonders, *Does Conrad know what's going on between these two?*

Outside the station, the women wait while Jack walks to the parking lot to bring his ride around, and the lull gives Harden time to question Allison. With a kindly smile, the older woman says, "I know this is very nosy of me, but I have to ask. Are you two having an affair?"

"What!?" sputters Giancarlo, taking a step back

in shock. "Me and Jack? Not just no, but hell, no! What the... Why would you ask that? I mean, not that he isn't attractive and all, but I'm happily married, and so is he!"

"Well, by the way you two were acting back there, it sounded like you were very close. I guess that's why Conrad said you and Stenhouse make a good team. And you're right; he is attractive. Too bad I'm old enough to be his mother!"

When Jack pulls up, Allison works hard at trying to forget that Alice thought she and Stenhouse were more than just partners. Without looking at Jack, she opens the passenger door and pulls the front seat up so Harden can squeeze into the back. When the women are buckled in, Jack gives his trademark honks and squeals the car away from the curb.

"Hey," asks Allison, "don't you get tired of hitting your horn twice every time you start this thing up?"

Piping up from the back seat, Ms. Harden declares, "Oh, come on, Detective, this is a Road Runner! Haven't you ever seen the coyote and roadrunner cartoons? The roadrunner *always* squawks when he runs away! You know, BEEP, BEEP?"

Jack smiles at Ms. Harden in his rearview mirror. Then, he gives two more quick beeps of the horn and points the car east, toward Long Island.

Thirty-five minutes later, he turns onto the Cross Island Expressway and exits at Jericho Turnpike East. Then, he turns south on Mineola Boulevard and pulls into an empty spot in the parking lot of the Nassau County Police Department.

On the drive over, Alice indicated her intent to question Sarah before they removed her from the custody of Nassau County PD, so the first thing Jack does is request the use of one of the police department's interrogation rooms. Request granted; the trio soon finds themselves sitting at a large table opposite their suspect.

Deferring to Alice, the detectives remain silent as the woman removes a digital recorder from her purse and introduces herself to Sarah as a representative of the New York District Attorney's office.

With the device turned on, Alice states, "Mrs. Cummings, your attorney will join you at the NYPD station in Manhattan. Is there anything you would like to say before we remove you from Nassau County's jurisdiction?"

Sarah stares at the ceiling for a long moment. Then, she looks directly at Alice. "Stanley was an ass," she states firmly. "He ruined our marriage with his constant gambling, and his stupid plan to steal the mob's cash is what got my Keith killed!" Fighting against the tears that well up in her eyes, she hisses, "That jerk wanted to reconcile and come back home, like nothing ever happened! Can you imagine that? After all those years alone, I was finally getting on with my life and planning to marry Keith! I couldn't believe it when Stan called and asked me to come to his place in Hammonton!"

Allison hands Sarah a tissue to wipe her eyes.

"What happened in Hammonton?" asks Alice.

"We have proof that you were there."

Sarah nods. "He said he was going to make our favorite meal, the same thing we had when we tailgated at the Jet's game the day he proposed. He wanted me to wear the Bills jersey I wore that day and to bring him the Jets jersey he wore. What a fool!"

"Did you do what he asked?" Alice inquires.

Sarah accepts another tissue and wipes her nose. "I wore my jersey, but I didn't bring his. I didn't want him back!"

"Okay. Then what happened?" probes Alice, surprised that Sarah is revealing so much.

"He forgot to get wine for dinner. I said we didn't need any, but he insisted. He said he wanted it to be just like the day he proposed. I guess he thought he was being romantic," sneers Sarah. "He told me to put some music on the stereo while he went to the store.

"When he left, I looked around the place and found some arsenic in a closet, and that gave me an idea." Sarah closes her eyes and shakes her head at the memory. After a deep sigh, she continues her recollection. "We always made two batches of chili when we tailgated. I'm not fond of spicy food, so one batch was plain, and the other was super spicy. I knew the hot peppers he likes would probably mask the taste of anything I put in his batch, so I poured a bit of the arsenic into the pot. I was so nervous that I spilled some on the floor. When Stan returned, we ate dinner, and he asked me to stay the night. I agreed, just to see if the arsenic worked."

At this point, Sarah stops and asks for a drink of water. While she takes a few sips, Jack and Allison confer quietly.

"Can you believe she's spilling her guts without her lawyer around?" asks Allison. "Yeah, it's weird," replies Jack softly. "He's not going to like this at all."

After Sarah accepts another tissue, Alice asks, "Are you ready to continue?" When Sarah nods in the affirmative, Alice says, "What happened after dinner?"

"Stan got awfully sick and started to vomit pretty violently. When I helped him into the bathroom, he threw up on my shirt. It was disgusting, so I took it off and threw it into his clothes basket. Then I found one of his tee shirts and put it on. He got much sicker around midnight, so I told him I would bring him to the hospital. He passed out before we could leave the house, and that gave me another idea. I decided to dump him at Memorial Park."

"The house was a mess when the police got there," states Alice. "Did you get into a fight before you left?"

"No. When I first got to his place, I saw that he was pretty beaten up, so I asked him about it. He said some of Vito Lucchese's guys had come over. So, before we left, I trashed the place to make it look like they did it."

"Why did you bring him all the way back into the city?"

"That piece of shit was supposed to have died at the Towers, so why not make it look like it happened there, just like it should have?" snaps Sarah. "He was semi-conscious when I put him into the van, and he remained that way until I pushed him out. I saw him stumble toward the pool when I drove away."

"Did you bring the van back to New Jersey?"

"Yeah. I had to get my car." At that point, Sarah drops her cuffed hands into her lap. "I'm tired," she sighs. "Let's get this over with."

Alice turns off the recorder. "We got all we need," she says, glancing at the detectives. "Let's go."

Pushing back his chair, Jack rises and helps Sarah stand. Then he unlocks her handcuffs, re-cuffs them behind her back, and steers her out of the interrogation room.

The ride to Manhattan is relatively quiet. When they arrive at Central Booking, Jack and Allison leave Alice Harden with Sarah and a couple of uniformed cops. Then, they drive over to Goldman Sachs to check in with Burley and Gomez about the roof jumper—their new case.

The CSI team is just about to wrap things up at Goldman Sachs when Stenhouse pulls his Road Runner into the sea of blue lights around the crime scene. As they walk toward the activity, Jack's cell phone rings, and he stops to listen. With a sigh, he responds, "Okay, we'll be right there."

Turning to Giancarlo, he says, "The grim reaper was busy today. We got another body at City Hall."

"Oh, crap," mutters Allison.

"Yeah, it never ends. I just hope this one won't involve political bullshit. I'm really tired of all that crap," says Jack. "C'mon, let's go. Burley and Gomez can handle this one."

As they turn to go back to Jack's car, Gomez catches sight of his colleagues.

"Hey, Jack!" calls Gomez. "The jumper was Officer Lester Smith, from the Evidence Room!"

"What...!?" exclaim the partners in unison, each of them shocked by the news.

"Bet he was on your uncle's payroll," declares Jack with a smug look at Allison.

"I don't know about that," says Allison, "but I do know that death seems to follow you around like a shadow."

CHAPTER FORTY-TWO

Michael Lucchese is a happy man. Now that he's in charge of the family business while his father is in prison, he's thoroughly enjoying his elevated status and the immense power it brings.

Seated at his father's table at the restaurant on Mulberry Street, he's blissfully digging into his favorite meal, pasta puttanesca, when Vito's consigliere sidles up to the table.

Rolling his eyes in annoyance, Michael grumbles around a mouthful of food, "Are you going to spoil my meal?"

"No, Mr. Lucchese, I have good news," responds his father's trusted counselor. "The money has been retrieved, and Smith has been taken care of. Is there anything else you would like me to do?"

Michael takes a sip of Peroni while he thinks. "No," he responds after a moment. "Just keep trying to get my dad out. Oh, wait, there is one thing. Dad wants to make sure Ally's kids are doing well. Keep an eye on them and set up a little something for them in his will. He has a soft spot for his niece."

"Very well, Mr. Lucchese. What would you like us to do about Sarah Cummings and Larry Grimes?"

Leaning back in his chair, Michael loosens his

belt and belches. "We got most of our money back, so let's let Sarah deal with the perils of prison life. As for Grimes, well, fuck him. We'll keep track of him and use him later, when we need a favor. Now, come and sit down; join me for dinner. Have some wine or beer. Let's enjoy tonight and leave all this shit for tomorrow."

"Looks like an easy one this time," says the Medical Examiner in front of City Hall. "From the color of this guy's eyes, I think it was liver failure. We found a half-empty bottle of Mad Dog 20/20 in his overcoat pocket. The fool must have drunk himself to death."

"Damn," mutters Jack when he notices the tattoo of a large skull on the homeless man's hand. "He was a Navy Seal. This doesn't seem right."

Allison aims her cell phone at the body so she can take a photo of the dead vet for later reference. "His military records will be on file," she says. "Remember, it's your turn to tell his family, Jack. And don't forget that you owe me a steak dinner for the last time."

"Yeah, I know. My mouth is cashing checks I can't afford. So is my temper. Come on; let's go back to the First to ID this guy. Maybe we can close the case before the city kills someone else."

On the walk back to the car, Jack says, "So for that dinner, I'm thinking Del Frisco's. Let me know when you can get a babysitter so your husband can join us. I'll ask Didi to make reservations."

"Okay, sounds good."

Just then, Jack remembers something and makes a soft moaning sound. Smacking a hand against his forehead, he exclaims, "Oh, no! I also owe dinners to Ellison, Burley, Gomez, and Stone. Shit! I think I need to ask Conrad for a raise!"

"Yeah, good luck with that!" laughs Allison.

When they are inside the car, Jack glances sideways at his friend. "Hey," he asks with one raised eyebrow, "you got an in at Ristorante di Cosenza, don't you? Can you get us the family discount?"

Allison gasps at the thought. "Not just no, but FUCK no!" she counters with several firm shakes of her head.

As the cherished Road Runner starts up, Jack adds two beeps to the outside sounds of big city life, but inside the car, his loud and raucous laughter is all that Allison hears.

No matter what happens, life goes on in the Big Apple.

CHAPTER FORTY-THREE

Keeping his promise, Jack drops over eight hundred bucks at Del Frisco's a few weeks later for all the steak dinners he promised to his crew and Sylvia Stone. Giancarlo and Joe Ellison have brought their spouses and Gomez brought his girlfriend, but each of the cops insists on paying for their individual guests.

Before leaving the restaurant, the group declares their intention to thank Jack for a great dinner by treating him to a nightcap. Jack accepts their offer but insists on going to a different establishment for the drink.

Keeping everyone, including Didi, in the dark as to where they are going, the convoy follows the Road Runner south on Seventh Avenue. When Didi spots the sign for a small sports bar known for its Karaoke nights, she grabs Jack's shoulder in a panic.

"Oh, no!" she moans. "You are *not* going to do this tonight!"

"Oh, yes, I am, Babe. Just wait," laughs Jack.

Luckily, the bar's staff is able to rearrange tables so the group can sit together, and after their drink orders are placed, they all sit back to listen to amateurs belting out their favorite tunes from the stage.

When the drinks arrive, Jack holds his glass aloft to salute his friends.

"Thanks a bunch for the nightcap!" he says with a smile for each of them. But Jack knows he won't stop at just one. "I have a designated driver tonight, so I'll take care of anything else I drink!"

As the evening progresses, Jack orders a second, third, and fourth Daniel's on the Rocks, all the while watching the singers for his chance to shine at the mic. As he finishes his fourth drink, he finally sees his opportunity. Bolting out of his chair, he sways back and forth on shaky legs but manages to make his way up the steps to the stage. Jack is in no pain tonight.

Back at the table, Jack's friends and colleagues watch with amusement as he strides toward the microphone.

"I can see it now," smirks Giancarlo. "Tomorrow's gonna be a coffee and coke morning for sure!"

Seated across from Allison, Didi cringes at what she knows is about to happen. Closing her eyes, she lowers her head into her hands and waits.

Up on stage, Jack also waits. When the strains of his chosen song begin, he brings the mic to his mouth and croons,

> *"Nothing could*
> *be finer than to be*
> *in Carolina in the*
> *mooorrroorrning..."*

As Jack's warbling continues, Sylvia looks over at Didi. Shouting to be heard, she declares, "I haven't known Jack very long, but this doesn't seem like a song he'd sing!"

"No one could be
sweeter than my
sweetie when I meet
her in the mooorr-
roorrning..."

Hearing Sylvia's comment, the rest of the team nods in agreement and turns expectantly toward Didi. Each of them seems to be asking for an explanation of Jack's song choice.

Didi knows that the friends don't understand what's happening, but she doesn't feel up to explaining. All she says is, "Just wait. You'll see soon enough."

When the tune ends, Jack remains at the mic. Looking out into the audience, he extends his hands to his wife and shouts, "Didi, my love, please stand!"

Glaring at Jack from her seat, Didi stares daggers at him and shakes her head in dismay. However, she knows her husband won't take no for an answer, so she grudgingly rises and stands next to the table with her arms folded across her chest.

Smiling happily at what he's about to do, Jack shouts into the mic, "This is for my wife, Didi, who is beautifully pregnant with our first child!"

While the patrons of the bar applaud the announcement, Jack goes down on one knee. In his best, or worst, Al Jolson imitation, he belts out one of the lines from the song he just sang:

"If I had Aladdin's
lamp for only a day
I'd make a wish

*and here's what
I'd saaayy..."*

Preparing for the worst, Didi closes her eyes as Jack ends the song as only he can:

*"...ohhh, nothing
could be finer than to
be in her vagina in the
moooooorning!"*

At the closing verse, the bar erupts in whoops, guffaws, and applause, prompting Didi to embrace the moment rather than dying from shame. Turning around, she waves in the direction of the bar and takes several low bows, showing off all she has. Then she turns toward Jack, who is also taking bows, and throws him a kiss.

While Jack walks cautiously down the steps of the stage, Allison puts her hand on Didi's shoulder and leans close to whisper into Didi's ear. "You *really* need to pray for a daughter!"

"I know," sighs Didi.

On the last step, Jack's legs suddenly betray him, and his alcohol-infused knees buckle, sending him face-first onto the floor. Worried that Jack has been hurt, John and Hector rush toward him, but they find him rolling around the floor, laughing happily. Looking on in amazement, they grab Jack's hand and pull him up.

"No prob, my friendsh!" says Jack drunkenly as Hector and John hold him steady. "Don't you know, drunksh neverr get hurt?"

At that moment, a cacophony of ring tones cuts

through the general noise of the barroom. Answering her phone, Allison listens intently and winces at what she's hearing.

"We got another body!" she announces to the assembled cops. Turning to Jack, she sizes up his condition. "I guess you're going to have to call in sick for this one!"

Standing on his own now, Jack cocks his head and rubs the side of his nose with his middle finger. Then, his face lights up with a lopsided grin.

"Let's roll!"